The Mill

The Millennial Detective

Essays on Trends in Crime Fiction, Film and Television, 1990–2010

EDITED BY MALCAH EFFRON

Foreword by Stephen Knight

McFarland & Company, Inc., Publishers
Jefferson, North Carolina, and London

The millennial detective : essays on trends in crime fiction,
   film and television, 1990–2010 / edited by Malcah Effron ;
   foreword by Stephen Knight.
        p.   cm.
   Includes bibliographical references and index.

   ISBN 978-0-7864-5851-6
   softcover : 50# alkaline paper ∞

   1. Detective and mystery stories, American — History and
criticism.   2. American fiction — 20th century — History and
criticism.   3. American fiction — 21st century — History and
criticism.   4. Detective and mystery stories, English — History
and criticism.   5. English fiction — 20th century — History
and criticism.   6. English fiction — 21st century — History and
criticism.   7. Detectives in literature.   8. Crime on literature.
9. Detective and mystery films — History and criticism.
10. Detective and mystery television programs — History and
criticism.   I. Effron, Malcah, 1982–
PS374.D4M55 2011
823'.0872090914 — dc23   2011025426

BRITISH LIBRARY CATALOGUING DATA ARE AVAILABLE

Front cover image © 2011 Shutterstock

Manufactured in the United States of America

*McFarland & Company, Inc., Publishers
   Box 611, Jefferson, North Carolina 28640
   www.mcfarlandpub.com*

Table of Contents

Foreword by Stephen Knight   1

Preface by Malcah Effron   5

Introduction by Malcah Effron   11

Crime Fiction and the Politics of Place: The Post-9/11 Sense of Place in Sara Paretsky and Ian Rankin (P. M. NEWTON)   21

A Normal Pathology? Patricia Cornwell's Third-Person Novels (BETH HEAD)   36

Inheriting the Mantle: Wallander and Daughter (SUSAN MASSEY)   50

"A Visitor for the Dead": Adam Dalgliesh as a Serial Detective (SABINE VANACKER)   66

Transforming Genres: Subversive Potential and the Interface between Hard-Boiled Detective Fiction and Chick Lit (SONJA ALTNOEDER)   82

The Poetics of Deviance and *The Curious Incident of the Dog in the Night-Time* (CHRISTIANA GREGORIOU)   97

"A Natural Instinct for Forensics": Trace Evidence and Embodied Gazes in *The Bone Collector* (LINDSAY STEENBERG)   112

"Post-Modern or Post-Mortem?" Murder as a Self-Consuming Artifact in *Red Dragon* (DAVID LEVENTE PALATINUS)   128

Revisiting Paranoia: The "Witch Hunts" in James Ellroy's *The Big Nowhere* and Walter Mosley's *A Red Death* (MAUREEN SUNDERLAND)   142

Table of Contents

A Detective Series with Love Interruptions?
The Heteronormative Detective Couple in Contemporary
Crime Fiction (MALCAH EFFRON)   157

Detective Fiction and Serial Protagonists: An Interview
with Ian Rankin (SIÂN HARRIS and MALCAH EFFRON)   173

About the Contributors   185

Index   187

Foreword

BY STEPHEN KNIGHT

Myths abound in crime fiction studies. They can be historical, like thinking Edgar Allan Poe started it all — what about E.T. A. Hoffman, whose work he knew, Eugène Vidocq whose *Mémoires* he almost certainly knew, and the Philadelphia *Gentleman's Magazine* crime writers he actually edited? Then there is national myth: English golden age fiction is, according to Americans, all cucumber sandwiches (overlooking the dark, often class-based, motives that drive the poisoned dart), while the American tough guys are decent democratic fellows (what about *Red Harvest* as Marxist melodrama, *The Big Sleep* as sexist hysteria?). The myths have gotten worse: today the fantasy of forensic science masks sado-masochism, the big sellers use conspiracy-myth to disseminate paranoia against the person — and some, like Patricia Cornwell, manage both those dubious maneuvers.

But wide as those gulfs between myth and reality might be, the largest and most disabling myth in crime fiction studies has been that it is not the same as literary studies. Just as the new crime novels are corralled in a column way down the literary pages, writing about crime fiction was for a long time connoisseurish, evaluative only in a personal way — Julian Symons was the best you could get. When by the 1970s critical habits and curricula changed across the arts faculties, crime fiction was still fugitive: it was twenty years after I first published on the subject that I was able to convince (or actually shame) a department into letting me mount a course. There have been developments: strong critical books have appeared in recent years — Tony Hilfer, Lee Horsley, Stephen Soitos, Priscilla Walton and Manina Jones — but they are all from North America (Horsley in British exile), where the myth of democracy has at least some benign pur-

Foreword

chase. Yet there is still, unlike science fiction, children's literature, even fantasy fiction, no major regular international conference in crime fiction, and there is only one dedicated journal, *Clues*, which had until very recently an uncertain career.

This curious case of absence, as criminographers might say, is actually twofold. First, there are no standard, recognized responses as there are in other fields. Journalists and teachers, let alone members of the public, will in large numbers remember what some feminist lecturer said or some serious tutor asserted about sexism or racism. But nobody has ever worked out what crimism might be. Authors like James Patterson can get away with a grotesque body count masked in a little liberalism (Alex Cross is not white) and with gestures towards science now and then — and people can lap up the blood and pain which he very lucratively promotes.

The second absence is inside the academy and among public intellectuals, ultimately causing the above-mentioned lack of public scrutiny about crimism, an intellectual disconnect. There has been a lack of impact on crime-fiction criticism from the high-level critiques that have been common parlance in what in the 1970s we called "the New Humanities" — or sometimes Cultural Studies goes to Theory College. Where theory has leaked into crime-fiction criticism, it has usually just admired Paul Auster and other exponents of post-everything self-admiration.

So criminography has mostly missed out on the last decades' very substantial advances of professional literary criticism — including discourse analysis, structuralism and post-structuralism, psychoanalytic criticism, reception theory, body studies, gay studies, gaze studies, Orientalism, Occidentalism, post-colonial analysis, whether socially focused as in subaltern studies or psychically internalized as in the line of Homi Bhabha. Feminists and black fiction scholars have drawn on these resources at times to handle crime fiction, but that is for their own very proper concerns. The tools of the modern intellectual analyst have hardly influenced crime fiction criticism as such, with the result that a recent writer like Charles Rzepka is basically speaking the same connoisseurish language as Julian Symons almost fifty years ago.

Stepping into the breach, *The Millennial Detectives* boldly addresses new directions in crime fiction and, like an Agatha Christie twist — you didn't spot the most familiar thing — its importance lies in the fact that the collective direction of the essays, very largely new to crime fiction, is in fact one that is now in literary criticism nearly half a century old, a knowing, well-read, conscious, and professional deployment of the skills and techniques of contemporary literary criticism. It is the context of the direction that is excitingly new.

This labile and often elegantly theorized set of critical essays on crime fiction ends with what seems like a very old direction — an interview with an author. But the author is the quicksilver Ian Rankin and the interviewers have written it up as an essay, a palimpsest of diegesis. When they ask him about theory in crime fiction, like Rebus he gives a double answer. The common man, or his appearance, says he never wants to seem "wanky," but then the subversive plain-man-as-thinker names Christie as "the supreme exponent of the form." There is, he is telling us — Siobhan would understand — theory in everything. These authors have shown that to be true, and also that when this is recognized and realized in sufficiently intelligent criticism, crime fiction becomes more fully and more thought-provokingly comprehensible, and crime-fiction criticism emerges from the mists of myth to take its long deferred place on the podium of contemporary intellectualism.

Stephen Knight is research professor in English literature at Cardiff University, Wales. He has written essays and books on a range of subjects, including *Form and Ideology in Crime Fiction* (1980) and *Crime Fiction Since 1800: Detection, Death, Diversity* (2010).

Preface

BY MALCAH EFFRON

This collection provides a wide array of critical analyses of detective fiction produced between 1990 and 2010. Working from the cultural importance of the change of millennia and the current events that surround it, these essays examine generic shifts in the crime fiction genre as published in the last twenty years, highlighting the ways in which crime fiction responds to millennial anxieties about the shifts in crime. With the rise of the Internet in the 1990s and the fall of the World Trade Center in 2001, the turn of the twenty-first century has experienced a new form of globalized crime not necessarily predicated on the World War rhetoric that influenced crime literature in the early twentieth century or the Cold War rhetoric that permeated the genre during its middle decades. The changes that appear in the crime fiction narratives during the final decade of the twentieth century and the first decade of the twenty-first call attention to the popular perceptions of shifts in crime culture, even if sometimes reminding us of the similarities and ubiquities of crime, rather than feeding into the eschatological fears that resurfaced at the dawn of the new millennium. By examining the new trends in crime fiction at the turn of the twenty-first century, this collection exposes, outlines, and articulates contemporary responses both to the new culture that responds to these interpretations of criminality and to the classic genre that has fictionalized it.

The idea of millennial changes is complicated in a genre known for — and even defined by — its conventionality. At the most basic level, this collection focuses on "what's new" simply in its selection of primary materials, as each essay focuses on texts published in the last twenty years, and often in the last five or ten. However, while a text's recent publication might guarantee its "newness," it does not necessarily guarantee changes in direction. The essays collected here approach the multiple challenges of the turn of the twenty-first century by considering texts produced by a diverse group of artists working in a variety of media as analyzed through several theoretical approaches. In this method, each one carefully identifies the new direction its primary material takes and the new critical approach that it contributes both to crime fiction studies and to contemporary textual analysis.

The essayists pull from a broad range of authors and styles to articulate the different directions that have branched off the classic path of the crime fiction genre. Ranging from the recent texts of comparatively old series (such as P. D. James's Adam Dalgliesh series or Sara Paretsky's V. I. Warshawski novels) to series that began with the turn of the twenty-first century (Janet Evanovich's Stephanie Plum series, for example, or Walter Mosley's Easy Rawlins books), the essays herein consider the millennial influences on crime fiction in terms of changes to pre-existing formulae as well as original paths. Furthermore, they approach depictions of crime through different media and narrative forms, including both written and visual, and both filmic and televisual. With essays that examine filmic adaptations (such as *The Bone Collector* and *Red Dragon*) as well as contemporary trends in television crime drama (such as the *CSI* franchise), this collection integrates discussions from many of the different routes that crime fiction narrative has taken, not only based on the changing nature of crime and the technology for its detection but also based on the changing nature of media available for fictional representation. The variety of forms in the primary sources thus illustrate that the contemporary shifts in crime narration are necessarily a function of both artistic inspiration and contemporary situation.

In addressing the vast field of primary texts available in the crime fiction genre from the past two decades, the authors of these essays have used a variety of different theoretical frameworks and critical techniques. Incorporating elements as seemingly diverse and as intimately connected as (but not limited to) cultural geography, feminist and postfeminist studies, linguistic analysis, and phenomenology, these arguments bring a range of texts into the conversation as well as a mixture of methods for their examination and interpretation. As Stephen Knight notes in the foreword, these chapters provide "a knowing, well-read, conscious, and professional deployment of the skills and techniques of contemporary literary criticism." The conversations explicit within the essays and implicit between them highlight how these critical analyses of crime fiction — insistently neither simply socio-historical accounts of popular culture nor simply exemplars of critical theory — come together in a cohesive mosaic to provide an image of both the aesthetic and the critical work of the crime fiction genre at the turn of the twenty-first century.

The diversity of these essays dwells not exclusively in their source texts and critical frameworks, as, importantly, it brings together the work of international scholars on crime literature. The essays thus not only illustrate globalized approaches to the genre both in terms of primary and secondary material but also in terms of the scholarly community engaged in this project. Incorporating the work and insights of scholars from across Europe, the United States, and Australia and featuring analyses of authors reading and interpreting material from outside their native languages, this collection illustrates the new direction crime fiction has to take in responding to a globalized community not only in terms of the events it narrates but also in terms of those who read it. So, with the plethora of social and cultural perspectives not only encapsulated in the texts here analyzed but also embodied in the authors working across cultural boundaries, the essays highlight the cross-cultural conversation that has become integral not only in crime fiction, but also in the study of the genre at the turn of the twenty-first century.

The present effort joins a wealth of edited collections on crime fiction, but its focus on turn of the twenty-first century texts indicates its position as an update to the collections that have preceded it. Also unlike its predecessors, the historic specificity of the present essays shifts the emphasis of the collection away from the theoretical, thematic, or national approaches common in other well-known collections, such as Jerome Delamater and Ruth Prigozy's *Theory and Practice of Detective Fiction* (1997), Stephen Knight's *Crime Fiction, 1800–2000: Detection, Death Diversity* (2003), or Renée W. Craig-Odders, Jacky Collins, and Glen Steven Close's *Hispanic and Luso-Brazilian Detective Fiction* (2006). The present work overtly declares its multi-faceted interests in an array of authors and media because, by putting these different approaches into one collection, the chapters generate new conversations about the genre. As such, this collection takes as its subject not only the shifts in crime fiction at the turn of the twenty-first century but also the new directions of crime fiction studies in the new millennium.

7

Introduction

BY MALCAH EFFRON

This collection, as with many collections of crime fiction criticism, began life as a conference, and the conference began with the observation that the aestheticization of crime fiction seems to have been largely influenced by Raymond Chandler's essay in the *Atlantic Monthly*, "The Simple Art of Murder" (1944). Unlike the wealth of crime fiction writers who had critically assessed the genre prior to Chandler, "The Simple Art of Murder" is not another apologia for the crime novel, defending its existence as popular literature and excusing its authors for producing non-literary texts. Instead, Chandler argues that the crime novel can be — and is — a form of literature when properly executed, and then he continues to explain how that execution should look. From the perspective of the twenty-first century academy, it initially appeared that crime fiction writers and crime fiction studies have latched onto the idea that the aesthetically appealing crime story is one that "gave murder back to the kind of people that commit it for reasons, not just to provide a corpse; and with the means at hand, not with hand-wrought duelling pistols, curare, and tropical fish" (Chandler 1988, 10). Investigating the validity of this assumption, the conference progenitor of this collection, for which we shamelessly cannibalized Chandler's title and came up with "The Literary Art of Murder," examined how fully Chandler's article had influenced both the production and the analysis of crime fiction.

In the course of this exploration, it became apparent that as much could be said of Chandler's influence on the aesthetics of the different aspects crime fiction at the turn of the twenty-first century as throughout the twentieth century. At the end of the millennium, crime fiction has begun reassessing and repositioning itself, reinterpreting Chandler's aesthetics in terms of the scientific, legal, and cultural advancements that have influenced crime and its narration at the end of the twentieth century and the start of the twenty-first. In some cases, these advancements might seem like a complete revision of Chandler's standards, in others simple modifications, and in some cases a return from paths that diverted from the Chandlerian aesthetic. Ultimately, however, what some of these pieces suggest is that Chandler, while influential, is not necessarily the point of origin for the literary and social agendas manifest in series newly produced or re-imagined at the turn of the twenty-first century.

The Literary Art of Murder

Of the many elements of Chandler's aesthetic philosophy challenged in this collection is the principal assumption that good crime fiction follows the protagonist "down these mean streets a *man* must go who is not himself mean, who is neither tarnished nor afraid. The detective in this kind of story must be *such a man. He* is the hero, *he* is everything. *He* must be a complete *man* and a common *man* and yet an unusual *man*" (18; emphasis added). Feminist evaluations and feminist crime novelists have already interestingly and effectively challenged the presumption of a male hero, particularly a white, Christian, male hero. To claim that this feminist challenge is the product of the turn of the twenty-first century would require a liberal definition of "turn," since authors such as Amanda Cross and Marcia Muller introduced their feminist detectives in the 1960s and 1970s, and the core texts of feminist crime fiction criticism began appearing in the 1980s, with texts like Kathleen Gregory Klein's *The Woman Detective* (1988) and Maureen Reddy's *Sisters in Crime* (1988). However, when considering the challenges — both in terms of the contemporary novels and the contributed criticism — to Chandler's masculine aesthetics of the detective figure, the chapters in this collection that engage in gendered exploration do so in the frame of *postfeminism*, which Sonja Altnoeder succinctly defines as a new direction in feminist theory that "aims critically — and, above all, self-reflexively — to assess the contemporary accomplishment of the feminist goals of the past three decades" (87–88). With this critical and self-reflexive approach to contemporary crime literature's implicit and explicit challenges to Western gender hierarchies, the re-reading of masculinity and femininity within this collection provides theoretical interpretations to such expressions in crime fiction at the turn of the twenty-first century.

10

Along with his masculine aesthetics, Chandler promoted a linguistic aesthetic of the vernacular, proposing that good crime fiction characters "talk and think in the language they customarily used for these purposes [and the hero] talks as the man of his age talks, that is, with rude wit, a lively sense of the grotesque, a disgust for sham, and a contempt for pettiness" (1988, 14–15; 18). For Chandler, "the language they customarily used for these purposes" implies a street lingo that deviates from standard English, whether of the American or British variety. As the articles in this collection suggest, the language used for describing and narrating crime has moved off the streets and back into the laboratories, as scientific advancements in genetic and microscopic technology have changed the nature of crime fighting and criminology. The influences of these scientific advancements on crime narration can be seen in the detective series of the turn of the twenty-first century, such as in the forensic focus of Patricia Cornwell, Jeffrey Deaver, and the *CSI* series. By exploring the increased use of forensic descriptions for criminal narration — moving beyond Sherlock Holmes's 140 varieties of tobacco — the chapters in this collection explore how the scientific advances in criminal forensics as well as audiovisual narration have allowed for new means of narrating the commission, investigation, and prevention of crime at the turn of the twenty-first century.

Just as the who and the how of the narratives have shifted between the beginning and the end of the twentieth century, the nature of the mean streets have themselves shifted in the intervening century. The empty spaces of Chandler's Los Angeles have been filled in, and, as this collection illustrates, the increasingly globalized culture of the turn of the twenty-first century has altered the understanding of setting and place in twenty-first century crime fiction. Certain chapters, especially those that work on texts that return to Chandler's Los Angeles, underscore how certain texts illustrate the French adage that *plus ça change, plus c'est la même chose*,[1] but the events of September 11, 2001, opened the twenty-first century to a new American and global self-conception in Western culture that needed to rethink itself in relation to other cultures. We can find parallels between the attack on Pearl Harbor (1941), which brought the United States into World War II and influenced Chandler's historical period, and the attacks on the World Trade Center (2001), which brought the United States into the War on Terror and can be considered one of the watershed events of the dawn of the twenty-first century. Nevertheless, World War II, which pitted nation against nation, significantly differs from the War on Terror, which pitted a nation against an international terrorist organization. This difference highlights the changes between the local rhetoric of crime and criminal activity accounted for in Chandler's descriptions of the mean streets and the global rhetoric of violence and criminality that characterizes settings at the beginning of the twenty-first century. This collection examines such transitions as they make themselves felt in the way crime is narrated at the end of the twentieth century and the start of the twenty-first. With their investigations into contemporary aesthetic evaluations in relation to cultural shifts at the turn of the twenty-first century, the chapters in this collection work together to highlight how the new directions in crime fiction narrative reflect, acknowledge, and anticipate the continued interest in and interpretation of crime and its detection.

Updates

Aside from the adjustment to the Chandlerian aesthetics of the crime story, this collection approaches general evolutions in crime narrative in texts published between 1990 and 2010. In many of these cases, the chapters refer to crime fiction series that span these two decades, considering the more recent texts in established crime series as they approach and enter the twenty-first century. In some cases, however, these chapters examine series of longer standing than the two decades around the twenty-first century, examining how series of long-standing in the twentieth century address their potential in the twenty-first. The material in these pieces predominantly examines how series develop both in terms of character development and in terms of historical shifts. By exploring character development and historical shifts, these chapters begin a discussion about series not simply as a means of maintaining the rules of the game, but also as a strategic means of illustrating generic growth through differentiation rather than repetition. Though some pieces focus on one text and others focus on the progress of series as a whole, they all draw upon the patterns established not only by the conventions of the genre but also by the individual authors in the series they cultivate. As such, these chapters use specific cases to examine public social change on personal conceptions.

In the pieces that examine updates to series rather than series that originate at the turn of the twentieth-first century, the arguments foreground the changes that appear in the social climate and the struggles faced from the inception of the series through the new material. In some cases, such as P. M. Newton's "Crime Fiction and the Politics of Place," these pieces examine authors' specialized responses to national and global events, such as the events of September 11, 2001, in the United States, or the events of July 7, 2005, in the United Kingdom. These pieces tend to focus on the textual examination of the unique nature of contemporary crime, its investigation, and its prevention. More than simply addressing one cataclysmic moment at the turn of the century, other chapters, such as Beth Head's "A Normal Pathology?," examine shifting narrative trends as a means of exploring endemic criminality and its social valuation in the twenty-first century. Other pieces reflect on how series in themselves have changed, rather than specifically in relation to geo-cultural events. Such shifts can be manifest either in the nature and life status of the detective protagonists, as in Sabine Vanacker's in-depth analysis of readership loyalty in relation to the evolution of P. D. James's Adam Dalgliesh from the 1960s to the 2000s, or through changes in the detective protagonist, as in Susan Massey's exploration of Henning Mankell's Wallander novels, as it shifts from father Kurt to daughter Linda as the key focalizer of the series.

By focusing on how series change over time, these pieces approach the concept of new directions by examining those taken within a series. In this sense, these pieces not only interrogate the contemporary contribution of these texts to our understanding of crime, criminality, and the way it is conceptualized and narrated at the turn of the twenty-first century, but also they investigate the nature of seriality and its effectiveness and affectiveness in relation to the crime genre as it moves toward a century beyond its Golden Age (1920s–1940s, cf. Howard Haycraft). The collection returns to this question of seriality in some of the other pieces that consider series not in terms of their recent interventions but in terms of the turn of the century narrative that they contain. These pieces also contribute to the dialogue between author and reader articulated in the conversation recorded in the appendix, an interview with Scottish celebrity crime writer Ian Rankin. Working with these chapters, the pieces that address updates to different crime fiction series as they enter the twenty-first century underscore the developmental process of series writing, allowing for the evolution of the crime fiction genre in relation to the evolution of crime, criminality, and its interpretation.

Adaptations

While many of the chapters in this collection deal with texts that fit the standard conventions of the crime fiction novel, several pieces investigate issues of adaptations of the form. The category of adaptation traditionally implies transferring a narrative from one medium to another. Some of the considered texts that are adapted from one medium to another deal with both written and visual sources from 1990 to 2010, but for some pieces, only the adaptation belongs to the appropriate decades, and for these texts, one of the interesting factors is that these earlier texts are adapted twenty years later. These pieces explore not only the adaptation from one medium to another, but also the transformation from one period to another. Moreover, adaptation refers to the ability of a form to alter itself to meet new criteria for survival. As such, the idea of adaptation equally applies to the evolution of generic forms, particularly as encountered in the mutation of subgenres. In this sense, adaptation comes to have an organic developmental logic in that, in addition to experimenting with textual modification, these adaptations show the shift in generic conventions in relation to cultural changes. By considering how crime narratives adapt, whether examining the same story told in new forms or contemplating the change in forms needed to tell new stories, these chapters highlight how media shifts at the turn of the twenty-first century encompass new ways of thinking about crime, its execution, and its investigation.

Some of these are adaptations that move between the written and the visual media of narrative, examining how the visual elements of media such as film and television allow for an aestheticization of crime and its investigation in a manner based on visual principles of art as well as literary ones. In some of these cases, the aesthetics discussed in the chapter identify new trends in cultural understanding of crime and its investigation, focusing on the fetishization of science and technology in their capacity to identify criminals and criminality unequivocally, as is the case in Lindsay Steenberg's "A Natural Instinct for Forensics." These chapters examine how scientific improvement has colored the expression of absolute truth, yet maintain a focus on how the human situation can be subsumed and overwritten by the technology, masking continuing problems within our treatment of others outside the quantitative diagnostic capabilities of turn of the twenty-first century technology. While some chapters tie science to art, for others, such as David Levente Palatinus's "'Post-modern or Post-mortem?,'" the aesthetics are themselves fetishized, and the spectacle, rather than being the means of detecting the crime, becomes the core of its perpetration. These chapters look at filmic dramatizations of crime fiction novels, but other pieces explore transformative genres. In particular, Sonja Altnoeder's "Transforming Genres" examines the fusion of the hard-boiled detective genre with the "chick lit" form that emerges as an identified genre at the turn of the twenty-first century. These discussions of different forms of adaptation indicate how texts can be altered to present concerns with different emphases that underscore the cultural shift — whether progression or regression — evident in the reformatting of the original tropes in a new narrative style.

Whether exploring the agendas in stories transferred from the initial narrative medium or the implications in generic mutations, these chapters consider a variety of permutations that advance the crime narrative to address new approaches to ideas as they evolve to deal with the new millennium. They indicate how the manner in which the criteria of detective fiction has influenced and has been influenced by other genres. By understanding adaptation not only as a shift from one medium to another but also as a conversion from one generic form to another, these pieces underscore how the nature of the genre has adapted to broader shifts in popular culture. In these analyses of the aesthetic renditions of popular attitudes toward changes in social and scientific methodologies for investigating and interpreting crime, these chapters offer new scope for understanding how these adaptations mark the new directions crime fiction takes when it translates similar stories between media and transfers similar structures between genres.

Revisions

While some chapters deal with how series have changed and others deal with how narratives have been adapted, others examine shifts in content in terms of revising the expectations of the crime fiction narrative. These revisions appear in terms of reconsidering historical assumptions, including those assumptions about race, gender, and developmental issues. All these queries can be found in the texts that deal with updates and adaptations, as is indicated in the theoretical frames used for the different chapters in this collection. As such, the new directions in crime fiction can be understood as examining these revisions to the classic form established in the different narratives of the trajectory of twentieth-century crime fiction, including but not limited to Chandler's "The Simple Art of Murder." With the pieces that focus on revisions, the chapters' arguments focus on the reformatting of a classic concept to address contemporary concerns. By highlighting the new approaches in new series, these revisions emphasize the developing forms of the genre in relation to socio-cultural progress.

In examining the revisions, the chapters take into consideration the present state of affairs as expressed in crime fiction narrative at the turn of the century. In some cases, the argument focuses on new areas of consideration that have been adopted into the generic modes to account for contemporary interests, such as mental disability, as is the focus of Christiana Gregoriou's linguistic analysis of the problematic correlation in contemporary culture between those who are designated as outsiders because of mental differences and those who are othered because of criminal activity in the chapter "The Poetics of Deviance and The Curious Incident of the Dog in the Night Time." Other chapters, such as Malcah Effron's "A Detective Series with Love Interruptions?," focus on the revisions to the detective form in relation to the narrative focus, namely from the investigation of the crimes and to the lives of the detectives, particularly commenting on the changes — or the lack thereof— in gendered criteria for criminal investigative success. Moreover, some chapters retell old stories from new perspectives, allowing the crime fiction genre to change its focus at the end of the twentieth century without necessarily changing the setting or register that establish its criteria at its beginning. Chapters such as Maureen Sunderland's "Revisiting Paranoia" examine how the changes anticipated between the beginning of the twentieth century and the start of the twenty-first share commonalities within its popular fiction that echo the similarities in its culture, all while using a perspective ignored in the literature of the first half of the twentieth century. As these chapters emphasize revisions to the detective genre rather than radical changes, they indicate that the problems perceived throughout the twentieth century follow us into the twenty-first. However, these problems appear in new forms that need to be recognized and understood in terms of their differences as well as their similarities.

The revisions outlined in this collection examine how current detective series have actively revised the standards of detective fiction established at the beginning of the twentieth century to accommodate differing cultural expectations nearly a century later. These pieces re-evalute the grand narratives proposed by both earlier studies of history and earlier studies of the genre, encouraging a reconsideration of national, historical, and generic constraints previously attributed to the detective genre. By reconsidering these constraints as they are re-interpreted and represented in the crime fiction literature at the turn of the twenty-first century, these pieces reveal the evolutionary nature of the understanding of crime and its associated social forces and consequences, as they explore both the similarities between social conditions and narrative forms during the twentieth century and those at the start of the twenty-first. As such, the new directions in crime fiction stem from revising the frameworks codified in the early twentieth century as a means of representing the scope of crime and crime studies at the turn of the twenty-first.

The Simple Art of the Collection

These dominant thematic elements of updates, adaptations, and revisions underscore how this collection presents the main ways in which contemporary crime fiction has developed in terms of the conventions of the genre. Elements that are updated look at changes within a series as they vary and adjust to new cultural climates, while adaptations reveal how way the crime genre has blended with other forms, including moving from written to visual media, and the revisions explore how classical tropes of crime fiction have been re-appropriated to address contemporary concerns and thus alter the generic expectations established in the first part of the twentieth century. While, as delineated above, certain chapters might focus more noticeably on updates, adaptations, or revisions than the others, all chapters incorporate certain elements of all these aspects in their response to new means of articulating — from both the creative and the critical perspective — the aesthetics of crime fiction. Considering the importance of seriality, the interview with Ian Rankin culminates this exploration of these aesthetics by presenting the author as both creator and critic, highlighting the critical work embedded in the primary, as well as secondary, analyses illustrated by this collection. In this regard, the collection as a whole works together to demonstrate the new directions taken in a manner that highlights the effects social conditions at the turn of the twenty-first century have exerted upon publishing trends and aesthetic critique of contemporary crime fiction.

Nevertheless, as is the case with most collections, the chapters in this collection contribute individual arguments and perspectives on various facets of the crime fiction genre without needing to address the same topics. While there is theoretical overlap — for instance Head, Altnoeder, and Steenberg all use a postfeminist perspective to analyze their texts and Newton and Sunderland both investigate the politics of place — this collection brings together diverse perspectives, seeking to highlight the disparate paths available within the genre of crime fiction narrative. Each chapter focuses on a different primary text, with a range of authors from different regions, ethnicities, and media. The texts span the two decades on either side of the third millennium, with some chapters addressing texts from the 1990s, some from the 2000s, and others series that span both decades. The diversity in both textual and critical perspectives allows this collection to explore more fully differing directions in crime fiction that appear at the turn of the twenty-first century. These differences that are foregrounded in the choice of texts, theoretical frameworks, and interpretive styles call more forceful attention to the similarities that appear across the pieces in this collection.

What truly comes to light across the pieces in the collection is that the real new directions in crime fiction stem from the perceived baseline assumptions about the progress of society. In perceptions of progress throughout the twentieth century — whether in terms of the rights of women, the rights of different races, the rights of the disabled, or the rights of humanity — these studies of crime reveal, through the generic underscoring of social conventions, that no quests for equality and egalitarianism have been achieved with complete success. In fact, these arguments about the new directions of crime fiction illuminate the new directions that crime takes to hide the injustices remaining at the start of the twenty-first century. Nevertheless, as these analyses suggest, the new forms of these crime fiction narratives offer a space for imagining how the future might be able to change, or at least pay attention to the ways in which it has not. As such, these new novels provide a means of encouraging the search for new ways in the twenty-first century to perfect those goals that remain unachieved at the end of the twentieth. Examining texts that focus on crime, its investigation, and its resolution, the chapters in this collection all call attention to the shifting images of criminality in a society that strives to adapt to changing legal, social, and scientific structures that dictate what constitutes what is permissible and what is criminal.

This collection examines generic shifts in the crime fiction genre as published in the last twenty years, highlighting both the changes in crime fiction in response to millennial anxieties and in response to the genre's critical coming of age. It brings together the work of international scholars on crime literature, illustrating the globalized approaches to the genre both in terms of primary and secondary material. By focusing on this specific period, this collection, while not ahistorical, breaks free from classic socio-historical approaches to crime fiction that have traditionally marked work in the field,[2] and instead provides a critical engagement with the genre in terms of its literary innovation. In considering these new directions, this collection examines the continued interest in narrating stories of crime and its resolution, which unites the crime fiction genre from its pre-twentieth-century origins to its twenty-first century manifestations. In an attempt to understand this interest, many critical arguments about crime fiction try to provide a progressive or developmental approach to the crime fiction genre throughout the twenty-first century.[3] While the chapters in this collection address the continuity at the turn of the twenty-first century established in these criteria enumerated throughout the twentieth, the experimentation illustrated in these arguments about the updated, adapted, and revised versions of Chandler's aesthetics indicates that the art of murder is becoming increasingly complex all while the basic appeal of crime fiction seems to remain so simple. The aesthetic treatments inherent in each of the primary texts considered contribute to the cultural understanding and social messages about crime and criminality as it enters the twenty-first century. This work thus follows and explains "the simple art of murder" into the complications and innovations of a new millennium.

Notes

1. The more things change, the more they remain the same.
2. Such texts include Gill Plain's *Twentieth-Century Crime Fiction* (2001), Stephen Soitos's *The Blues Detective* (1996), and Ralph E. Rodriguez's *Brown Gumshoes* (2005).
3. Examples include texts such as Howard Haycraft's *Murder for Pleasure* (1941), Julian Symons's *Bloody Murder* (1972), Stephen Knight's *Form and Ideology in Crime Fiction* (1980), and Lee Horsley's *Twentieth-Century Crime Fiction* (2005).

Works Cited

Chandler, Raymond. 1988. "The Simple Art of Murder." 1944. In *The Simple Art of Murder*, 1–18. New York: Random House.

Haycraft, Howard. 1974. *Murder for Pleasure: The Life and Times of the Detective Story*. 1941. New York: Biblio & Tannen.

Horsley, Lee. 2005. *Twentieth-Century Crime Fiction*. Oxford: Oxford University Press.

Klein, Kathleen Gregory. 1988. *The Woman Detective: Gender & Genre*. Urbana: University of Illinois Press.

Knight, Stephen. 1980. *Form and Ideology in Crime Fiction*. London: Macmillan.

Plain, Gill. 2001. *Twentieth-Century Crime Fiction: Gender, Sexuality and the Body*. Edinburgh: Edinburgh University Press.

Reddy, Maureen T. 1988. *Sisters in Crime: Feminism and the Crime Novel*. New York: Continuum.

Rodriguez, Ralph E. 2005. *Brown Gumshoes: Detective Fiction and the Search for Chicana/o Identity*. Austin: University of Texas Press.

Soitos, Stephen F. 1996. *The Blues Detective: A Study of African American Detective Fiction*. Amherst: University of Massachusetts Press.

Symons, Julian. 1985. *Bloody Murder: From the Detective Story to the Crime Novel: A History*. 1972. Harmondsworth: Penguin.

Crime Fiction and the Politics of Place: The Post-9/11 Sense of Place in Sara Paretsky and Ian Rankin

P. M. NEWTON

Critical reviews and academic studies of crime fiction recognize its powerful sense of place, a place often grounded in the authenticity of real streets and cities (Effron 2009). In fact, many crime writers and their characters have become identified with certain locales: Ian Rankin's Detective Inspector Rebus is synonymous with Edinburgh, Sara Paretsky's V.I. Warshawski with Chicago, Donna Leon's Commissario Brunetti with Venice, and James Lee Burke's Detective Dave Robicheaux with New Orleans. The existence of Rebus walking tours in Edinburgh and Inspector Morse tours in Oxford (Effron 2009, 331) might tend to support Stephen Knight's observation that some examples of crime fiction's sense of place are little more than "escapist" or "topographic fictionalization" (1995, 33–34), offering a conservative, sentimental regionalism. However, the representation of known landscapes can also be coupled with cultural anthropology to map a society at a specific place in time. Rankin and Paretsky, for example, develop a complex sense of place by entwining place with plot to such a degree that the characters and events of the narrative become inextricable from the place in which they occur.

Gary Hausladen uses the term "place-based police procedural" to define crime novels in which fiction and geography unite to create a place that is integral to plot (2000, 4). David Geherin widened the study of place from police procedural to crime fiction in general, focusing on "how setting informs a writer's fiction, and how these writers employ language to make the settings they choose come alive to the reader" (2008, 1). While Geherin's work contains a wider range of authors than Hausladen's, it concentrates on the language used to represent geographical settings rather than the integration of plot and place. Hausladen illustrates the distinction between place-based plot and place as backdrop by comparing the way Italy is used in the novels of Michael Dibdin and Donna Leon. Although Leon provides "excellent descriptions of Venice, these descriptions are not necessary plot ingredients," whereas Dibdin moves his Detective Aurelio Zen through various investigations in different regions of Italy where "location is absolutely necessary for the respective plots of each" (2000, 7). Dibdin's novels demonstrate that, for place to play a role beyond that of scenery, it needs to be entwined not only in the plot, but the plot itself needs to reveal something significant about the people, the society, and the culture of the place: the political pulse of a place.

The Politics of Place

The place-based plot identified by Hausladen occurs when place is "an essential — maybe the essential — plot element" in a narrative and "nowhere else could these kinds of murders have occurred; they are culturally and contextually specific" (2000, 4). To develop Hausladen's thesis a step further and develop a richer understanding of place in crime fiction, this chapter identifies two novels that display an essentially political sense of place. It examines the influence of culturally and contextually specific places on the writer and the way location creates a political sense of place within the novel. The terms *politics* and *political* are here used in the broadest sense of common understanding, as "the ways in which people gain, use, and lose power" and as a vehicle "for individuals to express their opinions, influence each other, and build institutions" ("Politics" 2002). This definition places politics at the heart of social and cultural activity, involving the basic operation of the power of the state, its institutions, the people who work in them and those affected by them. Crime fiction, a narrative containing some form of criminal act and its reverberations, lends itself to the political, as it interrogates and analyzes the way society operates and the struggles for power that take place within it. Murder is, essentially, the ultimate power struggle — the struggle between life and death. Murder is often the catalyst for a crime narrative, triggering the institutions of power — the police and the legal system — into an investigation where these institutions combine with economic, cultural, or social pressures and come to bear on the less powerful members of society. This motif of justice and injustice appears, for example, in the work of Dashiell Hammett's Depression-era America, Maj Sjöwall and Per Wahlöö's 1960s Sweden, and Sara Paretsky's contemporary America. By writing politics as the articulation of power in culture and society, the action of that power becomes intrinsic to both the plot and the place of a piece of fiction and renders the sense of place a political one. Developed in such a manner, place becomes more than just scenery; it is invested with agency over events and outcomes.

The politics of place requires the complex and dynamic interplay of various iterations of place. There is the political place of the author and the reader, defined as their ideological location on the political spectrum, which is engaged as they write and respond to texts. Each author and reader is a product of unique political, historical, social, and cultural features of place, a place that may not be the same place in which they now write or read. Sara Paretsky's *Blacklist* (2004) and Ian Rankin's *The Naming of the Dead* (2006) display tangible examples of the politics of place in the ways that authorial, geographical, political, and historical place and time shape the representation of the same global issue: the impact of terrorism on western liberal democracies.

A common political event resonating simultaneously across nations is rare; however, the terrorist attacks in America on September 11, 2001, were such an event. The attacks triggered joint international political responses, but prior to such action, major political choices were made at the national level. Paretsky and Rankin live in, and are products of, western liberal democracies — America and Scotland, respectively — and both writers position themselves on the progressive end of the political spectrum. While it may be expected that their books express similar political opinions, their works reveal that these political similarities remain culturally inflected and unique. *Blacklist* and *The Naming of the Dead* are examples of place-based plot in crime fiction, as the crime and the place are mutually dependent upon each other, and the politics of place appears in the way the culture and context of each location filters global events. For example, both *The Naming of the Dead* and *Blacklist* include scenes where security forces detain the chief protagonist, yet each evokes a highly specific sense of the cultural and historical politics of place. Paretsky uses the incident to have Warshawski declare her faith in the Bill of Rights, in an almost stereotypical portrait of American patriotism and pride in a nation founded on the ideal that "all men are created equal" (The National Archives and Records Adminsitration 2010). Similarly, when shadowy security forces illegally detain Rebus, Rankin's detective spends no time contemplating how the maxim of *habeas corpus* has been trampled, but immediately begins to plot (and eventually takes) violent illegal revenge on his kidnappers (Rankin 2006, 119–120). Like Warshawski, Rebus's reaction is also a seemingly stereotypical embodiment of the Scottish motto of *Wha daur meddle wi' me?*[1] However, as will be seen, Rebus has a more complex relationship with the rule of law than this incident would initially suggest.

The Plots

Paretsky's *Blacklist* is set in Chicago at a time and place defined by historical events; America is at war in Afghanistan and anticipating a second war in Iraq, the Patriot Act (Uniting And Strengthening America By Providing Appropriate Tools Required To Intercept And Obstruct Terrorism ([USA Patriot Act] Act Of 2001) has passed into law with only one senator voting against it (Feingold 2010). When Paretsky's protagonist, Warshawski, investigates the death of a journalist, Marcus Whitby, her inquiry uncovers secrets dating back to the anti-communist fervor of the McCarthy era of the 1950s. Simultaneously, Warshawski is confronted with a moral dilemma when she is asked to assist a teenage Egyptian dishwasher who is on the run from Homeland Security and who may have a family connection to extremist Islam. Warshawski experiences the reach and power of the Patriot Act as she attempts to solve Whitby's murder, protect the boy, and maintain her faith in American democracy.

Rankin's *The Naming of the Dead* takes place during the 2005 meeting of the G8 in Edinburgh. Sidelined from investigating the apparent suicide of Ben Webster, a Member of Parliament, at a G8 event, Rebus takes on an investigation that none of his colleagues care about: the serial murders of three sex offenders. Eventually these two investigations connect but the plot unfolds to pose questions not only of whodunit, but also about what constitutes the rule of law.

The Acts of Patriots

The politics of place include the personal place of the author and his or her geographical, historical and ideological place. Paretsky was a volunteer for Martin Luther King's organization during the civil rights marches of the 1960s in Chicago, and the experience shaped her personal politics of place and underpins the political philosophy espoused in *Blacklist*, namely that of progressive politics that show an awareness of the historical issue of race in America and the power of legislation to guarantee or curtail rights. *Blacklist* is an elegiac novel that captures Paretsky's "fierce nostalgia for the sixties" and for its "noblest moments" (2007, 47) when, in the face of violence on the streets, judgments were made in the courts and laws were made in the White House to end segregation. In *Writing in an Age of Silence* (2007), Paretsky recalls the political events of the summer of 1966 that "shaped the way in which I looked at the world around me" (xv). Paretsky's presence in Chicago at such an historic place and political time clearly influenced her representation of America in the aftermath of the terrorist attacks of 9/11, as she addresses the contemporary fears propelling a traumatized American society into hunting for enemies and eroding civil liberties. Paretsky correlates these fears to those that led many Americans to accept the politics of McCarthyism and segregation. In *Blacklist*, Paretsky laments the lost nobility of the Civil Rights Movement while demonstrating what seems a distinctively American sensibility given voice through Warshawski's statements of her profound love and respect for American political institutions and history. At first glance, it might appear that Warshawski is a caricatured American; however, hers is not the patriotism of "my country right or wrong." Instead, she grieves at the betrayal of the spirit of the founding fathers.

Paretsky's self-confessed "despair" with the Bush government (2007, 48) establishes her personal politics of place, which manifests in *Blacklist*, a book in which most of the heroes are either dead or disgraced. Liberal heroes are established, only to be demolished, whilst the real hero, the reporter Whitby, is discovered dead in the opening pages. Whitby is the noble and bittersweet counterpoint to the real politics of place occurring in Paretsky's world during the writing of *Blacklist*. He is characterized as a professional reporter who investigated, who checked his sources, and whose diligence in pursuing the truth ultimately cost him his life. At the time Paretsky was writing, the politics of place in America were such that those determined to implement a policy of preemptive war rested the case for war in Iraq on disputed facts and little of the investigative rigor shown by Whitby.

The contemporary politics of place in America after 9/11 provided Paretsky with a parallel to the historical politics of place of the civil rights era. Although Paretsky draws on both McCarthyism and the civil rights struggle to build the historic world of Warshawski's investigation and to provide analogies with the contemporary situation, she does not shy away from coming to grips directly with the real and specific events of post-9/11 America. The Patriot Act is a concrete example of Paretsky's thesis that the spirit of the Bill of Rights was under attack by the politics of the post-9/11 world. Paretsky notes that "[d]uring the 18 months it took me to write the book, the powers of the Patriot Act and the actions of the U.S. attorney general began frightening me almost as much as Al Qaeda" (2003). When Warshawski runs afoul of Homeland Security and is suspected of harboring a possible terrorist, the Patriot Act itself becomes an actual foe that Warshawski has to outwit. Warshawski sets up strategies, including a routine of calls at set times so that her friends will know if she is picked up and held *incommunicado*. Whilst Warshawski is no stranger to threats and violence, as in previous novels she has been beaten, burnt, and broken, there is a qualitative difference to the incidents in *Blacklist*.

In past novels, Paretsky has held various aspects of America's social and institutional structures accountable for criminal acts and the suffering of the powerless. In *Bitter Medicine* (1987), for example, the American health care system and the insurance industry are held culpable, whilst in *Tunnel Vision* (1994), suburban gentrification fueled by greed results in homelessness and the corruption of institutions. Similarly, in *Hard Time* (1999) the destructive ethos of small government is exposed through the privatization of prisons. In all of these novels, despite the corruption and debasement of certain individuals and institutions, Warshawski believes that if she can prove her case, then she may be able to hold someone accountable — culpable — before the law. However, in *Blacklist*, the law itself has been distorted, since there is no individual Warshawski can pursue, or charge, and there is no appeal against the Patriot Act, an all powerful perversion of the law. When Warshawski finally hands herself in to the authorities who have been pursuing her, she is at the mercy of a law she regards as unjust, and her response to her inquisitors expresses the politics of place that shaped Paretsky and *Blacklist*. Like Paretsky, Warshawski responds as an American liberal patriot who recognizes the power of the law to either perpetuate injustice, as in the various Jim Crow laws, or to remedy injustice, as in the Civil Rights Act.

Confronted by the power of the Patriot Act, Warshawski says, "I think this is the most serious thing that has happened in my lifetime. Not just the Trade Center, but the fear we've unleashed on ourselves since, so we can say that the Bill of Rights doesn't matter anymore" (Paretsky 2004, 248). Of all Warshawski's battles, she states this is the most serious. The politics of place operating in America at the time of Paretsky's creation of the book are on display at this point, since Warshawski's position highlights that the country is terrorized, on the brink of a second war, and Warshawski is at the mercy of a law that could see her detained indefinitely, yet it is the threat to America's most fundamental institution that is her major concern. The analogy Paretsky chooses to explain this fear is potent: Warshawski tells her interrogators that if her lover (a reporter in the field in Afghanistan) were to die her heart would break, but "if the Bill of Rights is dead my life, my faith in America, will break" (Paretsky 2004, 248). In *Blacklist*, it is not the loss of a case or a failure to solve a crime that has Warshawski contemplating a loss of faith. Here the stakes are higher: the loss of belief in America. Paretsky's twin sensibilities, her abhorrence of the crushing of civil liberties by bad laws and her ingrained faith in American institutions such as the Bill of Rights, are proclaimed through Warshawski, while Paretsky identifies the real threat to America not in terrorism but in the response to terrorism.

Warshawski's personal experience of the Patriot Act depicts the powerlessness of the individual and the sacrifice of liberties the anti-terror laws demand. The near unanimous cross-party support the Patriot Act received is a good barometer of the level of fear in America at that time (Feingold 2001). Warshawski observes that fear is "holding the horse's reins in America" (Paretsky 2004, 208), but when this fear is analysed in *Blacklist*, race not terrorism is identified as the driver. Paretsky draws direct lines between race and fear, referring to McCarthyism as an analogy of the contemporary paranoia: "'America in 1956, baby,' Amy said. 'Communist? Black? You only needed to whisper it once'" (2004, 258). Warshawski reflects on the young Egyptian she is protecting and concludes that the security agencies and police who are hunting him "don't like his race, creed or place of national origin" (2004, 215). When Whitby's death is finally confirmed as a murder, after having been dismissed by racist county police as misadventure, the journalist's sister grieves that he has succumbed to "[t]he black man's disease [...] Murder [...] It doesn't matter if you're educated and live a decent life, it's still going to get you" (Paretsky 2004, 354). Paretsky thus cites fear of the other that led to laws that enshrined discrimination, such as the anti-miscegenation laws, as leading, in the contemporary era, to laws that strip away rights. In *Blacklist*, Paretsky indicts racism and the climate of fear it instills by charting its pernicious influence through the historical and cultural politics of place in America as she draws a line from slavery to the present.

The Rule of Law

Just as Paretsky's work is the product of a specific politics of place, so too is Rankin's. The politics of place in Rankin's books involve charting his homeland, Scotland, as it devolves from England and rediscovers its national identity. Like Paretsky, Rankin has taken a public interest in politics, writing about Scottish elections for newspapers and examining the national identity of his "mongrel nation" in *Rebus's Scotland* (2005), which he describes as a "a small proud and ancient country with a confused and fragile sense of its own identity" (2005, 28–29). In *The Naming of The Dead*, Rankin explores not only Rebus's sense of national identity but also his response to an ethical challenge to his sense of justice.

When interviewed about *The Naming of the Dead*, Rankin claimed, "I think the contemporary crime novel can now take on some of the larger themes we face. With issues like 9/11 or terrorism, or racism, I think you're more likely to find some answers in good crime fiction than in any other form" (*News Wales* 2008, par. 5). The larger themes about the rule of law that Rankin takes on in *The Naming of the Dead* occur in Scotland but have global resonance. Rankin questions whether the rule of law applies universally and if revenege can be justified. He then engages with the argument by incorporating it into real events, such as the G8 and the London Tube bombings:

> [W]hen I started thinking about writing the book, I had nothing in mind like that. But because it actually happened in the real world, it had to become part

of the storyline. And I didn't want it to vicariously become part of the storyline, so I had to find a way of actually making sure that it was intrinsic to
everything that I was going to say [Hansen 2007, par. 24].

Rankin's ambition to make real events intrinsic to the narrative in *The
Naming of The Dead* exemplifies the workings of a place-based plot. This
is more than just reportage; it is the politics of place where the crime, plot,
and place are embedded into the narrative and infused politically in ways
that resonate with the moral complexity of the post–9/11 world. This complexity is established in the opening pages, where security forces have
locked down Edinburgh and Rebus tests their legitimacy and utility. However, by the end of the book, after the bombing of the London Underground and the deaths of scores of commuters, the question becomes one
of whether more, not less, power is required by the security forces to keep
the public safe, thus capturing the moral complexity of the place and
time.

Two themes become apparent early in *The Naming of the Dead*: invasion and the fragility of the rule of law. Rankin knew Rebus "would hate
other cops from outside Edinburgh trespassing on his patch" (Hansen
2007, par. 18) and develops this atmosphere of invasion through Rebus's
reactions. In so doing, this establishes Rankin's second theme, a sophisticated and subtle case for the primacy of the rule of law. The politics of
place in Edinburgh during the G8 meant that vast numbers of security
personnel came into the city, the normal rule of law was suspended, movement was constrained, and roadblocks were set up to check identities. The
operation of the rule of law and the Bill of Rights provide clear examples
of the way culture and history shape the politics of place in Rankin and
Paretsky's representation of their respective society's response to the threat
of terrorism. Whereas Paretsky can clearly identify what she asserts to be
a violation of the Bill of Rights by the Patriot Act, the legal situation in
the United Kingdom is one of Common Law rather than statue law. Common Law is a rule of law built up by court decisions, not by legal instru-
ments such as a Bill of Rights (Law and Martin 2009). Scotland operates
under a mixed judicial system based on Roman Law, Canon Law and,
since the 1707 Union with England, elements of English Common Law
(Cairns 2010). This historical, cultural, and political sense of place means
that Rankin cannot point to one specific law, as Paretsky can, and declare
it to be under threat. Instead, he demonstrates in various ways that the

rule of law is disintegrating, for instance by showing the security forces flouting the road rules and beating protesters.

The Edinburgh G8 drew numerous protesters, many of them against the 2003 invasion of Iraq, and Rankin develops this theme of invasion. The signs of Edinburgh's occupation appear early, as barriers go up. Security forces and police arrive from across the United Kingdom with "visible strength" and "[v]isors and truncheons and handcuffs; horses and dogs and patrol vans" (Rankin 2006, 24–25). At a roadblock, Rebus reacts to the invader's accents: "'This route's closed,' the man stated. English accent, maybe Lancashire" (Rankin 2006, 37). Similarly, when David Steelforth, an English government security agent, tells Rebus, "You see all this as an incursion. Edinburgh is *your* town, and you wish we'd all just sod off back home" (Rankin 2006, 41), the detective can only agree and eventually obey when the invader orders him off the case of the dead M.P., Ben Webster. Rebus reacts to the specific cultural and historical politics of place in Edinburgh, recalling the city's long history of invasion and its inhabitants' tactic of hiding: "leaving the city empty and the victory hollow" (Rankin 2006, 25). The word *hollow* recalls the place and time of writing, as "hollow" victories came to define the War on Terror: the invasion of Afghanistan had failed to locate Osama bin Laden or to establish security; invasion had failed to establish security in Iraq; and the invasion of Edinburgh by massive security forces had failed to protect London from terrorism.

While Rebus's reaction to the invaders could appear to be just the hypersensitivity of the Scottish to the English, those local politics of place are only one aspect of the G8 landscape of invasion, nationalism and the global issues. The context of these scenes highlights a wider sense of the politics of place in which the historical tension between England and Scotland metaphorically explores the international politics of the post–9/11 world. Rebus's increasing bitterness and sense of outrage invites parallels with other places and other people invaded not by politicians, protestors, and high security, but by bombs, soldiers, and "shock and awe" (Ullman and Wade 1996). When Rebus goes to the university, where the out of town police are billeted, Rankin gives a detailed description of a privileged group of outsiders, exempted from the normal rules of life and living apart from the society they have come to police:

> There wasn't a single Scottish accent in the cafeteria. Rebus saw uniforms from the Met and the London Transport Police, South Wales and Yorkshire [...] He

decided to buy a mug of tea, only to be told there was no charge [...] "You from round here then?" one of the other uniforms asked, placing Rebus's accent. "Bloody beautiful city you've got. Shame we had to mess it up a bit." His laughter was shared by his colleagues [Rankin 2006, 189].

The visiting police, who mock the local man and joke about the damage they will inflict on his city, could be read just as symbolic of the cultural resentment between Scotland and England. However, this episode lends itself to an allegory of the Green Zone of Iraq, where the coalition forces were also quartered in an artificial environment, sealed off from the place they had invaded, emerging only to patrol and control a resentful population by force.

As fellow police officers, Rebus and Siobhan Clarke ought to feel at one with the security forces, as they share a role in the exercise of power. However, Rankin provides an explicit incident to show they, too, are vulnerable when unmarked security vans on the wrong side of the road nearly collide with them:

"Welcome to the police state," Rebus added. "[...] they pulled that little stunt just because they could."
"You say 'they' as if we're not on the same side."
"Remains to be seen, Siobhan" [Rankin 2006, 100].

The choice of the phrase "police state" is deliberate and provocative, particularly coming from a policeman. The discussion of sides reinforces Rebus's suspicion that, as locals, they are not on the same side as the invaders. With this minor traffic incident, Rankin displays the abuse of power of the invaders and establishes an atmosphere of bitterness and distrust, depicting a world where the rule of law no longer seems to apply.

Rankin develops this argument for the primacy of the rule of law through Rebus's investigation into the murders of the sex offenders. The most cursory exposure to crime headlines in the media, particularly in the tabloid media, suggests that along with terrorists, sex offenders are among the great pariahs of the new millennium. Rankin's choice of such "undeserving" victims, on whose behalf Rebus pursues justice, challenges the reader in a way that Paretsky does not. *Blacklist* explores the effect of bad law on the lives of innocents, whereas *The Naming of the Dead* tackles the rights of the guilty. Rebus's pursuit of justice on behalf of the murdered sex offenders is a subtle challenge to the rationalization of lawmakers in western liberal democracies that, after 9/11, weakened various laws — such as access to legal representation — parsed the meaning of torture, endorsed the use of water-boarding to extract confessions, and flouted *habeas corpus*. By using such unsympathetic victims, namely criminals, to test Rebus's integrity, Rankin challenges western democratic legislators' post–9/11 justifications that terrorists have no rights. *The Naming of The Dead* provocatively suggests the potential extension of such legal precedents to other undesirables, such as rapists and pedophiles. However, Rankin argues for the rule of law, as he does explicitly in Rebus's conversation with Ellen Wylie, a detective who has been exacting her own personal revenge on behalf of her sister, a victim of sexual assault. Wylie has been reluctantly investigating the sex-offender case with Rebus, so the placement of their conversation is critical, as it occurs only a few hours after the terrorist bombings of the London Tube. The dead are still being brought out and counted, and the fear of terrorism is high, causing Wylie to express her doubts about the value of their work. Rebus tells her:

> "It was still the right thing to do, Ellen. Time like this, we need to feel we're doing *something*."
> "Say they were bombers instead of rapists..."
> "What's the point in that?" he asked, waiting until she'd given an answering shrug [Rankin 2006, 292–293].

Again the specific politics of place of Scotland, with rule of law rather than a Bill of Rights, means that Rebus has difficulty in articulating to Wylie why a policeman is duty-bound to investigate a crime against criminals. Unlike Warshawski, Rebus does not have a codified set of rights to point to; he has only the rule of law and his role as a policeman to guide him. The London Tube bombings are the event Rankin said he wanted to make "intrinsic to everything that I was going to say" (Hansen 2007, par. 24), so it is significant that they catalyze Rebus's defense of a rule of law that extends even to rapists and bombers. The politics of place here may be rooted in the local, but they reverberate with the wider political debates about human rights in the post–9/11 world.

The Naming of The Dead charts the disintegration of a society under invasion, as the rule of law breaks down, leaving individuals seeking their own justice and revenge. Many characters in the novel take the law into their own hands, and most of them are police. Ellen Wylie seeks justice for her sister's assault; Siobhan Clarke seeks justice for her mother's bashing at the hands of a riot squad police officer; and Stacey Webster seeks murderous justice for her mother's death. Rankin has said that this novel is about "personal responsibility [...] the difference that we think we make to the world" (Hansen 2007, par. 19). At the conclusion of *The Naming of the Dead*, Rebus has indeed had little impact on the bigger picture. Despite identifying Webster as a murderer, assisted by the security agencies, she eludes him and disappears into the chaos following the London Tube bombings.

Similarly, *Blacklist* also concludes with no optimism that justice will prevail. Marcus Whitby, a man of integrity, is murdered to preserve the reputation of an unworthy man, and the only witness is shot dead by Whitby's murderer. The killing is justified as the righteous killing of a suspected terrorist, which allows the world of the Patriot Act, not the Bill of Rights, to triumph. The final scenes of *The Naming of the Dead* are poignant as Rebus, the policeman who has upheld the rule of law and exposed the unaccountability of the security forces, finally extracts his own personal and illegal revenge on the security agent who had abducted him. Rebus's abduction echoed an "extraordinary rendition," the term given to the abduction of terrorist suspects and their illegal transfer from one state to another by security forces (American Civil Liberties Union 2005). After taking his revenge, Rebus is shown taping missing persons notices of Stacey Webster to telegraph poles in what appears a futile gesture to bring a murderer to justice.

In this coda to *The Naming of The Dead*, Rankin seems to ask a subtly different question to the usual "what if" of crime fiction. The reader is asked to contemplate the consequences of Rebus's abandonment of the rule of law and to consider, perhaps, that if one man who cares about the rule of law can respond to such events vengefully, then *what if* his rage is magnified to Iraq or Afghanistan. Though the politics of place in *The Naming of the Dead* may have their roots in Rankin's geographical, historical, and cultural place in Scotland, they also resound with the politics of the wider post–9/11 world concentrated into Edinburgh during the G8 conference.

Conclusion

For Sara Paretsky and Ian Rankin, the local is the starting point through which they see the world, as their regional representations metaphorically address politics that reflect and implicate a much wider sense of place. Paretsky's Warshawski embodies American idealism with its faith in institutions, while she simultaneously exposes the nation's specific and enduring legacy of racism. The politics of place in Paretsky's crime fiction result from the dynamic amalgamation of place, politics, history, and lived experience. The young Paretsky, who watched Martin Luther King, Jr., face riots in Chicago with only his faith in the Bill of Rights to support him, now writes crime fiction that indicts America's response to 9/11 as yet another link in the chain of American history, a history formed as much by slavery as by the founding fathers.

Writing about Edinburgh, Rankin's politics of place draws on the culture of an ancient nation that lost identity through invasion and occupation and is now in the process of rediscovering it. Yet, by depicting Edinburgh's invasion by the G8, Rankin illustrates just how fragile a civilized identity based on the rule of law can be. Rankin uses this specific moment in the post–9/11 environment to pose an essential ethical question regarding the rights of the guilty to protection of the rule of law. Posing this question in a contemporary climate of fear evokes a very specific sense of the politics of place in liberal democracies post 9/11, where legal protections and rights have been stripped from state-designated enemies by societies who have been literally terrified.

In Paretsky and Rankin, the politics of place embraces the geographical, the historical, the social, the cultural, the political, and the personal to create a place that is integrated and implicated in the narrative and events. This is not place as background; it is the politics of place, in all its iterations, permeating plot, character, and theme. These politics provide the key to that rich and powerful sense of place that characterizes contemporary crime fiction.

Notes

1. This is the motto of the Order of the Thistle, which in Latin is, *Nemo me impune lacessit*, meaning "No one attacks me with impunity" (Thornber 2009, par. 1).

Works Cited

American Civil Liberties Union. 2010. "Fact Sheet: Extraordinary Rendition." Accessed May 3, 2010. http://www.aclu.org/national-security/fact-sheet-extraordinary-rendition.
Cairns, John W. 2010. "Scottish Law." In *The New Oxford Companion to Law*, edited by

Peter Crane and Joanne Conaghan. Oxford Reference Online, Oxford University Press, 2010. Accessed September 24, 2010. http://www.oxfordreference.com/views/ENTRY. html?subview=Main&entry=t287.e1956.

The National Archives and Records Adminsitration. 2010. "Declaration of Independence." 1776. Accessed September 24, 2010. http://www.archives.gov/exhibits/charters/declara tion_transcript.html.

Effron, Malcah. 2009. "Fictional Murders in Real 'Mean Streets': Detective Narratives and Authentic Urban Geographies." *Journal of Narrative Theory* 39.3: 330–346.

Feingold, Russell. 2010. "Statement of U.S. Senator Russ Feingold On the Anti-Terrorism Bill." 2001. Accessed May 2, 2010. http://feingold.senate.gov/speeches/01/10/102501at. html.

Geherin, David. 2008. *Scene of the Crime: the Importance of Place in Crime and Mystery Fiction*. Jefferson: McFarland.

Hansen, Liane. 2007. "Author Ian Rankin Makes Crime Pay Nicely, Thanks." National Public Radio, April 22. Accessed January 6, 2008. http://www.npr.org/templates/story/ story.php?storyId=9745872.

Hausladen, Gary J. 2000. *Places for Dead Bodies*. Austin: University of Texas.

Knight, Stephen. 1995. "Regional Crime Squads: Location and Dislocation in the British Mystery." In *Peripheral Visions : Images of Nationhood in Contemporary British Fiction*, edited by Ian A. Bell. Cardiff: University of Wales Press.

Law, Jonathon, and Martin, Elizabeth A. 2009. "Common Law." In *A Dictionary of Law*, Oxford Reference Online, Oxford University Press, 2009. Accessed September 24, 2010. http://www.oxfordreference.com/views/ENTRY.html?subview=Main&entry=t49.e715.

News Wales. 2008. *Confessions of a Crime Novelist*. Accessed March 6, 2008. http://www. newswales.co.uk/?section=Culture&F=1&id=13498.

Paretsky, Sara. 1987. *Bitter Medicine*. New York: William Morrow.

_____. 1994. *Tunnel Vision*. New York: Delacorte Press.

_____. 1999. *Hard Time*. New York: Delacorte Press

_____. 2003. "For Those Who Wish To Dissent: Speech, Silence And Patriotism." *Chicago Tribune*, September 21, 2003.

_____. 2004. *Blacklist*. London: Penguin.

_____. 2007. *Writing in an Age of Silence*. London: Verso.

"Politics." 2002. In *Dictionary of the Social Sciences*, edited by Craig Calhoun. Oxford: Oxford University Press. Accessed March 12, 2010. http://www.oxfordreference.com/ views/ENTRY.html?subview=Main&entry=t86.e1042.

Rankin, Ian. 2005. *Rebus's Scotland : A Personal Journey*. London: Orion.

_____. 2006. *The Naming of the Dead*. London: Orion.

Thornber, Ian. 2009. "Scotland's Noble Thistle." *Scottish Field*. Accessed March 12, 2010. http://www.scottishfield.co.uk/article/140-Scotlands_noble_thistle.html.

Ullman, Harlan K., and James P. Wade. 2010. *Shock and Awe: Achieving Rapid Dominance*. The Command and Control Research Program, Department of Defense, 1996. Accessed April 20, 2010. http://www.dodccrp.org/files/Ullman_Shock.pdf.

U.S. House of Representatives. 2001. "Uniting And Strengthening America By Providing Appropriate Tools Required To Intercept And Obstruct Terrorism (Usa Patriot Act) Act Of 2001. Public Law 107 — 56." Accessed April 30, 2010. http://www.gpo.gov/fdsys/pkg /PLAW-107publ56/content-detail.html.

A Normal Pathology?
Patricia Cornwell's
Third-Person Novels

BY BETH HEAD

Patricia Cornwell's *Postmortem* (1990) signifies a new branch of detective fiction, as since then "forensic fiction" has become ubiquitous in contemporary culture, experiencing a staggering degree of popularity. Writers such as Kathy Reichs, Jeffrey Deaver, and Tess Gerritsen are rarely out of the best-seller list, and their narratives are strewn with scientific explanations of violence and the body. These texts appear to feed an insatiable cultural appetite for science-led crime narratives that incorporate graphic reproductions of violence. The term "forensics" has been absorbed into popular culture, manifest in films and television series such as *CSI: Crime Scene Investigation* (USA) and *Silent Witness* (UK). Patricia Cornwell is widely acknowledged to be the pioneer of this genre and the success of *Postmortem*, which won the Edgar, John Creasey, Anthony and MacAvity awards and the Prix du Roman d'Adventure in the same year, remains unsurpassed. It has generated one of the longest-running detective serials in the United States, as Cornwell has produced seventeen novels over a period of twenty years. These texts have generated wide-ranging critical debate, but the Scarpetta series is most commonly critiqued for its overtly conservative nature. I instead concentrate on the changes in narrative format in the novels published over the past five years,[1] *Predator* (2005), *Book of the Dead* (2007), *Scarpetta* (2008), and *The Scarpetta Factor* (2009). The simple shift from first-person to third-person narration has had a significant impact upon the series, allowing images of graphic violence to infiltrate the texts and altering the dynamic of these texts to a staggering degree.

36

Cornwell shifts from first-person to third-person narration in the novel *Blow Fly* (2003), so the texts, originally first-person narratives that use Scarpetta's empathic point of view to contain violence, henceforth become dialogic. These more recent texts reveal Cornwell's determined search for the origin of sadistic behavior, as a plurality of voices releases multiple forms of violent behaviors into the texts. This enables Cornwell to blur certain boundaries effectively, specifically the boundary between the normal and the pathological, which manifests in various forms. Members of the police force are often also depicted as criminals, and the scientific — and previously sanctified — process of autopsy is "abjectified"[2] in the dialogic narratives, resulting in the possible exposure of the female corpse to degradation and abuse. This blurring indicates that the origin of violent behavior remains elusive, but I suggest this is directly linked to the shifting parameters of what is deemed "normal." I further contend that the United States is presently a society wherein the structures defining "normal" are currently in a state of flux, due to necessary re-adjustments after the impact of the traumatic events of September 11, 2001.

Cornwell's first novel, *Postmortem*, exemplifies her use of a monologic first-person narrative, aptly demonstrating how the use of monologic first-person narrative contains the violence of the genre, evident throughout the first eleven Scarpetta novels. The text introduces Kay Scarpetta, the Chief Medical Examiner for the Commonwealth of Virginia. She is teamed with Pete Marino, a brash and sexist detective who resents Scarpetta's position of power, and Benton Wesley, a profiler with the Federal Bureau of Investigation (FBI), as they investigate a serial killer who brutalizes and strangles women in their bedrooms. Scarpetta attends to the bodies at the crime scene and also performs the autopsies herself, a staple aspect of "classic" Scarpetta. Using Scarpetta as narrator enables a discursive hygiene, as the autopsies and violence are played out *through* her and her commentary, effectively purifying the narrative. The primary violence, or the crimes enacted upon the victim, remain outside the narrative, or "off screen," and are reconstructed for the reader by Scarpetta. She acts as a filter, cleaning the narrative, as the following scene from *Postmortem* demonstrates:

> An uneasy silence returned as I sat at my desk trying to dictate Lori Peterson's autopsy report. For some reason, I couldn't say anything, couldn't bear to hear the words out loud. It began to dawn on me that no one should hear these words, not even Rose, my secretary. [...] Rape and murder were no longer

enough for him. It wasn't until I'd removed the ligatures from Lori Petersen's body, and was making small incisions in suspicious reddish-tinted areas of skin and palpating for broken bones that I realized what went on before she died. [...] The incisions revealed the broken blood vessels under the skin, and the patterns were consistent with her having been struck with a blunt object, such as a knee or a foot. Three ribs in a row on the left side were fractured, as were four of her fingers. There were fibers inside her mouth, mostly on her tongue, suggesting that at some point she was gagged to prevent her from screaming. [...] He must have deliberately broken her fingers one by one after she was bound. [...] I began typing the autopsy report myself [Cornwell 1990, 36–7].

Scarpetta's clinical language and reluctant monologue contain the evident brutality, and her respect for Lori Peterson is demonstrated through the act of naming her as opposed to using the term "victim." Scarpetta is compassionate, clearly abhorring the sadism her report reveals. As Scarpetta begins to type the autopsy report herself, she indicates that the crimes uncovered are only to be scrutinized and narrated from her position as a pathologist, and furthermore, a *female* pathologist. The early novels illustrate Scarpetta's mistrust of fellow *male* colleagues who may create a spectacle out of the often displayed female corpse. For example, while at the scene of Lori Petersen's murder, Scarpetta confides:

The dead are defenseless, and the violation of this woman, like the others, had only begun. I knew it would not end until Lori Petersen was turned inside out, every inch of her photographed, and all of it on display for experts, the police, attorneys, judges and members of a jury to see. There would be thoughts, remarks about her physical attributes or lack of them. There would be sophomoric jokes and cynical asides as the victim, not the killer, went on trial, every aspect of her person and the way she lived, scrutinized, judged and, in some instances, degraded [Cornwell 1990, 10].

This passage has usually been cited as a demonstration of Scarpetta's feminist sentiments, and I further suggest it illustrates how the potentially degrading thoughts of "experts, the police, attorneys, judges and members of a jury" (1990, 10) have been prevented from infiltrating the narrative, as the graphic content is merely implied by Scarpetta and not specified. These lesser secondary pathologies, those of the deviant sexualities of men in positions of authority, have been diluted by Scarpetta's hygienic monologue.

In stark contrast, writing in the third person opens the text, creating a dialogic narrative by allowing a plurality of voices to bleed together. The violence that has previously existed outside of the narrative and been retold by Scarpetta is now graphically described without her filtering consciousness. *Predator* (2005), *Book of the Dead* (2007), *Scarpetta* (2008), and *The Scarpetta Factor* (2009) enable multiple pathologies to infiltrate the texts through voices whose points of view resist and oppose Scarpetta's perspective. This narratological explosion has created an "excess," as Gill Plain explains:

> Crime fiction no longer occupies a stable position in relation to contemporary cultural desires. Where once it sought to allay the anxieties of its readership, it now seems designed only to satisfy their appetites. Crime fiction has become the pre-eminent genre of the consumer age. It is bigger, better, and comes with 25 per cent extra free. That excess is largely comprised of variously dismembered, decomposed, displayed and eroticised bodies. Contemporary crime fiction is unflinching in its confrontation of the corporeal, and its readership [...] is remorseless in its consumption of that excess [Plain 2001, 245].

Switching to third-person narration feeds the demands of the consumer. In these later novels, multiple killers provide multiple victims and the medical brutality is more explicit, with more uninhibited graphic reconstructions and recreations of the crimes. Scarpetta's point of view is thus blurred with polarized views and the narrative becomes dominated by a violent, masculine voyeurism.

In the dialogic text, vulnerable woman are collectively and perpetually threatened, and the source of this threat is often those who abuse positions of power, the experts. For example, in *Scarpetta* (2008), detective Mike Morales brazenly displays his voyeurism when positioned on a rooftop with Investigator Marino. Observing the neighboring building wherein a murder had been committed, Morales and Marino discuss the installation of a camera to capture footage of the killer should he return. However, Morales is more concerned with watching the other inhabitants:

> [Morales] indicated the apartment where the woman in green pajamas was still on her couch, gesturing and talking.
> "Amazing how many people don't pull down their shades," Morales said. [...]
> "The window to the left? Lights are off now, but maybe thirty minutes ago, blazing as bright as a movie premier, and there she was."
> Marino stared at the dark window as if it would suddenly light up again and show him what he'd missed.
> "Out of the shower, off came the towel. Nice tits, I mean real nice," Morales said. "Thought I would fall off the fucking roof. God, I love my job" [Cornwell 2008, 223].

Morales anchors his opportunistic voyeurism in his profession, and his profession enables the indulgence of his scopophilia. He thus reveals himself to be one of the "experts, the police" (1990, 10) who would degrade the victim, as Scarpetta indicated through her contained monologic discourse. In *Postmortem*, these "remarks about [women's] physical attributes" remain outside of the narrative, whereas in *Scarpetta*, a dialogic text, Morales's predatory sexuality is freely incorporated into the text. Morales performs the standard detective-killer mimesis — re-building and re-enacting the crime are typical investigative actions — but with skewed motivation. Instead of maintaining focus upon the identification and apprehension of the killer, Morales exploits the situation for his own pleasure. He manifests the erosion of binary systems that have underpinned the traditional detective genre; instead of detective *versus* criminal, Morales is detective *and* criminal. Cornwell's dialogic texts thus refuse conventional functions of the detective genre.

As critics such as Joy Palmer have previously observed, detective fiction provides a particularly useful and often reassuring arena within which to enact societal anxieties concerning issues of identity, religion, gender, violence, and sexuality. It is the role of genre, she argues, to "smooth over" these contradictions to re-establish the *status quo*.[3] Cornwell's dialogic texts, however, depict an ambiguous *status quo*, a society in which there are no certainties or security. The removal of Scarpetta as discursive protector has revealed levels of corruption in society and very few archetypal heroes. The multiple discourses of the later texts produce a string of disreputable officials, again revealing an uncertain state of normality. For example, Dr. Joe Amos, a male pathologist, is Scarpetta's polar opposite:

> [Dr. Amos] imagines [Jenny] dead. He imagines her in a pool of blood, shot dead on the floor. He imagines her naked on the steel table. One of life's fables is that dead bodies can't be sexy. Naked is naked if the person looks good and hasn't been dead long. To say a man has never had a thought about a beautiful woman who happens to be dead is a joke. Cops pin photographs on their corkboards, pictures of female victims who are exceptionally fine. Male medical examiners give lectures to cops and show them certain pictures, deliberately pick the ones they'll like. Joe has seen it. He knows what guys do [Cornwell 2005, 62].

His perspective implies that an almost necrophilic masculine desire is now laced through the text whereas before it was channeled through Scarpetta's non-sexualized gaze. Dr. Amos encourages experts, in this instance the police, to be degrading — behavior Scarpetta had previously sought to diffuse. Dr. Amos's abuse of power reveals the permeable nature of positions of trust, implicating that everyone is a suspect.

A Normal Pathology? (Head)

Martin Priestman argues that *Postmortem* (1990) signifies a shift in focus in terms of the suspect. He suggests the text "is a good example of the way in which the contemporary procedural uses classic whodunit procedures to identify a criminal who is no longer "in here" — one of a closed circle of known suspects — but "out there" — identifiable only through the gradual narrowing-down of possibilities which potentially include the whole society" (1998, 31). Cornwell's dialogic texts allow these suspects a voice, exploding the structure of classic detective fiction. Without the containing qualities of Scarpetta's monologue, Cornwell's later texts refuse a fixed narratological origin for serial killers and struggle to control what is deemed as monstrous or abject. The plurality of voices allows abject narratives to circulate unchecked within the text, which unsettles the genre on a fundamental level. The abject is that which is neither subject, nor object; it is that which repulses us, but its identification and eradication are essential for the stability of order. As Julia Kristeva explains:

> What is *abject* [...] is radically excluded and draws [Kristeva] toward the place where meaning collapses. A certain "ego" that merged with its master, a super-ego, has flatly driven it away. It lies outside, beyond the set, and does not seem to agree to the latter's rules of the game. And yet, from its place of banishment, the abject does not cease challenging its master [Kristeva 1982, 2].

To re-establish the *status quo*, detective fiction identifies and eradicates the abject, as Plain suggests:

> Crime fiction depends upon an illusion: it categorically states that death can be confronted and explained. But such a premise is impossible. [...] Crime fiction is a literature designed to contain, and celebrate 'mastery' over the abject, and it attempts this through identity, system and order" [2001, 245].

However, given the excess of dismembered bodies and necrophilic officials in Cornwell's forensic fiction, "identity, system and order" become unrecognizable, as all forms of normality are persistently destabilized. Dr. Amos's necrophilia, for example, now echoes throughout the "normal" monologic series, corrupting other scenes depicting examinations of female corpses by male doctors or investigators. The body, therefore, in almost every condition, is at risk.

Within the genre of forensic detective fiction, the body is most exposed and vulnerable during autopsy. The portrayal and performance of autopsies have always been problematic, as Elizabeth Klaver explains:

41

> We speak of autopsy as deploying a *penetrating* or *piercing* gaze [Klaver's italics], made possible by phallic instruments that expose the interior of the body for the benefit of our knowledge. Indeed, this particular *habitus* of Westerners, arguable in place since the Renaissance, toward the dead body as a sexual object has been unpacked in many interpretations of representations of the corpse [2005, 140–141].

The corpse as "a sexual object," or rather a deviant masculine desire, haunts the narratives of forensic detective fiction. Cornwell's series positions a woman as pathologist to rectify this gaze: to control and to neutralize it. As a female pathologist, Scarpetta therefore combats the implied voyeuristic autopsy and averts the assumed desire of male police officials from the victimized female body. As autopsy is the very nucleus of forensic detective fiction, there is a worrying potential for the eroticization of the corpse, as the body must be subjected to the gaze of the criminal and detective as well as displayed for the reader. Scarpetta's reluctant monologic narrative contained these images, but as the texts become dialogic, her gender alone is not enough to deflect the inherently voyeuristic nature of autopsy. Readers cannot escape the penetrating gaze even when the pathologist is a woman. Cornwell therefore must contain the generic desire to eroticize the victimized body even more so when using the third person, as the autopsy without the presence of Scarpetta, and acts of violence that resemble autopsy, are unsettling in Cornwell's dialogic texts.

Within Cornwell's series, Scarpetta's performance of autopsy is the "master" narrative, unchallenged until now. Cornwell has released the violence of autopsy by removing the presence of Scarpetta. By switching from first-person narration to third-person narration, Cornwell has enabled a sexually-fueled, masculine, arguably abject narrative to seep into the text, which radically destabilizes the genre. The two opposing narratives now exist alongside each other, reflecting what each is *not*. Consequently, each autopsy now resists a naturalistic reading, as the underlying aspects of macabre have been revealed, so previously "safe" scientific discourse is unsettled by images of brutality. Each abject autopsy implies that every medical procedure performed in this genre has a sinister, sexual undercurrent, which radically destabilizes "the norm." Forensic science becomes a battleground between generically legitimate and illegitimate discourses.

Perhaps the best example of this is found in *Book of the Dead* when Marino gives his girlfriend, Shandy Snook, a tour of the morgue. This scene is interesting for a number of reasons — not least because the entire

episode is captured on camera and watched by Scarpetta's niece, former
FBI Agent Lucy Farinelli, and Benton Wesley on their computers in separate locations — but mainly because of Marino's inappropriate state of
arousal in Scarpetta's morgue. Marino's sexual interplay with Shandy
encroaches upon Scarpetta's sanctity of procedure, as the corpse is neg-
lected. Furthermore, Lucious Meddick, an undertaker, signs the morgue
log, a legal document handled only by Scarpetta. The disruption of procedure displaces the corpse, and without the *performance* of procedure,
the morgue becomes a vulnerable space subsequently filled by Marino's
intrusive masculinity.

As Lucious delivers a corpse to the morgue, the scene is dominated
by Marino's flirtations with Shandy, rather than the actual function of the
morgue, the systematic processing of the body:

> Marino and Shandy [...] pay [Lucious] no mind as he enters the autopsy
> suite unattended. Marino wraps his huge arms around [Shandy's] waist [...]
> He slides his hands up and fondles her.
> "Good God," Lucy says in Benton's ear. "He's got a hard-on in the fucking
> morgue" [Cornwell 2007, 76].

Their behavior, offset by Lucy and Benton's vulgar commentary and the
prolonged nature of the scene, completely disrupts the text. Marino's
arousal is referred to repeatedly:

> Shandy says to Marino, "See, it's not hard being in here. Well, maybe it is."
> Reaching back, grabbing him. "You sure know how to cheer a girl up. And I
> do mean up. Whoa!"
> Benton says to Lucy, "This is unbelievable" [Cornwell 2007, 76].

Benton also "thinks [Marino and Shandy] might have sex in the hallway
[76]," and as Marino moves around "his arousal is apparent [76]" and
remains evident when he is handling the gurney carrying the cadaver. The
corpse in this scene is not a "turn off," as, rather than dampening his
arousal, the corpse and the morgue heighten the intensity of the experience.
This scene demonstrates perverse sexuality performed by the heroic male
detective, so Cornwell here indicates that there is no definitive narrative
origin for deviant sexuality, evoking a universal paranoia of sexual preda-
tion.

The problematic notion of the eroticized autopsy is a prevalent concern given the disruption of Scarpetta's clinical gaze. Cornwell contains
the assumed narrative of desire for the dead or victimized body again in

Predator when three men, namely Benton, Dr. Lonsdale, and Detective Thrush, view the autopsied body of Kristin Christian. As Dr. Lonsdale wheels the body out of the refrigerator, he comments: "'We need to make this quick [...] I'm already in deep shit with my wife. It's her birthday'" (2005, 34). The usual respect afforded the corpse is absent here; rather the absence of intense scrutiny is used to de-eroticize the viewing. Dr. Lonsdale is inattentive rather than too attentive, and the reference to his wife indicates that his desire is focused elsewhere. The men in the scene attempt to view Kristin's body as anything other than a *female* body. For example:

> "Saved the best for last," Thrush says. "What do you make of it? Reminds me of Crazy Horse."
> "You mean the Indian?" Dr. Lonsdale gives him a quizzical look as he unscrews the lid from a small glass jar filled with a clear liquid.
> "Yeah. I think he put red handprints on his horse's ass" [Cornwell 2005, 35].

Comparing Kristin to a "horse's ass" effectively de-eroticizes her, but the necessity of this neutralization emphasizes that the perceived threat of masculine voyeurism already haunts the text.

In the later novels, perverse desire is not ascribed exclusively to the othered serial killer, but instead is evident in doctors, police officials, and other officers of justice responsible for protecting society. The absence of Scarpetta's monologic clinical discourse implies that the corpse is no longer "safe." To eradicate this paranoia, investigative energy must be split to focus upon the identity of the killer and the source of the underlying pathology, as Cornwell searches for the origin of violent desire.

Forensic fiction must always return to the physical body, as it is the pivotal site of investigation. Cornwell's texts, therefore, enact a discursive contestation through questioning the intrinsic, gendered source of violence rather than the identity of the single violent perpetrator. This questioning appears from the outset of *Predator*, wherein Scarpetta vets potential patients for Benton's government-funded research project entitled PRED-ATOR (Prefrontal Determinants of Aggressive-Type Overt Responsivity). The study attempts to determine biological reasons behind compulsive violent behavior, as Benton explains:

> The reason [Basil Jenrette] is getting his brain scanned in a 3-Telsa MRI machine that has a magnetic field sixty thousand times more powerful than the earth's is to see if there is anything about his gray and white matter and how it functions that might hint at why. Benton has asked him why numerous times during their clinical interviews [Cornwell 2005, 6].

Basil is a violent, compulsive murderer who abducted women to "stab them in the eyes, keep them alive a couple days, rape them repeatedly, cut their throats, dump their bodies and then pose them to shock people" (2005, 11). Most significantly, Basil's means of abduction exemplifies the conflation of criminality and professional power; as a police officer he would "arrest" women and force them into his car. By using his recognized position of power, Basil is enabled to act out violent fantasies. As Basil represents both detective and criminal, his character again merges these two identities. He defies classification, as throughout the study he both behaves as a typical subject pleading repeatedly to see the photographs of his victims and also uses "cop jargon" (2005, 8), thus performing his identity as policeman. His identity remains split and fractured — he is neither detective nor criminal — thus the failure of the PREDATOR study reflects the text's transgression of boundaries. Basil's brain scan reveals that his body encompasses two polarized identities. Benton reveals that "so far, the structure of Basil Jenrette's brain is unremarkable except for the incidental finding of a posterior cerebella abnormality, an approximately six-millimeter cyst that might affect his balance a little, but nothing else" (2005, 7). Basil has a cyst that is "incidental" and "unremarkable"; in other words, his body falls into the category of "normal," yet his psychopathology is well documented. Basil therefore epitomizes Cornwell's blurring of normal and pathological, since both identities exist within him. The medical classification of Basil's brain as "normal" therefore reveals that "normal" is a structured and measured status and that Cornwell's search for pathology actually locates it within the "normal."

Georges Canguilhem defines "normal" as "a dynamic and polemical concept" (1989, 239). He uses the example of "man's normal weight" to illustrate that in some cases, "normal" is also that which is considered to be for our "own good" (1989, 238). For example, man's normal weight, "bearing in mind sex, age and height, is the weight 'corresponding to the greatest predictable longevity" (1989, 238).'" The "normal" therefore holds a position of reference, casting all that lies beyond its parameters in a negative light and using itself as an ultimate measure. The position of the "normal" is reified by the existence of "what does not meet the requirement it serves" (1989, 239). The "normal," then, is "at once the extension and the exhibition of the norm" (1989, 239). Normalization is not, therefore, an inert or static concept, but a process. The images of Basil's brain, for example, define a normal brain only after years of research and development and the integration of scientific norms into pedagogical institutions.

The blurring of the pathological and the normative reveals a genre and society wherein the structure of "the normal" is unstable. Cornwell's recent texts point to a society, the United States in post–9/11, where paranoia questions the state of normality. As demonstrated in Cornwell's *Book of the Dead*, Will Rambo, a soldier returning from Iraq whose already fragile psychology is deeply affected by the traumas of war, becomes a dangerous serial killer. His unpredictability is compounded by his surname, which, since Sylvester Stallone's iconic role in the film of the same name, is now a generic term for a morally lost, itinerant soldier. Will Rambo, Cornwell's soldier, becomes a threat, as instead of the country's protector, he becomes a predator. In this dialogic narrative, those in authority become risks to the *status quo*. The police, for example, are menacing, and doctors and other professionals, "experts" placed within governments, are not to be trusted. Cornwell firmly expresses that the "threat" to society is located upon American soil and exemplifies this in characters and scenarios. In *Book of the Dead*, Marino sexually assaults Scarpetta, and Dr. Self, a narcissistic woman who first appears in *Trace*, uses her influence as a therapist to persuade people to commit suicide. Furthermore, Will Rambo, Dr. Self's son, is both victim and product of an abusive environment.

In *The Scarpetta Factor*, however, Cornwell's deployment of the serial killer motif appears to respond to contemporary anxieties in a different way. Cornwell's texts reveal the real threat to be the perversion and cruelty embedded within contemporary society, not the "War on Terror." Cornwell's main concern is that, after 9/11, the government focuses on foreign terrorism rather than (re)turning their attentions towards home-grown dangers such as the serial killer. She expresses this view in *The Scarpetta Factor* through the character of Benton Wesley, who comments:

> "Law enforcement for the most part has turned its attention to other international troubles. Al Qaida, Iran, North Korea, the global economic disaster. Jean-Baptiste, the surviving child, seizes the opportunity to take over, to start his life again and do it better this time" [Cornwell 2009, 424].

Cornwell thus reintroduces Jean-Baptiste Chandonne, the "werewolf" serial killer of *Black Notice* (1999) and *The Last Precinct* (2000), who had uncharacteristically escaped. In a complete reversion of form, *The Scarpetta Factor* marks Cornwell's return to an unequivocal closed-narrative format, as, in the absence of "law enforcement," Scarpetta and her team must maintain order. Chandonne's resurrection during the aftermath of 9/11 bizarrely enables the text's unquestionable victory over him; his defeat reassures the reader that society does in fact retain some heroes. In an attempt perhaps to reduce levels of paranoia generated by mass media (including Cornwell's own work) and popular culture, Cornwell has produced a traditional detective narrative, one that attempts to alleviate the fears and anxieties of its readers through confrontation and resolution.

Historically speaking, it is unsurprising that the return to a closed-narrative format has occurred in a postwar climate, given the causal link outlined by Frederick Whiting between detective fiction, psychiatry, and postwar societal anxieties. As Whiting explains in his essay on post-war detective fiction, psychoanalytic discourse enabled the definition of the sexual psychopath, and in turn, this othered identity fueled detective narratives:

> As an aberration of the human form, the psychopath precipitated an interrogation of the period's ideas about ordinary erotic identity. And detective fiction, as one of the pre-eminent products of postwar popular culture, translated this interrogation into narratives for the public imagination [Whiting 2005, 151].

Whiting here refers to the ease with which the detective genre lends itself to the expression of emerging societal anxieties. The merging of psychoanalytical thinking and the detective genre encapsulated "a revision of popular conceptions of criminal motivation and a redrawing of what were taken to be boundaries of normal human identity" (2005, 150). These developments influenced the construct of normality as related to human identity within popular consciousness, further illustrating Canguilhem's concept of the normal.

Deviant sexualities were thus identified through their measure against the norm. Terms and labels were provided by science, for example, "psychopath," and this new concept was slowly absorbed into common lexicon. It has now become the norm to refer to any psychosexual killer who repeatedly offends as a "serial killer," but this marriage of psychoanalytical thinking and detective fiction also prompted changes within detective narratives. Whiting illustrates how the new psychoanalytical ideas were absorbed into crime narratives. The popular psychoanalytic revision, Whiting explains, "amounted to a shift in investigative emphasis from the identity of the criminal (the name of the perpetrator) to the criminal's identity (the struc-

ture of the perpetrator's desire)" (2005, 151). This is arguably the beginning
of an infinite regression in detective fiction, as the focus in investigative
emphasis continually shifts backwards over time. Early twentieth-century
crime fiction sought mainly to identify the killer, but as time has passed,
focus has shifted to the identity of the body, the cause of death, and more
recently, the motivations behind the perpetrator's actions and/or behavior.
Cornwell's search for the source of violent behavior is therefore a natural
regression, seamlessly in line with the development of crime fiction.

Furthermore, within the context of a post–9/11 world, Cornwell's
return to the serial killer parallels, albeit with a new inflection, the post-
war crime fiction's response to alterations within the American landscape
in the twentieth century. As Whiting observes, "The large-scale loss of
jobs and the rapid rise of a transient population of rootless men created
anxieties about the unattached male drifter, a figure of economic and sexual
chaos uncontained by workplace and home" (2005, 154). This figure of
the "unattached male drifter" resurfaces in the aftermath of each war to
date. For example, Sally Satel, M.D., predicted that the return of approximately 130,000 American troops from Afghanistan and Iraq in 2004 would
"renew a debate over post-traumatic stress disorder" (2004, 1). The delayed
variation of this illness, identified in the 1970s, was thought to be the root
of the problematic reintegration of American soldiers post–Vietnam.
Symptoms included "alienation, depression, an inability to concentrate,
insomnia, nightmares, restlessness, uprootedness, and impatience with
almost any job or course of study" (2004, 2). The transient population of
itinerant men therefore remains a concern in popular consciousness because
the rogue soldier, a negative image of a normal soldier, evokes the image
of a time bomb. The soldier's potentially explosive, unidentified pathology
represents the tensions simmering within an already unstable *status quo*.

Within post-9/11 thinking in the United States, Cornwell's search for
the source of pathology reveals the shifting parameters of normality. Cornwell's attempt to locate the formations of social and cultural abnormalities
has determined that to discover pathology, a concept of normal must first
be secured. However, in the current United States climate, it is arguably
impossible given the vast degree of cultural, societal, economic, and political change recently experienced. Therefore, in this text specifically and in
direct opposition to Plain's assertions that crime fiction merely satisfies the
appetites of the reader, Cornwell reverts to the traditional function of the

crime genre by seeking to alleviate the anxieties of the reader. She achieves this with the emphatic silencing of Jean-Baptiste Chandonne and by extending Scarpetta's network to incorporate heroic members of New York Fire Department's Bomb Disposal Unit who disarm an explosive device found in Scarpetta's apartment. An easy professional relationship develops, forging links between disparate agencies and demonstrating positive results of teamwork. As Martin Priestman suggests, "teamwork is the result of the influence of realism and an attempt to rectify the negative image [police procedurals] often present of society" (1998, 32). Cornwell therefore reassures the reader that normality will be regained through the depiction of a vision of harmonious camaraderie.

Notes

1. At the time of writing.
2. Defined on page 41.
3. "I argue that neither gender nor technology are stable categories of meaning, and that it is precisely the anxiety surrounding both that accounts for their overdetermined association in medical, criminal, and cultural representation. In turn [...] genre fiction takes up the cultural work of glossing and smoothing over these contradictions" (Palmer 2001, 55).

Works Cited

Canguilhem, Georges. 1989. *The Normal and the Pathological.* Translated by Carolyn R. Fawcett and Robert S. Cohen. New York: Urzone.

Cornwell, Patricia. 1990. *Postmortem.* London: Time Warner Paperbacks.

_____. 2005. *Predator.* London: Little, Brown.

_____. 2007. *Book of the Dead.* London: Little, Brown.

_____. 2008. *Scarpetta.* London: Little, Brown.

_____. 2009. *The Scarpetta Factor.* London: Little, Brown.

Klaver, Elizabeth. 2005. *Sites of Autopsy in Contemporary Culture.* New York: State University of New York Press.

Kristeva, Julia. 1982. *Powers of Horror: An Essay in Abjection.* Translated by Leon S. Roudiez. New York: Columbia University Press.

Palmer, Joy. 2001. "Tracing Bodies: Gender, Genre, and Forensic Detective Fiction." *South Central Review* 18: 54–71.

Plain, Gill. 2001. *Twentieth-Century Crime Fiction: Gender, Sexuality and the Body.* Edinburgh: Edinburgh University Press.

Priestman, Martin. 1998. *Crime Fiction: From Poe to the Present.* Plymouth: Northcote House.

Satel, Sally, M.D. 2004. "Returning from Iraq, Still Fighting Vietnam." *American Enterprise Institute for Public Policy Research (AEI).* Accessed May 28, 2010. http://www.aei.org/doc Lib/20040309_16466Satelgraphics.pdf.

Whiting, Frederick. 2005. "Bodies of Evidence: Post-War Detective Fiction and the Monstrous Origins of the Sexual Psychopath." *The Yale Journal of Criticism* 18.1: 149–178.

Inheriting the Mantle: Wallander and Daughter

BY SUSAN MASSEY

In Britain, the last decade has witnessed a boom in sales of crime fiction in translation, the appetite of readers for which seems to defy the usual Anglo apathy towards translated literature. According to figures cited by *Crime Time*, only 3 percent of United Kingdom reading matter is in translation, compared with 40 percent in Holland and Spain and 14 percent in both France and Germany (Hopkinson 2004, 37).[1] While foreign literature as a whole does not, therefore, seem to find a receptive audience in Britain, crime fiction in translation has, in recent years, carved out a successful niche for itself, spearheaded by independent publishers such as The Harvill Press. Although now part of the Random House conglomerate (but still continuing as the Harvill Secker imprint), The Harvill Press provided the impetus for the current wave of crime in translation when, in 2000, it published *Sidetracked* by the Swedish writer Henning Mankell. The text introduced Anglophone audiences to the irascible policeman hero Kurt Wallander. Already a huge commercial success in his homeland and across Europe, *Sidetracked* quickly established Mankell as major presence in the British crime market, earning its author the prestigious Crime Writer's Association Gold Dagger Award in 2001. A further seven novels followed, all set in the small coastal town of Ystad and spanning seven years in the life of Wallander, as he attempts, not just to fight crime, but also to come to terms with a rapidly changing Swedish society.[2] Together, these books have sold just under one million copies in the UK, with worldwide sales — Mankell's work has been translated into some thirty-five languages — in the region of twenty-five million (Nestingen 2008, 224). It is testament to Mankell's popularity in Britain that the BBC recently screened adaptations of six of his novels, starring Kenneth Branagh as Kurt Wallander.

In 2002, Mankell returned to Ystad with *Before the Frost.* Although marketed as "a Linda Wallander mystery" and written, principally, from the perspective of Wallander's daughter, a new recruit to the Swedish police force, the novel still includes Kurt Wallander in a prominent role. In interviews, Mankell has spoken of his intention of writing more Linda Wallander novels, but in recent years his work has focused on the AIDS epidemic in Africa, where he is now based, and on stand-alone thrillers, rather than the Wallanders. While Linda Wallander is a compelling heroine, the real significance of the text lies in how Mankell uses it to manipulate the dynamics of serial fiction, introducing a new protagonist and offering a fresh insight into an existing serial character. Although written in the third person, the original eight novels in the series employ Wallander as a focalizer, and the reader is thus forced to witness events purely from his point of view. *Before the Frost* alters this comfortable perspective, affording a chance to see Wallander from the outside, which challenges existing assumptions about the series as a whole and Wallander in particular. In this respect, the text builds upon Mankell's series-wide objective of presenting Wallander in ambivalent terms, a technique that resists any attempt to read his protagonist as a straightforwardly heroic character. Glenn Most argues that the detective in crime fiction "is himself a figure of far deeper and more authentic mystery" (1983, 343) than the crime he is investigating, and, as such, *Before the Frost* can be read as an attempt to unravel some of the mystery of Wallander's character. Because of this unraveling, a previously well-known protagonist gains depth and the series itself is given a new trajectory, with a female character moving center stage. This is not unparalleled in contemporary crime fiction. Ian Rankin, too, in his John Rebus novels, features a female investigator, Siobhan Clarke, who initially occupies little space in the narrative but gradually comes to be seen as the true inheritor of her mentor's skills and position within Scotland's Lothian and Borders' CID.[3] While Rankin, therefore, treads similar territory, he is much less successful at writing from a female perspective than Mankell. Rankin's characterization of Clarke draws heavily upon on cliché and, on occasion, Clarke is presented as little more than a version of Rebus in drag. Linda, by contrast, possesses a personality distinct from that of her father and is deftly and realistically drawn by Mankell.

Mankell's Narrative Strategies

From the outset, Mankell characterizes Kurt Wallander as a man entirely defined by his vocation. When first introduced, Wallander is Ystad's most senior police officer and, although ostensibly part of a small, efficient team, Wallander feels an intense personal responsibility to apprehend criminals himself. Wallander tends to withhold crucial information from his colleagues, even though he is aware that this reticence is "a cardinal sin for a police officer" (Mankell 1994, 28). He also benefits from a relatively flexible approach to the law he represents. For Wallander, the law is not set in stone; rather, it is something to be negotiated:

> In recent years his experiences as a police officer had taken place in a no man's land where any good he might have been able to do had always involved *his having to decide* which regulations to abide by, and which not [Mankell 1994, 238; my emphasis].

Despite — or perhaps because of— his idiosyncratic approach, Wallander is a gifted detective. Armed with a capacity for intuition that is almost preternatural and an ability to detach himself from everything except the case he is investigating, Wallander is almost always successful within the professional sphere. But, the necessary consequence of Wallander's all-consuming drive is domestic misery. In the first novel in the series, Wallander, at forty-two, has just been left by his wife, Mona. In an early instance of his characteristic emotional myopia, Wallander expresses surprise at Mona's departure, although later he concedes that he was aware of problems in the relationship but chose to ignore them, privileging instead his much more manageable work commitments over his familial responsibilities. In *The White Lioness* (1993) he ruminates:

> I devote myself to trying to catch and then put away criminals guilty of various crimes. Sometimes I succeed, often I don't. But when one of these days I pass away, I'll have failed in the biggest investigation of all. Life will still be an insolvable riddle [Mankell 1993, 94].

For Wallander, human relationships are problems of almost impossible complexity, especially when compared with his professional life, over which he has more control.

Ironically, given the insight she will later provide into him, Linda poses the biggest riddle to Wallander. Linda's attempt to kill herself when she was fifteen, combined with the divorce of her parents, opens up a gulf between father and daughter. Thus, in the first few novels of the series, Linda, at this point in her early twenties, is a minor character, occupying a peripheral space in the narrative. Wallander clearly longs for contact with his daughter but is baffled as to how to approach her. Instead of reaching out, he remains passive, waiting for her to communicate with him. When Linda is mentioned in these early texts, she is usually referred to simply as "Wallander's daughter." By choosing not to use her first name, Mankell confines Linda to the role of emotional baggage for her father, rather than a character in her own right.

By contrast, Wallander is on surer ground within the professional sphere. The frequently isolated nature of police work, with its emphasis on analytical thought, calms Wallander, affording him an opportunity to exercise control in at least one area of his life. For example, in *Faceless Killers* (1991), "Wallander felt a great sense of security in th[e] methodical and meticulous scrutiny of details" (Mankell 1991, 220). With his obsessive interest in his work, his repeated failure to form and sustain relationships with actual people — Wallander's closest companion in the series is his dead mentor, Rydberg — and his inability to express his own emotional needs, coupled with his lack of sensitivity to those of others, Wallander comes across as a figure who could register on the autistic spectrum.[4] Although perceptive about criminal behavior, Wallander seems relatively impervious to anything that falls outside the professional arena, and the novels are replete with examples of him conspicuously failing to read emotional and social situations correctly. Autism is frequently characterized by lack of awareness of reality, and given that Wallander displays this autistic tendency, his reliability as a series focalizer becomes questionable. While the device of an unreliable narrator is not without precedent in crime fiction — see, for instance, Agatha Christie's *The Murder of Roger Ackroyd* (1926) — Mankell bases an entire series upon the perspective of a man whose judgment becomes increasingly questionable. Not only does this strategy reflect how Mankell pushes the boundaries of the form, but also the ambiguity at the heart of Wallander's construction renders him a complex character about whom the reader can never quite be sure.

Mankell subtly hints at Wallander's lack of perspicacity throughout the series with a few incidents that suggest his protagonist's judgment might not be completely reliable. The most telling of these involves Wallander's junior officer, Martinsson. In *Firewall* (1998), Wallander is shocked to discover that Martinsson, far from being a loyal foot soldier and potential protégé figure, is actually "going after the throne" (Mankell 1998, 383), by conspiring against Wallander in a bid to succeed him. Wallander himself does not actually notice Martinsson's duplicity but has to have it spelt out to him by another member of the Ystad police force, Ann-Britt Höglund. An exasperated Höglund, seemingly seeking to protect Wallander from Martinsson's scheming, tells him, "Sometimes you really surprise me [...] You see and hear everything. You're a great policeman and you know how to keep your investigative team motivated. But at the same time it's as if you see nothing that's going on around you" (Mankell 1998, 382). Höglund seems to have a point: to Wallander, Martinsson's act of betrayal is almost impossible to believe, despite his obvious desire for professional advancement, and Wallander's ignorance here seems almost self-deceptive. Once again displaying behavior suggestive of autism, Wallander exhibits an almost unshakeable trust in Martinsson and reacts like a child when this trust is abused. Martinsson, young, ambitious, and at home with the technological side of modern policing in a way that Wallander is emphatically not, seems an all too obvious threat. Yet when Wallander does consider who amongst his colleagues might be after his position, he suspects Ove Hansson, the station's inveterate gambler and a man who cannot handle any form of responsibility.

Mankell uses several other occasions throughout the series to suggest that Wallander's judgment may not always be shrewd. In the novels, Wallander frequently makes pessimistic pronouncements on the state of contemporary Sweden. Yet, the texts suggest the astute reader should not necessarily take Wallander's word at face value. Upon returning from Latvia in *The Dogs of Riga* (1992), Wallander refers to his own lack of awareness regarding the situation in the former Soviet Union:

> He knew that he was not the kind of man who consciously surrounded himself with lies, but he had begun to ask himself whether his ignorance of what the world actually looked like was in itself a sort of lie, even though it was founded in naivety rather than a conscious effort to cut himself off [Mankell 1992, 321].

These lines suggest Wallander suffers from damaging tunnel vision and an important issue raises its head: if Wallander is genuinely ignorant of "what the world actually looked like," how can the reader trust his assessments of Sweden? Just as Wallander's perception is undercut, Mankell frequently places his protagonist into situations in which he literally cannot see. As Andrew Nestingen has observed, "Fog figures prominently as a symbol throughout the series" (2008, 237) and is regularly used by Mankell to obscure Wallander's vision (Mankell 1999, 238). Given this, and the insularity suggested in the quotation above, it seems reasonable to question the clarity of Wallander's wider vision.

From this perspective, other small inconsistencies appear in the texts. Although Wallander constantly strives to understand the world in which he lives, he appears hopelessly out of touch with the *zeitgeist*. Even as a young man, in the short story "Wallander's First Case," surrounded by long-haired hippies and peace protesters in 1969, the neatly-presented and straight-laced Wallander can only think of his career with the police. In *Before the Frost*, Wallander says, by way of reaction to the killing of Birgitta Medberg: "I can't see that you'd get murdered for knocking on the wrong door" (Mankell 2002, 118). Yet, this is exactly what happened in one of his earlier cases. In *The White Lioness*, the estate agent Louise Åkerblom becomes lost and stops at a house occupied by the killer Anatoli Konovalenko to ask for directions — "I can always knock, she thought. That doesn't cost anything" (Mankell 1993, 8) — and Konovalenko shoots her in the head.

While Mankell has admitted to the presence of textual discrepancies throughout the series (Mankell 1999, 1), it is impossible to know when and where these mistakes are deliberate and are supposed to be on the part of Wallander rather than his creator. However, since Mankell deploys various strategies to undercut his leading man, his work clearly indicates a degree of intentionality. Just as the reader is invited to doubt Wallander through the interjections of Höglund and Linda, Mankell himself occasionally mocks Wallander. In *The Dogs of Riga*, for example, Wallander is lost when attempting to negotiate an investigative procedure without a handy piece of advice from his dead mentor, Rydberg: "He ransacked his memory to try to recall any words of wisdom from Rydberg about the difficulties of tailing people, but was forced to conclude he had not expressed any views on the art of shadowing" (Mankell 1992, 169). Here, Mankell exposes Wallander's co-dependence on his deceased colleague for dry comic effect.

Mankell further undercuts his leading man by introducing an air of almost comic ineptitude to his characterization. Without impinging upon his professional credentials, Mankell makes Wallander into something of a walking disaster. Not only is he accident-prone, regularly showering himself with scalding beverages and foodstuffs (Mankell 1994, 66; 1998, 207), but also he is the kind of man who forgets to bring his wallet when he eventually finds time to go to the supermarket (Mankell 1998; 327). By subtly undercutting Wallander's judgment, seriousness, and vision, Mankell presents him as a relatively un-heroic hero. Wallander is not a super-cop, and his occasional tendency to read a situation incorrectly emphasizes that he is flawed and fallible. However, once Mankell starts to question Wallander, it is difficult to decide where to stop.

Linda Wallander and a New Direction?

Wallander's fallibility as a focalizer is, however, thrown into sharpest relief when his daughter, Linda, moves to the center of the narrative. At the conclusion of *Firewall*, Linda announces her intention to become a police officer to her somewhat amazed father, and the surprise with which Wallander greets the news again calls his observational powers into question, given that Linda's career choice is hinted at as early as *The Fifth Woman* (Mankell 1996, 138, 223). Despite his shock, Wallander is enthusiastic, telling her, "I think you'll be just the kind of police officer we're going to need in the future" (Mankell 1998, 533). As well as feeling pleased, Wallander also experiences a sense of personal vindication at Linda's news, interpreting her decision to follow in his footsteps as an endorsement of his own choice of career. Whereas in the past his job has kept him from his family, work now unites him with his daughter.

Where father and daughter immediately diverge, however, is in their attitude to Ann-Britt Höglund. Höglund makes her first appearance in *The Man Who Smiled* (1994). Introduced as "an usually promising police officer" (Mankell 1994, 45), Höglund's youth and talent immediately ruffle the feathers of Ystad's male detectives. Wallander is initially uncomfortable with Höglund's attempts to cast him as a mentor figure, yet he slowly warms to the role and realizes that he, too, can learn from Höglund. He immediately benefits from discussing casework with someone capable of offering a fresh perspective, and his confidence in Höglund legitimizes her presence on the team. The two gradually develop a close rapport. Though Wallander struggles to form relationships, after working with Höglund for three years, he is cautiously optimistic that she might be "on her way to becoming his new partner" (Mankell 1997, 137). Höglund seems to have attained this position by *Before the Frost*, in which Linda Wallander notes with distaste that Höglund is always at her father's side (Mankell 2002, 105).

Seeing Wallander and Höglund through Linda's eyes offers a fresh perspective both on Höglund's character and on her relationship with Wallander. In the novel, Wallander seems heavily reliant upon Höglund, specifically requesting her presence at a crime scene (Mankell 2002, 120), while Höglund appears confident and self-assured, untroubled by the antipathy that characterizes her interaction with Linda. At one point, Linda suggests that things between Höglund and her father were once more than platonic: "I still wonder what my father saw in you when he courted you a few years ago" (Mankell 2002, 239). This internal thought offers a tantalizing glimpse of a relationship Mankell otherwise chooses not to detail, although, in *The Man Who Smiled*, Wallander does note that Höglund is attractive (Mankell 1994, 87, 173). Mankell similarly chooses not to explain the origins of Höglund and Linda's obvious mutual dislike. The two barely speak in *Before the Frost*, as Höglund tends to ignore Linda's presence (Mankell 2002, 166, 260), and Linda takes refuge in a series of (unspoken) bitchy observations about Höglund's weight and heavy make-up (Mankell 2002, 120, 239). Linda is clearly jealous of the closeness between Höglund and her father, which supports the idea that they may at one time have been romantically involved.

While Linda's dislike of Höglund may owe something to jealousy, it also seems to be motivated by a desire to protect her father. Rather than accepting Höglund as her father's confidante, Linda sees Höglund as a cunning manipulator who is herself looking forward to Wallander's retirement, hopeful that she might succeed him. In light of Linda's suspicions, Höglund's behavior in *Firewall*, when she alerts Wallander to Martinsson's treachery, can be re-examined and understood as Höglund working to her own advantage, rather than Wallander's. With typical guilelessness, Wallander never actually sees Höglund as a specific danger to his leadership, and in this respect, he perhaps underestimates her. In *Firewall*, Höglund exacerbates the tension between the two men by reporting Martinsson's derogatory comments to Wallander. While Mankell does not choose to discuss any possible agenda behind Höglund's behavior other than loyalty to her boss, the incident can be interpreted less generously if we accept Linda's assessment of Höglund. Höglund has the ear and confidence of both men; arguably, she benefits most from the disintegration of their relationship. By the end of the novel, Martinsson is isolated from Wallander and, by *Before the Frost*, Höglund has become Wallander's right-hand woman.

However, before accepting the veracity of Linda's viewpoint, we should consider if she is any more reliable than her father. Mankell's depiction of Linda suggests that she possesses an emotional well-roundedness that her father conspicuously lacks, and her (painful) awareness that Wallander prioritized work over his family implies that she is unlikely to make the same mistake of over-investing in her job at the expense of everything else in her life. As Linda states in *Before the Frost*, "I don't want to be like Dad, who can never find the right house and the right dog and the wife he needs" (Mankell 2002, 134). Unlike Wallander, Linda seems aware both of her own personal needs and also the importance of fulfilling them.

Linda also seems to have a more realistic outlook than her father. The Sweden that appears in Mankell's fiction is not the socially enlightened idyll of popular European (mis)conception, but is instead a country that seems to be teetering precariously on the edge of anarchy. Throughout the series, Sweden is variously shown to be a territory ripe for exploitation by criminals from the former Soviet Union, a center for international terrorist conspiracies, a country with an enormous immigration problem and a resulting escalation in racism and right-wing militias. This is in addition to home-grown serial killers and psychopaths. In Mankell's Sweden, crime is almost endemic, and Wallander is a law enforcement officer in an increasingly lawless society. As a result, Wallander frequently eulogizes the Sweden of the past as "a lost paradise" (Mankell 1991, 232)" and seems to hold similarly idealized notions about policing when he was a younger officer (Mankell 1991, 135 and 1993, 33). Martinsson, too, is convinced that times have changed for the worse and that Sweden is in inexorable decline. However, when Linda joins the force in *Before the Frost*, she gives short shrift to this kind of rose-tinted sentimentality:

> She had never heard of a positive "state of affairs," there was invariably something to lament. A shipment of sub-standard uniforms, detrimental changes in patrol cars or radio systems, a rise in crime statistics, poor recruitment levels and so on. In fact, this continuing discussion of the "state of affairs," of how

this era was different from the era before, seemed to be central to life on the force [Mankell 2002, 37].

As Linda observes, constant complaining seems to be a key component of being a police officer.

Linda, thus, possesses a clear-sightedness that her father lacks, and, of the two Wallanders, she is the more mature and balanced. Following Wallander's breakdown in *The Man Who Smiled*, Linda provides the curative female company he desperately seeks, restoring her father's mental and physical health. As occurs frequently through the series, it here appears that the roles of parent and child have been reversed, since Linda provides a stable source of unconditional love and support for her troubled and emotionally needy father. Wallander displays an almost childlike enthusiasm when Linda contacts him, which she notes and appreciates, telling him, "That's the best thing about you [...] you're always so glad to see me" (Mankell 1995, 142). Wallander sleeps better when Linda stays with him in his flat (Mankell 1992, 225, 267), and she also energizes him: "He was rested, his fatigue was gone and his thoughts rose easily and soared on the updraughts inside him" (Mankell 1995, 270). Wallander only seems to abandon his characteristic dour pessimism when near Linda, and her physical presence in *The White Lioness* makes him feel secure (Mankell 1993, 200).

While there are benefits to the Wallanders' closeness, Mankell suggests that there are negative consequences to such intense emotional reliance on one's children. Because of his dependence upon Linda, Wallander is devastated when she returns to her normal life after visiting Ystad. After putting her on a train back to Stockholm, Wallander's mood immediately deteriorates: "The station seemed terribly desolate. For a moment he felt like someone who was lost or abandoned, utterly powerless. He wondered how he could go on" (Mankell, 1996 226). Linda is also aware of the possible dangers of being stifled by her father's affections:

> Linda wondered if following in his footsteps and becoming a police officer was going to be the greatest mistake of her life. Why did I do it? she asked herself. He's going to crush me with all the kindness, understanding and love — even jealousy — he should really be giving to another woman and not to his own daughter [Mankell 2002, 223].

The relationship between father and daughter here takes on an almost incestuous intensity that is born of the fact that Linda is the only outlet

Wallander has for his emotions. Wallander experiences "a pinch of irritation and jealousy" (Mankell 1998, 53) at the thought of Linda with a boyfriend, which implies unhealthy undertones in his interaction with his daughter. This is matched by Linda's jealousy of Höglund.

While Wallander finds it uncomfortable to consider his daughter's romantic interactions, Linda frequently contemplates the kind of woman who may be a suitable partner for her father, although her resentment of Höglund indicates that she might prefer to speculate about an ideal partner, rather than deal with a genuine competitor for her father's affections. As Linda is represented as being more mature than her father, she seems to have a better idea about what Wallander needs than he himself does. Although Wallander has little or no insight into his daughter's private life, he acknowledges, "she sees right through me [...] I'm an open book" (Mankell 1998, 52). While Linda provides reassurance and security for her father, he is, by contrast, a source of concern for her. Linda frequently worries about her father's loneliness (Mankell 2002, 17, 106), to the extent that she berates him for his non-existent sex life (Mankell 2002, 228). From Linda's perspective, the Wallander of *Before the Frost* seems quite a different character from that depicted in the earlier novels. Linda ruminates on her father, thinking:

> I used to look on him only as a big friendly man who was not too sharp, but stubborn and with pretty good intuition about the world. I've always thought he was a good policeman. But now I suspect he's much more sentimental than he appears, that he takes pleasure in the little romantic coincidences of everyday life and hates the incomprehensible and brutal reality he confronts through his work [Mankell 2002, 83].

The idea of Wallander as "a big friendly man who was not too sharp" contradicts Mankell's earlier portrayal of his protagonist as an intelligent, yet socially-awkward figure. By using Linda's perspective, Mankell can draw out aspects of Wallander's character that were oblique. Hence, although the reader is already aware of how Wallander dwells on the memory of the deceased, such as his mentor Rydberg and several criminals he would have arrested had they not died, Mankell develops this sense of attachment further when Wallander shows Linda his "cemetery," an area of forest in which Wallander has assigned trees in memory of those no longer living (Mankell 2002, 72). Linda's presence in the narrative, therefore, emphasizes both Wallander's emotional vulnerability and his sentimentality.

Although Linda is more expressive and self-aware than her father, the two Wallanders have much in common. These shared characteristics suggest that Linda, like her father, will be a talented detective, but the differences between them also indicate that she will be more skilled at establishing a balance between her work and her private life. Even from Linda's early infrequent appearances, Mankell emphasizes the parallels that exist between father and daughter. In *The Dogs of Riga*:

> It dawned on him [Wallander] that Linda was very much like her father. He couldn't put his finger on it, but he had the feeling he could hear his own voice as he listened to her. History was repeating itself: he recognised his own complicated relationship with his father echoed in his conversation with his daughter [Mankell 1992, 104].

Although this is a perceptive comment, Wallander is wrong to see his relationship with Linda as an echo of that between him and his father's. Wallander's father never approved of his son's decision to join the police and, as a result, their relationship throughout the series is tempestuous. Wallander, by contrast, endorses Linda's career choice, and Linda's character is marked by variations from the pattern established by Wallander.

In *Before the Frost*, Linda's similarities with her father become most striking. In terms of temperament, the two are so alike that living together quickly becomes a strain. Following one particularly intense confrontation, Linda tells a friend, "My father and I are like two fighting cocks" (Mankell 2002, 220). It quickly becomes apparent that the two are evenly matched. When Wallander disparagingly compares Linda's presence to "having a ball constantly bouncing up and down by my side," Linda sharply retorts, "At least I can still bounce. More than some people I know" (Mankell 2002, 258–59). Both Wallanders are irritable and impatient, and both demonstrate a propensity towards violence. When her father makes her cry, a frustrated Linda throws an ashtray at him, hitting him on the head and drawing blood (Mankell 2002, 344). Throughout the series, Wallander's own domestic violence toward his ex-wife Mona is rendered ambiguous. Both *Faceless Killers* and *Sidetracked* imply that, while Wallander may have harbored violent feelings during his marriage, he did not act on them. However, in *The Fifth Woman*, Wallander admits to having struck Mona, causing her to fall and hit her head on the doorframe (Mankell 1996, 193). Here, context is crucial, as *The Fifth Woman* examines unpunished male aggression. It features a serial killer, Yvonne Ander, who establishes herself as judge, jury, and executioner towards men who have abused their partners. It therefore seems fitting that Mankell would choose this novel in which to reveal more about Wallander's own marital violence. Ander targets "respectable" men whose domestic violence is at odds with their public image. By thus linking the detective with the criminals, the text underlines the pervasiveness of male violence.

Linda also takes after her father in other, less negative ways. At the conclusion of *Firewall*, a novel in which the issue of Wallander's heir is addressed, Linda announces that she intends to join the police. Her timing suggests that, despite Martinsson's intrigues and the steady progression of Höglund, Linda will assume Wallander's spiritual mantle once he retires. In *Before the Frost*, Linda, the newly qualified cadet, displays many of the attributes that have made her father such a success. Like Wallander, Linda has a keenly developed intuition (Mankell 2002, 71, 301), and she shares his sharp powers of observation (Mankell 2002, 150). She also demonstrates a disregard for proper procedure, breaking and entering on two separate occasions, and a tendency to be too self-reliant. At three points during the novel she puts herself in danger by acting alone (Mankell 2002, 183, 216, 346), much to her father's chagrin. Linda admires her father's ability to handle information (Mankell 2002, 261), and she, too, seems to possess this gift of being able to unpack the often complicated details of a case. Employing a phrase that could equally be applied to her father, Mankell writes, "Linda picked up her story with both hands and unfolded it as carefully as she was able; all in the right order" (2002, 121). Like Wallander, Linda is able to focus closely on the minutiae of an investigation, but Mankell's choice of words also suggests a possessiveness over information that indicates Linda may share an element of her father's tendency towards obsession.

Linda inherits many of her father's personality traits, but rather than just straightforwardly replicating self-destructive behaviors, she is characterized by a Butlerian sense of possibility. In *Gender Trouble* (1990), Judith Butler argues that gender is a performance that people are individually compelled to repeat. Butler states that "all signification takes place within the orbit of a compulsion to repeat; 'agency,' then, is to be located within the possibility of a variation on that repetition" (1990, 185). Within this framework, Linda's potential is clear, for rather than offering a male successor who simply replicates Wallander's damaging example, Mankell eschews masculinity, turning instead to a female inheritor, whose variations in reiterative practice offer a space for "reconfiguration and redeployment" (Butler 1990, 185).

Conclusion

With his technique of delayed disclosure, Mankell is able to draw the reader in, gradually revealing more about his leading character and under-cutting any sense of certainty. He further maintains ambiguity in his texts by offering two viewpoints that sometimes conflict. Although Linda may seem like the more reliable witness, her version of events and opinion of characters are not definitive, and there are no guarantees that she herself will not be undermined if Mankell ever returns to Ystad. In addition to muddying the water, Linda's perspective softens and humanizes her father, as it emphasizes Wallander's vulnerability. This corresponds with the way in which the other novels in the series constantly question Wallander's heroic stature. Wallander is brave and cowardly, sympathetically drawn and yet still capable, on occasion, of alienating readers. Although he excels at his job and privileges it above everything else, he remains wracked by professional insecurity. A highly intuitive and emotional policeman, Wal-lander is manifestly unable to deal with the complexities of his personal life, repeatedly failing to articulate his needs and desires. Wallander's char-acter, therefore, is full of inconsistencies and contradictions. Glenn Most has stated that "detective stories are, for many readers, installments in the fragmentary biographies of their heroes, each displaying his familiar virtues under a new and surprising light" (1983, 345). *Before the Frost* achieves this. Slavoj Žižek has noted the potential implicit in Mankell's use of Linda:

> This appears to be something new in the history of detective fiction: a series of novels that take place in the same locale, but in which the principal investiga-tor, the focus of the reader's identification, shifts from father to daughter, then to another colleague [Stefan Lindman in *The Return of the Dancing Master*]. The effect is again that of parallax: the perspective shifts, and in being deprived of a single point of view, the reader gains a whole family, a collective identification bound together by a dual sense of vulnerability and solidarity [2003, 24].

Žižek's words recall how Mankell works against generic norms in his novels. He deprives his audience of easy certainties and, by doing so, destabilizes masculine authority in his texts. Against the semi-apocalyptic backdrop that Mankell presents, it seems appropriate that the position of Wallander as focalizer and, thus, guiding presence, should be compromised. Mankell's novels map out new ground for series fiction, which has the capacity to evolve into something unexpected and potentially radical.

Notes

1. In the United States, consumption of translated fiction is on par with that of the United Kingdom. The University of Rochester's online resource page for international literature states that only 3 percent of fiction published in the United States every year is translated. According to the website Publishing Perspectives, 85 percent of this translated material is published by small, independent presses, who lack the financial resources necessary to market their stock aggressively. Although Mankell is published in America by Vintage, part of the Random House group, his sales, while respectable, have not achieved the same kind of market dominance he has realized in Europe.

2. In chronological order, the series includes *Faceless Killers, The Dogs of Riga, The White Lioness, The Man Who Smiled, Sidetracked, The Fifth Woman, One Step Behind* and *Firewall*. The novels were published non-sequentially by Harvill, who also published the short story collection *The Pyramid*, which charts Wallander's early career, in 2008, although it originally appeared in Sweden in 1999.

3. Carefully groomed by Rebus, and possessing many of his "unique" talents, Clarke succeeds where male protégé figures, such as Brian Holmes, fail. The last few Rebus novels feature Siobhan prominently, and when Rebus is pensioned off in *Exit Music* (2007), the way seems clear for Siobhan to move into the leading role. Rankin has spoken of his desire to return to the character of Siobhan Clarke, although since publishing *Exit Music* he has moved away from serial fiction, perhaps wary of committing to a single protagonist following twenty years of John Rebus.

4. It is not my intention to medically diagnose Wallander. He is a fictional character and Mankell makes no explicit reference to autism or any other psychological impairment in the texts. Whether he is autistic or not is outside the scope of this essay, which merely intends to suggest that Wallander displays behavior that could register on a wide autistic spectrum

Works Cited

"About Three Percent." The University of Rochester. Accessed June 16, 2010. http://www.rochester.edu/College/translation/threepercent/index.php?s=about.

Butler, Judith. 1990. *Gender Trouble: Feminism and the Subversion of Identity*. London: Routledge.

Chernaik, Warren, Martin Swales, and Robert Vilain, eds. 2000. *The Art of Detective Fiction*. Basingstoke: Macmillan.

Christie, Agatha. 1926. *The Murder of Roger Ackroyd*. London: HarperCollins.

Hopkinson, Amanda. 2004. "Niche No Longer." *Crime Time* 37: 36–38.

Mankell, Henning. 1991. *Faceless Killers*. Translated by Steven T. Murray. 2000. London: The Harvill Press.

_____. 1992. *The Dogs of Riga*. Translated by Laurie Thompson. 2002. London: Vintage, 1992.

_____. 1993. *The White Lioness*. Translated by Laurie Thompson. 2002. London: The Harvill Press.

_____. 1995. *Sidetracked*. Translated by Steven T. Murray. 2000. London: The Harvill Press.

_____. 1996. *The Fifth Woman*. Translated by Steven T. Murray. 2001. London: The Harvill Press.

_____. 1997. *One Step Behind*. Translated by Ebba Segerberg. 2002. London: The Harvill Press.

_____. 1998. *Firewall*. Translated by Ebba Segerberg. 2003. London: Vintage.

_____. 1999. *The Pyramid: The Kurt Wallander Stories*. Translated by Ebba Segerberg and Laurie Thompson. 2008. London: Harvill Secker.

_____. 2000. *The Return of the Dancing Master*. Translated by Laurie Thompson. 2003. London: The Harvill Press.

_____. 2002. *Before the Frost*. Translated by Ebba Segerberg. 2004. London: The Harvill Press.

Most, Glenn W. 1983. 'The Hippocratic Smile: John le Carré and the Traditions of the Detective Novel." In *The Poetics of Murder: Detective Fiction and Literary Theory*, edited by Glenn W. Most and William W. Stowe. New York: Harcourt, Brace, Jovanovich.

Most, Glenn W., and William W. Stowe, eds. 1983. *The Poetics of Murder: Detective Fiction and Literary Theory*. New York: Harcourt, Brace, Jovanovich.

Nestingen, Andrew. 2008. *Crime and Fantasy in Scandinavia: Fiction, Film, and Social Change*. Seattle: University of Washington Press.

Priestman, Martin. 2000. "Sherlock's Children: the Birth of the Series." In *The Art of Detective Fiction*, edited by Warren Chernaik, Martin Swales and Robert Vilain. Basingstoke: Macmillan.

Rankin, Ian. 2007. *Exit Music*. London: Orion, 2007.

"Want More Rights Deals and Translations? Try Taking Editors and Publishers Overseas." Accessed June 16, 2010. Publishing Perspectives. http://publishingperspectives.com/?p=1 6157.

Žižek, Slavoj. 2003. "Parallax." *London Review of Books*, November 20.

"A Visitor for the Dead": Adam Dalgliesh as a Serial Detective

BY SABINE VANACKER

> Reading a series involves a special relationship between reader and writer which the reader has made a conscious decision to sustain. It is an advanced kind of play; the rules are slightly different, and the pleasures are acknowledged and savoured.... [F]iction can provide a complex variety of profoundly private pleasures, and [...] these pleasures are repeatable and entirely within the reader's control [Watson 2000, 1].

The Pleasures of the Series Reader

In his discussion of series reading, Victor Watson emphasizes readerly pleasure and reader activity. Readers of a series, he underlines, make an active choice to continue with a specific narrative context, a specific group of characters, and a specific plot type. While Watson's comments concern the series reading of children and young adults, he immediately points out that this readerly pleasure — this "advanced kind of play" — is a narrative attitude we carry with us for the rest of our lives. The prevalence of the series format is a typical feature of crime fiction, too. Although infrequently discussed by critics, it plays a central role in reader experience and in the audience's engagement with the genre. In her introduction to a collection on the first novels of various detective series, Mary-Jean DeMarr is categorical about its importance: "The appeal of mystery series is indisputable" (1995, 1). As William Crisman emphasized, the "father" of detective fiction, Edgar Allan Poe, chose to center his three canonic tales of ratiocination on the same returning series character, Chevalier Auguste Dupin (1995).

Arthur Conan Doyle's huge popular appeal, likewise, is attributed to a canny narrative strategy, the introduction of returning series characters Sherlock Holmes and Dr. Watson. P. D. James's series detective, the policeman Adam Dalgliesh, constitutes a similar enduring contract — forty-eight years so far — with the reader. He is a constant figure whose characterization is fundamental to the prolonged appeal of the series and to its enduring atmosphere and mood. As the central character, Dalgliesh has added a particular modality — measured, introspective, and coolly contemplative — to James's representation of murder and violence.

Inevitably, commercial value is of prime importance in the creation of a series, more specifically the marketing opportunities delivered by the series formula to both publisher and author. A reader who stumbles on a series novel and likes it typically goes back to the beginning of the series and reads the novels in chronological order. Consequently, sales of an author's backlist can make a considerable commercial impact. In their brief discussion of this topic, Priscilla Walton and Manina Jones emphasize that the series has a "self-sustaining function, since the backlist of a reputable author's previously published work in a continuing series promise[s] consistent, cumulative sales" (1999, 26). Publishers consequently see good market sense in promoting series:

> For producers, the advantage of serialization is that it essentially creates the demand it then feeds: the desire to find out "what happens next" can only be satisfied by buying, listening to, or viewing the next installment. And ... methods of maximizing serial profits have been progressively refined as industrial capitalism developed [Danielsson 2002, 142].

Equally important, moreover, is a very specific type of reading behavior. As Watson reminds us, when starting a new non-series novel, readers frequently experience "wariness," "a degree of watchfulness," and a "cautious reconnoitring curiosity" as they sense their way into the plot and assess new, untested characters (2000, 1). The detective series, on the other hand, promises a comfortable return to a community of well-known friends and to recognizable places and situations. Martin Priestman has similarly pointed to "the unique, personal interest drama of the individual episode and the reassuring repetition of the continuum" (2000, 57). As a result, series reading is, as Watson says, "always conscious and always deliberate" (2000, 1): nobody reads a series of ten or fifteen books by accident. John Fiske tellingly highlights that series readers treat the novels as a resource

(1991, 106). Indeed, series reading can be pleasurable not in the least because of the sense of control that the readers can thus exercise over their engagement with the author's fictional world.

The P. D. James Brand

The continued success of a series is also dependent on the author's ability to establish a *brand*, a recognizable set of features that characterize "the James novel" for the reader. As Walton and Jones put it, "The serial form generates a relationship of trust and identification between the reader and both the series protagonist *and* her author" (1999, 55). Danielsson links this form of "community building" with the growth in "special interest" crime fiction (lesbian, gay, feminist, academic, historical), where readers include or exclude themselves on the basis of an interest in a certain set of themes or a shared ideological perspective (2002, 16). As a result, the readers commit, emotionally and intellectually, both to a series character and to the atmosphere, themes and mood of the series. Here, Scott McCracken suggests, the reader's complicity with the underlying ideological implications of the series is essential (1998, 101).

A small selection of reviews and articles on James's work quickly demonstrates the clarity with which readers, reviewers, and interviewers recognize the James brand. A number of features emerge clearly, helping to establish how James's writing is perceived and what characteristics are considered to be typical of her formula. Many critics and reviewers, for instance, note the gothic flavor of her novels. They comment on the set-piece mansions and country houses, now no longer home to upper-class families but to institutions, such as the publishing house that resides uneasily within a patrician, Thames-side mansion in *Original Sin* (1994). Similarly, in her review of *The Murder Room* (2003), Nicola Upson refers to the many working communities featured in her fiction, the nurse training schools, private nursing homes, barristers' chambers, forensic laboratories, schools and seminaries: "Fascinated by institutions — churches, hospitals, publishing houses and now museums — she evokes the tensions and alliances that underpin tight-knit communities" (2003). Critics comment positively on James's evocation of her settings, her treatment of nature, and on the many descriptions of churches and historical homes: "Her writing on architecture is exceptional, and *The Murder Room* is enriched by descriptions of London's parks and churches" (Upson 2003), and these remarks are supported by Mark Lawson's perceptive characterization of James's "passion for classical architecture" (2003).

However, as discussed more extensively by critics such as Susan Rowland (2002) and David Schmid (2000), some reviewers also note a more persistent dynamic in James's fiction between an engagement with modernity and an inherent conservatism that limits this modernization. Thus, Peter Guttridge highlights "a wonderfully, comfortingly old-fashioned and narrow world peopled mostly by posh traditionalists" (2003), and Mark Lawson comments more extensively on the same tension: "*The Murder Room* finds James moving towards a final position on a subject that has dominated her novels: conservatism. The attitude behind James's writing is fundamentally Christian and Tory, although these allegiances are gently expressed" (2003). At the same time, he notes that this novel "proves to be a surprisingly modern book, or at least one that is arguing with modernity" (2003). James's many references to topical events — from political correctness and nuclear power in *Devices and Desires* (1989) to plastic surgery and civil partnerships in *The Private Patient* (2008) — maintain a background state of the nation argument that many readers, especially those of a more conservative frame of mind, may find appealing.

As a more central feature, reviewers regularly acclaim James's project of enhancing the classical tradition by merging the detective story with the literary novel. Thus, Lawson affirms that James's locations "echo the settings of the classic British whodunnits [sic], and her life's mission has been to reclaim that genre for serious writing" (2003). Reviewers focus on the novels' style and the quality of the writing, her leisurely, careful descriptions, and the many literary references. For instance, emphasizing the literary qualities of *Death in Holy Orders*, Roy Hattersley highlights a possible contradiction between the narrative speed of the thriller and the more measured approach of the literary novel:

> A thriller it is not, nor is *Death in Holy Orders* intended to justify that description. It proceeds at a pace appropriate to the speed of life at St Anselm's, the Anglican theological college at which most of the plot — "action" being quite the wrong word — is set. But P D James is able to meander with a sense of urgency. [...] Not once, as I read the description of Father Martin's bedroom, the paraphrase of Archdeacon Crampton's homily or any of the other vignettes of clerical life, did I think, "For God's sake, get on with it!" This is a novel of time and place as well as a detective story [2001].

Similar sentiments appear regularly: "James's books largely succeed as a bridge between the murder mystery genre and literature" (Shreve 2003). In the same way, John Harrison evokes an author trying to rise above the genre format: "P. D. James is a career gymnast, entertaining us with her inventive mastery of that limiting apparatus, the classic English mystery novel" (2008, 10). In these comments, the reviewers appear keen to maintain the binarism of two incongruous literary blocks in their continued separation of the "popular" and the "literary." In James's case, they frequently invoke her transformative powers, turning the base metal of genre fiction into the alchemist gold of the literary novel. This crossover status appears to be important to James's perception by readers, critics, and publishers alike, regarding her as a practitioner of genre fiction and simultaneously as a literary novelist transcending the perceived restrictions of the genre.

"A Visitor for the Dead"

An equal part of our enjoyment of a series is what Umberto Eco calls "redundant information" (1979, 118). There are, for instance, the much-loved and much-repeated eccentricities of many detectives. Agatha Christie persistently reminds us of Hercule Poirot's fussiness and franglais or of Miss Marple's knitting and her woolly, apologetic speech. Sara Paretsky regularly invokes her feminist detective's love for red high-heeled shoes and the tragic past of her dead mother. The reader expects these features to return in every story, as "their reappearance is an essential condition of its reading pleasure (1979, 118):"

> The reader continuously recovers, point by point, what he already knows, what he wants to know again: that is why he has purchased the book. He derives pleasure from the non-story ... in a withdrawal from the tension of past-present-future to the focus on an *instant*, which is loved because it is recurrent [1979, 119–120].

As readers of series fiction, we have "a hunger for redundance" (1979, 120). Although Adam Dalgliesh does not have any outstanding physical features, a number of redundant facts about this detective are repeated in almost every novel: his rectory childhood, his melodramatic past with the loss in childbirth of a wife and son, his essential duality as both a policeman and a poet, his professional eminence, and the speed of his investigations.

In fact, James's first novel *Cover Her Face* (1962) presents a composite picture of Dalgliesh that will remain his core personality:

> Five pairs of eyes swung simultaneously to the taller stranger in fear, appraisal or frank curiosity.
> Catherine Bowers thought, "Tall, dark and handsome. Not what I expected. Quite an interesting face really."
> Stephen Maxie thought, "Supercilious-looking devil. He's taken his time coming. I suppose the idea is to soften us up. Or else he's been snooping round the house. This is the end of privacy."
> Felix Hearne thought, "Well, here it comes. Adam Dalgliesh, I've heard of him. Ruthless, unorthodox, working always against time. I suppose he has his own private compulsions. At least they've thought us adversaries worthy of the best."
> Eleanor Maxie thought, "Where have I seen that head before? Of course. That Dürer. In Munich was it? Portrait of an Unknown Man. Why does one always expect police officers to wear bowlers and raincoats?" [...]
> When he spoke it was in a curiously deep voice, relaxed and unemphatic [2005, 59].

Here, in a nutshell, is the Dalgliesh mystique, typically focalized through the eyes of observers, suspects, or his own staff. In this passage, James uses Conan Doyle's strategy of outside narration, creating a heroic image for her detective through the eyes of others, with the different witnesses fusing their impression of Dalgliesh with their own expectations and worries. The resulting composite picture is contradictory and paradoxical. Lonely, romantic Catherine Bowers sees the detective as heroic, tall, dark and handsome; the surgeon Stephen Maxie on the other hand notes his arrogance. The serene murderer of the story, Eleanor Maxie, sees an intriguing enigma, a man with a painterly, sublime face significantly reminding her of Dürer's portrait of an *unknown* man. Felix Hearne links Dalgliesh with his war-time experiences of Nazi torture, emphasizing danger, ruthlessness, and an absence of mercy. This is Dalgliesh, the adversary and agent of authority and oppression. But contradictorily, and for a series reader tantalizingly, we can see, through Hearne's eyes, a potentially fraught and agonized man "with his own private compulsions." The net result of these contrasting perspectives is a character whose final definition and characterization is withheld and whose personality is subtly moveable and changeable. The riddle of Dalgliesh keeps the reader hooked with a set of characteristics suggestive of a more psychologically rounded and changeable character and open to future narrative possibilities.

James still maintains this representation of her detective in her recent novel, *The Private Patient,* where she constructs a similar opposition between the troubled witnesses and suspects and the disquieting presence of the detective: "All their eyes turned to him [the owner of the house], although Benton was aware that their thoughts were with the tall dark-haired man on his right. It was he who dominated the room" (2008, 161). Moreover, even Benton, Dalgliesh's subordinate, still reflects on the mystery of Dalgliesh: "He thought, *I wish I knew who you are.* But that was part of the fascination of this job. He served a boss who remained an enigma to him, and always would" (2008, 205; original emphasis).

Within this representation of the central detective, however, a certain dynamic is at work throughout the Adam Dalgliesh series, a tension that encompasses many of the other characters. Inevitably, the mood and the psychology of the detective feature largely in the readers' attachment to a series. Upon his arrival in *The Black Tower* (1985), Adam Dalgliesh is announced as "[a] visitor for the dead" (46), a description that immediately suggests a dark, elegiac quality. As Bernard Benstock points out, while the reader has no clear image of the physical Dalgliesh, his mindset and his mood stay with us: "Interestingly enough, Adam Dalgliesh is almost unrecognisable *except* for his inner feelings" (1982, 112; original emphasis). He is at once "pragmatic and austere" (1982, 115), reticent and self-sufficient to the point of paranoia, characterized by melancholia, and nostalgia for his youth. He always appears considering corpses, suspects, and murderers with a gloomy detachment. The perpetual present of the series novel involves the constant reiteration of this redundant information, so Dalgliesh is always-already bereaved, particularly with the repetition of the deaths of his wife and child in each novel. In the end, the reader continuously hopes, Dalgliesh's will be a comforting life story and that nothing too terrible will happen to him because of what already has.

Similarly, the suspects and witnesses introduced are often equally introspective, reticent, and unhappy. They are often failed or failing human beings, such as Dr. Kerrison, the pathologist in *Death of an Expert Witness* (1977) and Dr. Staveley in *The Lighthouse* (2005), both doctors who have fled their profession after the death of a child. They reflect on being imperfect parents for their unhappy children, on their loneliness and enforced self-sufficiency as single, aging men and women (*A Taste for Death* [1986]), on their creaking marriages (*A Certain Justice* [1997]), or on their lack of efficiency and confidence in the modern world (*The Private Patient*). James's revision of the classical detective novel effectively dispenses with the comedic mode of the Golden Age detective novel and resituates the action in an altogether gloomier universe.

So why do the readers undertake a prolonged identification with this muted and moody series detective, surely a masochistic enterprise? As Benstock remarks, "Diagnosing the trouble with Dalgliesh is no easy matter" (1982, 115). Above all, Dalgliesh and the many other suffering, stoic characters represent a central comforting model, the Jamesian ideal of discipline and self-control. John Harrison discusses this feature extensively: "The themes — of privacy, modesty and self-control — are present and correct, recognisably Jamesian" (2008, 10). Likewise, the supporting series characters in these novels are equally thoughtful, equable, cautious, and wary of giving offence or embarrassment: his lover Emma Lavenham, the police officer Kate Miskin, and especially Dalgliesh's redoubtable aunt Jane Dalgliesh, who is a monument to emotional self-sufficiency.

Linked with this internal discipline, Dalgliesh also demonstrates the Foucauldian "totalizing social control" that Priestman has identified in Sherlock Holmes (2000, 54), and this characteristic, too, is a central feature of the detective. When he takes on a case, Dalgliesh considers the people in the case "his" suspects (2005, 189). When the detective, his fingerprint specialists, photographers, and interviewers descend on the Steen clinic in *A Mind to Murder* (1963), the staff feel caught up in "the inexorable machinery of justice and being ground forward to God knew what embarrassments and disasters" (2005_d, 23). Unlike Holmes's scientific positivism, rationalism, and scopophiliac surveillance, Dalgliesh's mastery mainly focuses on his consummate skill as an interviewer. His patient, probing questions are a consistent feature, as is his superior ability to read the witnesses, as in *A Mind to Murder*: "And so it went on: the patient questioning, the meticulous taking of notes, the close watch of suspects' eyes and hands for the revealing flicker of fear, the tensed reaction to an unwelcome change of emphasis" (2005_d, 80).

In *The Lighthouse*, there are numerous similar examples of Dalgliesh's finely tuned sensitivity to the involuntary responses of his interviewees. Repeatedly, he notes minute changes in the reactions of his witnesses: "Dalgliesh sensed a small tremor of unease" (2005_c, 180); "Dalgliesh could sense a change, subtle but unmistakable, in the tenor of the questions and in their response" (2005_c, 205);" "And now he sensed a change, subtle but

73

unmistakable, in Dr Speidel's response" (2005, 225). In the same novel, he becomes aware of the distraction of one of the suspects: "But it seemed to Dalgliesh that there was no link between those familiar actions and her thoughts" (2005$_c$, 293). A little later, he catches another barely noticeable response: "He thought he detected the quick look of relief" (2005$_c$, 295)." Elsewhere, his receptiveness as an interviewer tells him to hold back: "Instinct told him the moment was not propitious" (2005$_c$, 226). Likewise, his inferiors comment on his endless reserves of patience when he senses a suspect needs more time: "Kate knew that Dalgliesh could be patient when patience could best get results" (2005$_c$, 179).

Such moments illustrate that Dalgliesh has such supreme skills of observation in common with Sherlock Holmes, but James's work does not display the triumphant optimism evoked in Conan Doyle's writings. Unlike the late-Victorian fictional universe, the world of Dalgliesh cannot be easily set to rights. As P. D. James reiterates repeatedly, both the murder and the police investigation permanently disrupt and infect the societies she describes. For instance, in *A Certain Justice*, Dalgliesh considers the effect on the house of a murder victim: "If this were murder the house would never escape its contamination, but it would be felt less here than in those desecrated Chambers of the Middle Temple. More had been lost there than a friend or colleague" (James 1997, 343). Frequently, it seems, the appearance of Dalgliesh at a crime scene has all the joy and optimism of the arrival of an undertaker, called in to pick up the pieces while striving to be as tactful and discreet as possible.

The Enduring Detective

In his discussion of television series, Glen Creeber has considered the peculiar relationship of television audiences with the characters in long-running television series. He suggests that the time duration of long-form drama brings an extra dimension to characterization and character psychology that is beyond the scope of single films or novels. Creeber's claims about television apply to the Dalgliesh series, as what readers remember about Dalgliesh, the redundant information, turns them into initiated readers. Equally important, moreover, is what readers forget: as we dip into the Dalgliesh novels over the four decades of the series, we develop an illusion of continuity, of "character density" (2004, 5). While maintaining Dalgliesh's core personality, James has over the years subtly altered minor features of her detective. For instance, the Dalgliesh we encounter at the start of the series is more irritable and has a more troubled relationship with his subordinates. Additionally, over time, he sheds the sexist comments of the earlier novels. In *The Private Patient*, conversely, the detective notes with mild surprise that he has come to like Victorian genre painting (2008, 317). However, Dalgliesh's status as a character of long duration prevents us from seeing these minor changes as inconsistent. He resembles his readers, and his creator, in the sense that he appears to have slowly changed and aged over the decades, thus suggesting that he is a richer, "biographical," fully rounded character in a manner uncommon in other fictional characters. Moreover, Dalgliesh and his officers exist in opposition to the characters in the individual crime novels. James effectively inserts characters with "temporal progression" (Eco 1979, 116) and psychological development into classical novels that typically celebrate discrete, snapshot, and temporal elements: the order is disrupted, the disruption is investigated, and the order is restored. As a result, amid the more limited characterization of the crime plot characters — the suspects, the victim, the criminal — the series detective and his entourage become more colorful and more resonant. Dalgliesh has a different status to Felix Hearne, Stephen, and Eleanor Maxie in *Cover Her Face*. Their lives "freeze" once the novel is over; for Dalgliesh, we expect, "life" continues.

In this way, James follows a trend in contemporary crime fiction also noted by Karin Danielsson (2002), whereby features of both the "series" and the "serial" are combined. A typical series, on television for instance, will return the same central characters in each installment, operating in the same or similar settings for a number of discrete episodes rounded off with their own individual conclusion. As such, the individual episodes can be broadcast in any order "without losing narrative coherence" (Creeber 2004, 8). James's Adam Dalgliesh novels mostly fall into this category. They can be read in any order, with reader satisfaction depending on narrative closure within the confines of the individual novels and the discrete crime detection plots. The serial, on the other hand, typically forms "a continuous story set over a number of episodes that usually comes to a conclusion in the final installment (even if a sequel follows)" (Creeber 2004, 8). Consequently, the serial is characterized by a narrative arc that goes beyond the discrete crime and detection plots of the separate book installments, "a distinct narrative trajectory over a number of limited episodes" (9). Over the decades, and more clearly in the most recent novels, James has increasingly moved towards this hybrid structure, linking her individual crime novels together by a more explicit, overarching narrative that spans all the novels. Typically, the later novels will refer to events in earlier installments, while the detectives themselves age, rise in their professional careers, and, in some cases, become progressively disenchanted with policing and detection.

The plot of James's novel *The Black Tower*, for instance, structurally highlights this serial arc by using the detective's life to frame the detection plot (1985). The novel opens and closes with Adam Dalgliesh in hospital. In the first chapter, he is recovering from a potentially lethal disease, and more seriously, from the perspective of the series reader at least, he has decided to quit his profession. In the final pages of the novel, now wounded because of the case and returned to hospital, a disoriented Dalgliesh assumes that he never left. By this stage, moreover, the readers have been reassured that the detective, and his series, will continue.

Where classical detective fiction continually performed the disruption and recreation of order, in many modern crime fiction series, this ritual re-enactment of ordering is no longer the sole function of the crime novel. Adam Dalgliesh and his entourage of junior detectives, exist, to borrow Danielsson's phrase, "in a world which goes on between books, a world in which actions in book number one have an effect in books number two and three" (2002, 13). In this way, the reader of this hybrid, the series with serial features, simultaneously experiences a pleasurable sense of closure — the resolution of the crime plot — and a renewed awareness of narrative openness and promise — the assurance of further cases, a prolonged life for their protagonists, and the promise of further novels to come.

Likewise, *A Taste for Death* features Dalgliesh's younger colleagues, John Massingham and Kate Miskin, both maintaining an uneasy balance between work and family and both hindered by the emotional and physical needs of elderly parents and relatives (2005$_b$). Kate's emotional struggles with her impoverished and unhappy childhood feature prominently in this novel, and the subplot developed around the detectives' personal lives threatens to overwhelm interest in the search for the criminal. At the end of this novel, too, Kate's continuation as a longstanding series character has been ensured.

More recently, starting from *Death in Holy Orders*, James has been developing an ongoing, if sedate, love life for her detective, with the introduction of Emma Lavenham as Dalgliesh's love interest (2003). The discovery of a burning corpse in *The Murder Room* interrupts a romantic date between them, with a Hollywood-style ending as Dalgliesh races back to London to declare his love. The promise of an engagement duly follows in *The Lighthouse* (2005) and, disconcertingly, *The Private Patient* features a meeting with Emma's father and a dignified, if uneasy, request for her hand in marriage (2008, 110). Their wedding, in the final pages of the novel, ominously suggests the denouement of the serial narrative arc and indeed the potential closure of the series. It may possibly indicate that, like Dorothy L. Sayers before her, James is domesticating her detective in the end, giving him a typically feminine ending with marriage.

Like Sayers, James marries her detective off to another advanced reader, a Cambridge academic rather than an Oxford-trained author. But where Sayers' marital ending was triumphant with feminist spinster Harriet Vane donning "cloth of gold" for her wedding (Sayers 1974, 11), Dalgliesh's marriage makes distinctly uncomfortable reading. Both Harriet and Emma fuss around their respective husband's sensitive psyches, but Dalgliesh's marriage causes a certain diminishment, forcing him to set up house and undermining the perception of his power. "An Inspector Palls," as M. John Harrison's review of *The Private Patient* calls it, and he suggests that the narrative urgency of the romantic ending is more vivid and memorable than the crime and detection plot of this novel:

> For most of the novel you wish someone would murder the lot of them. Then, at the very end, with the crime almost solved and the unsolveability of human beings confirmed, something strange happens. Baroness James, one of Europe's most distinguished mystery novelists, renews her interest in her own book. Scenes and characters leap into focus, dialogue livens, and a weirdly affectionate final act plays itself out. Lovers are united [Harrison 2008].

This "renewed interest" highlights the shift in interest in the series from Dalgliesh's series function as a "the Great Policeman" (Dove 1982, 9) to his serial life as a man.

Significantly, the novel in which Dalgliesh marries contains intimations of narrative closure for both series and detective. To a certain extent it feels indulgent, as if James is providing a romantic ending for a character whose "glorious isolation" had previously been a core feature. Indeed, as with the feminine marriage ending for the nineteenth-century heroine in Rachel Blau DuPlessis' famous book title, there are a number of suggestions that the author may not write "beyond the ending" (1985). While the romantic lives of two detectives and two suspects are neatly tied up, the novel avoids a definitive and conclusive closure of the detection plot. The murderer in this novel not only escapes Dalgliesh's arresting grip — this has occurred in earlier novels contributing to James's realism — but there are also strong suggestions that one potential culprit is allowed to benefit from the crime. In the closing chapters, Dalgliesh visits a frail, elderly solicitor who effectively absolves him from further efforts:

> Commander, there is nothing you can do and nothing you need to do. This will could only have been challenged by Robin Boyton, and Boyton is dead. Neither you nor the Metropolitan Police have any *locus standi* in this matter. You have your confession. You have your murderess. The case is closed. The money was bequeathed to the two people who had the best right to it [2008, 369].

More seriously, *The Private Patient* increasingly accrues a certain elegiac quality with several suggestions that this may be Dalgliesh's final case. Early on, Kate Miskin speculates on her own future with the growing rumors that Dalgliesh may retire or be promoted out of the force. The body of Rhoda Gradwyn, moreover, feels summative of all the corpses previously viewed by the detective: "This was not the most horrific corpse he had seen in his years as a detective, but now it seemed to hold a career's accumulation of pity, anger and impotence. He thought, *Perhaps I've had enough of murder*" (2008, 138; original emphasis). Towards the end of the novel, Dalgliesh again ruefully considers a potential *fin de carrière*: "This one might well be his last" (2008, 360). Indeed, the detective's love affair and imminent marriage feel inimical to his detection. This is emphasized several times, with both Dalgliesh and Kate Miskin considering that Dalgliesh's life with Emma must remain separate from his cases: "Hadn't his job been ring-fenced with an invisible sign, *Keep out?*" (2008, 306; original emphasis). Also during the Gradwyn investigation, he regards Emma as "distanced by the complicated emotions and unexpressed inhibitions which kept them apart when he was on a case" (2008, 309). When Emma does appear in the middle of the case, upset by her friend's assault and rape, she is clearly transgressing an unspoken rule. In a slightly awkward scene, she quickly agrees that she should not intervene and allows herself to be ushered away. Finally, unlike

Sayers' joyful wedding scene, the wedding ceremony here is understated, shown only indirectly, from the perspective of Emma's two friends Annie and Clare reflecting back on the wedding service.

P. D. James may very well decide to continue the Dalgliesh series beyond *The Private Patient*; undoubtedly there is scope for further narrative development. Her crime fiction series has had a long-lasting appeal in its fluctuation between redundancy and narrative innovation and between an engagement with modernity and a more conservative world view. Taking part in this advanced play for grown-ups, the reader has enjoyed a continuing relationship with the series and the "brand" — its typical and expected themes, mood, atmosphere, and detective — vacillating pleasurably between narrative openness and closure. Always existing in the present and yet enduring over time, James's detective is a visitor for the dead who tries to contain and control the living and whose utopian presence, with its promise of cool introspection, measured rationality, self-control, and discipline, forms a central part of the reader's pleasure.

Works Cited

Benstock, Bernard. 1982. "The Clinical World of P. D. James." In *Twentieth-Century Women Novelists*, edited by Thomas Staley, 104–129. Totowa: Barnes & Noble.

Danielsson, Karin Molander. 2002. *The Dynamic Detective: Special Interest and Seriality in Contemporary Detective Series*. Acta Universitatis Upsaliensis, Studia Anglistica Upsaliensia (AUUSAU): 121. Uppsala: Uppsala University.

Dove, George N. 1982. *The Police Procedural*. Bowling Green: Popular Press.

Campbell, Sue Ellen. 1995. "The Detective Heroine and the Death of Her Hero: Dorothy L. Sayers to P. D. James." In *Feminism in Women's Detective Fiction,* edited by Glenwood Irons, 12–28. Toronto: University of Toronto Press.

Creeber, Glen. 2004. *Serial Television: Big Drama on the Small Screen*. London: BFI.

Crisman, William. 1995. "Poe's Dupin as Professional, the Dupin Stories as Serial Text." *Studies in American Fiction* 23.2: 215–29.

Du Plessis, Rachel Blau. 1985. *Writing Beyond the Ending: Narrative Strategies of Twentieth-Century Women Writers*. Bloomington: Indiana University Press.

Eco, Umberto. 1979. *The Role of the Reader: Explorations in the Semiotics of Texts*. Bloomington: Indiana University Press.

Fiske, John. 1991. "Popular Discrimination." In *Modernity and Mass Culture*, edited by James Naremore and Patrick Brantlinger, 103–117. Bloomington: Indiana University Press.

France, Louise. 2008. "Dastardly Deeds among the Dahlias? Call for Dalgliesh." Review of *The Private Patient*, by P. D. James. *The Observer*, September 7, 22. http://www.guardian.co.uk/books/2008/sep/07/crime1.

Guttridge, Peter. 2003. "Gosh, This is Posh. Even the Cleaning Lady's Called Tallulah." Review of *The Murder Room*, by P. D. James. *The Observer*, June 29. http://www.guardian.co.uk/books/2003/jun/29/crimebooks.features/print.

Harrison, M. John. 2008. "An Inspector Palls." Review of *The Private Patient*, by P. D.

James. *The Guardian*, August 30, 10. http://www.guardian.co.uk/books/2008/aug/30/fiction1.

Hattersley, Roy. 2001. "Clerical Terrors." Review of *Death in Holy Orders*, by P. D. James. *The Guardian*, March 10. http://www.guardian.co.uk/books/2001/mar/10/fiction.crimebooks/print.

James, P.D. 1985 (1975). *The Black Tower*. London: Sphere Books.

_____. 1986 (1977). *Death of an Expert Witness*. London: Sphere Books.

_____.1989. *Devices and Desires*. London: Faber and Faber.

_____.1995 (1994). *Original Sin*. London: Penguin.

_____.1998 (1997). *A Certain Justice*. London: Penguin.

_____.2003 (2001). *Death in Holy Orders*. London: Faber and Faber.

_____.2004 (2003). *The Murder Room*. London: Faber and Faber.

_____.2005$_a$ (1962). *Cover her Face*. London: Faber and Faber.

_____.2005$_b$ (1986). *A Taste for Death*. London: Faber and Faber.

_____.2005$_c$. *The Lighthouse*. London: Penguin.

_____.2005$_d$ (1963). *A Mind to Murder*. London: Sphere Books.

_____.2008. *The Private Patient*. London: Faber and Faber.

Kotker, Joan G. 1995. "P. D. James's Adam Dalgliesh Series." In *In the Beginning: First Novels in Mystery Series*, edited by Mary Jean DeMarr, 139–153. Bowling Green: Popular Press.

Lawson, Mark. 2003. "Bricks and Slaughter." Review of *The Murder Room*, by P. D. James. *The Guardian*, July 5. http://www.guardian.co.uk/books/2003/jul/05/crime.pdjames/print.

Marg B. 2007. "The Readaholic Review of Shroud for a Nightingale." Last modified June 28. Accessed September 18, 2008. http://thereadaholic.blogspot.com/2007/06/shroud-for-nightingale-p-d-james.html.

Maslin, Janet. 2003. "Foul Play Even as the Teakettle Humms." Review of *The Murder Room*, by P. D. James. *The Times*, December 2, E7. http://www.nytimes.com/2003/12/02/books/books-of-the-times-foul-play-even-as-the-teakettle-hums.html.

McCracken, Scott. 1998. *Pulp: Reading Popular Fiction*. Manchester: Manchester University Press.

Nixon, Nicola. 1995. "Gray Areas: P. D. James's Unsuiting of Cordelia." In *Feminism in Women's Detective Fiction,* edited by Glenwood Irons, 29–45. Toronto: University of Toronto Press.

O'Conner, Patricia T. 2003. "Grisly Picture from an Institution." Review of *The Murder Room*, by P. D. James. *New York Times*, December 7, 743. http://www.nytimes.com/2003/12/07/books/grisly-pictures-from-an-institution.html.

Priestman, Martin. 2000. "Sherlock's Children: The Birth of the Series." *In The Art of Detective Fiction*, edited by Warren Chernaik, Martin Swales, and Robert Vilain, 50–59. Basingstoke: Macmillan, St. Martin's with Institute of English Studies, School of Advanced Study, University of London.

Priestman, Martin. 2002. "P. D. James and the Distinguished Thing." In *On Modern British Fiction*, edited by Zachary Leader, 234–57. Oxford: Oxford University Press.

Rowland, Susan. 2002. "The Horror of Modernity and the Utopian Sublime: Gothic Villainy in P. D. James and Ruth Rendell." *In The Devil Himself: Villainy in Detective Fiction and Film*, edited by Stacy Gillis and Philippa Gates, 135–146. Westport: Greenwood.

Sayers, Dorothy L. 1974 (1937). *Busman's Honeymoon*. London: New English Library.

Schmid, David. 2000. "The Locus of Disruption: Serial Murder and Generic Conventions in Detective Fiction." In *The Art of Detective Fiction*, edited By Warren Chernaik, Martin Swales and Robert Vilain, 75–89. Basingstoke: Macmillan; St. Martin's, with Institute of English Studies, School of Advanced Study, University of London.

Shreve, Anita. 2003. "Murder, times 3." Review of *The Murder Room*, by P. D. James. *The Boston Globe*, November 30. http://www.boston.com/ae/books/articles/2003/11/30/murder_times_3/.

Siebenheller, Norma. 1981. *P. D. James*. New York: Frederick Ungar.

Soloski, Alexis. 2003. "Paper Clips." Review of *The Murder Room*, by P. D. James. *The Village Voice*, December 16. http://www.villagevoice.com/2003-12-16/books/paper-clips/1.

Upson, Nicola. 2003. "Behind the Scenes at the Museum." Review of *The Murder Room*, by P. D. James. *New Statesman*, July 28. http://www.newstatesman.com/200307280033.

Walton, Priscilla L., and Manina Jones. 1999. *Detective Agency: Women Rewriting the Hard-Boiled Tradition*. Berkeley: California University Press.

Watson, Victor. 2000. *Reading Series Fiction: From Arthur Ransome to Gene Kemp*. London: Routledge Falmer.

Transforming Genres:
Subversive Potential and the Interface Between Hard-Boiled Detective Fiction and Chick Lit

BY SONJA ALTNOEDER

Popular culture opens up sites of contestation, sites upon which the meanings of cultural signs and symbols are perpetually de- and re-constructed and upon which society negotiates its values. It thus not only participates in the complex signifying processes that are constitutive of contemporary culture but also obtains subversive potential in that it provides indispensable strategies for undermining dominant power relations. As John Fiske argues, popular culture constitutes a hybrid terrain, which, on the one hand, inherently depends on the artists' inventive creativity, but which, on the other hand, is always-already interspersed with traces of the hegemonic structures that the artist seeks to overcome and alter in the process of production (cf. Fiske 2001, 32). Popular culture thus revolves around a postmodern play with power relations and their subversion. Accordingly, Joke Hermes (2005) celebrates popular culture as a domain of resistance to existing hegemonies. Indeed, it often relies on strategies like irony and humor and therefore yields to a manifold of opportunities for facets of identity to be borrowed, to be merged in ever-shifting arrays, and, finally, to be assessed with regard to their performative potential.

Yet, at the same time, less favorable assessments often disapprove of popular culture's inherent conservatism. After all, popular genres — ranging from literature to TV shows to music — not only are designed to entertain and please a mass audience but also are marketed within the prevalent capitalist structures of supply and demand. In fact, from a feminist point of view, these structures are seen as representative of patriarchal mass culture (cf. Hollows & Moseley 2006). From this disapproving stance, popular culture does not exhibit any of the features mentioned above — neither inventive creativity nor subversive irony — but rather reinforces hegemonic structures and, in consequence, confirms the status quo. In other words, popular culture is deemed too easy to consume and too entertaining to be critical. Arguably, it is not immediately obvious how these schemes may yield to critical, let alone subversive, interventions or negotiations of the (patriarchal) powers that be.

This study, however, rejects any monolithic reading for or against popular culture and seeks to examine, instead, contemporary phenomena according to their discursive, political and real-life implications.[1] In particular, this chapter explores some dynamic intersections of two popular genres, the literary genres of hard-boiled crime fiction and chick lit, from a postfeminist perspective on the gendered body to reveal their transformative potential. Hence, in the following, the main features of hard-boiled detective fiction and chick lit will be discussed and, ultimately, merged into a theoretical approach. The subsequent discussion of the first two novels from Janet Evanovich's Plum series, *One for the Money* (1994) and *Two for the Dough* (1996), are intended to provide examples of how these transformations may yield to new directions in crime fiction.

Hard-Boiled Detective Fiction

At first glance, crime fiction's subgenre of detective fiction may seem to constitute a conservative genre in the most basic and literal sense of that word. The sleuth's professional task generally revolves around tracking down felons to restore a moral status quo that has previously been disrupted by a crime. The story of the crime, however, remains unknown to the reader and must be revealed in the course of the detective's investigation. Hence, detective fiction revolves around a double narrative, in which the unknown story of the crime is gradually reconstructed in the story of the investigation.[2] In this framework, the detective proceeds to make sense of the crime, to discover the criminal, and, subsequently, to eradicate his or her disruption until, finally, the status quo is restored. In most examples, the detective is male, representing such stereotypically masculine character traits as overdetermined individualism and the ultimate triumph of logical, rational thought (cf. Makinen 2001).

This fairly conservative and gender-biased form appears as early as Edgar Allan Poe's ground-breaking invention of the detective story and has retained its significance throughout the Golden Age of the 1920s and 1930s, when so-called brilliant men and women were represented in their endeavors to solve baffling mysteries by means of rational deduction. By contrast, women's roles in the popular genre of hard-boiled detective fiction, both as authors of detective fiction and as characters, are rather one-dimensional. As characters, their sexuality is represented as a site of social disruption and crime, hence rendering them either villains or victims, but hardly agents. As authors, women have had a difficult standing throughout literary history and particularly in the male-dominated canon of the hard-boiled subgenre.

These traditions notwithstanding, detective fiction has been subjected to various strategies undermining its conservative and gender-biased implications. Hard-boiled detective fiction, for instance, constitutes one of the subgenres in which the means employed to achieve the goal of solving a mystery may be regarded as a challenge to the social order. Hence, this subgenre embraces a transformative potential that can be traced most concisely in the literary figure of the hard-boiled detective. Instead of solving mysteries intellectually, hard-boiled detectives rely chiefly on their intuition and frequently employ physical force in their encounters with felons. Above all, they venture into dangerous territory and exhibit a remarkable disposition to survive the most threatening situations, often emerging barely harmed. Raymond Chandler outlines the characteristics of the hard-boiled genre, including the detective figure, setting, and content, most succinctly in his essay "The Simple Art of Murder," first published in *Atlantic Monthly* in 1944. In contrast to the Golden Age tradition outlined above, the founding father of the hard-boiled tradition, Dashiell Hammett, "took murder out of the Venetian vase and dropped it into the alley [and] gave murder back to the people who commit it for reasons and with the means at hand" (10). Accordingly, hard-boiled detective fiction is characterized chiefly through its setting in the so-called mean streets, "a world [...] where no man can walk down a dark street in safety because law and order are things we talk about but refrain from practicing" (18). This dangerous territory is the site of many violent crimes and, above all, compels the detective to take the law into his own hands to restore a precarious moral status quo.

Hard-boiled detective fiction thus draws attention to the intricate overlaps between place and identity. After all, the detective is deeply influenced by his life in these "mean streets." Chandler spells out a wide variety of characteristics that result from the detective's practices of inhabiting the "mean streets." The hard-boiled detective is a common, though unusual, man who, despite living in the "mean streets," has retained a sense of honor and a sense of character. His methods of investigation are unconventional, and he is generally portrayed as a solitary figure who ignores socially accepted norms. This characterization positions hard-boiled detectives outside of prevalent social hierarchies. Nonetheless, this brief outline has already indicated that, in the canon of crime fiction, hard-boiled detectives are generally male figures.[3] However, with the two specific features of setting and of detective personality, the hard-boiled form emerges as a highly adaptable genre for social criticism, and especially for negotiating feminist and postfeminist matters.

One of the most recent and widely-read examples of such new directions in crime fictions is the protagonist of Janet Evanovich's detective Stephanie Plum series. As hard-boiled detective, Plum operates in the "mean streets" of her hometown, Trenton, New Jersey, which she describes in rather dreary terms:

> Trenton's placement on the banks of the Delaware River made it ripe for industry and commerce. Over the years, as the Delaware's navigability and importance dwindled, so did Trenton's, bringing the city to its present-day status of being just one more big pothole in the state highway system [Evanovich 1996, 42].

In keeping with the "mean streets" of hard-boiled detective fiction, Janet Evanovich locates her novels in a setting intrinsically characterized by the ubiquity of corruption and crime. These circumstances affect the entire population without regard for gender roles. Plum grows up in a neighborhood where women discuss the assets of different types of guns at the hairdresser's (cf. Evanovich 1996, 150 f.). Men, on the other hand, are rough characters like cousin Vinnie, who runs a bail firm, and his clientele. Against this spatial and cultural background, Plum begins her career as fugitive apprehension agent, or bounty hunter. When she loses her job as lingerie buyer, she feels compelled to blackmail her cousin Vinnie to force him to employ her as bounty hunter in his firm. Even in this first step into her new job, Plum exhibits some of the pertinent characteristics of a hard-boiled detective. Not only does she use unconventional methods to find a job, exploiting her knowledge that Vinnie enjoys "kinky sex" (Evanovich 1994, 18), but also bounty hunter is a fairly eccentric career choice. Having grown up in the "mean streets" of Trenton, she is both common and unusual, a solitary investigator who seeks to restore law and order, if only to make decent money.

Plum's job involves tracking down criminals who have failed to appear for a court hearing, which is apparently a profitable business. Yet, she quickly realizes that this new business also involves considerable risks, as her clientele habitually dwell in the darker corners of the "mean streets" of Trenton. So, her tasks take her into dangerous territory for a woman, and particularly for a white woman. Pondering her gendered and racialized position, she asserts: "I was berating myself for being the wrong sex and the wrong color to operate effectively in over half the neighborhoods in Trenton" (Evanovich 1994, 103).

These "mean streets" are juxtaposed with "the burg," the residential area where Plum grew up and where her family still lives. These two living areas starkly contrast one another, as "the burg" represents a haven of safety and normality for Plum. This is illustrated in her response to her mother's invitation for dinner after a rough day:

> I wanted temporary respite from adulthood. I wanted to feel unconditionally safe. I wanted my mom to cluck around me, filling my milk glass, relieving me of the most mundane responsibilities. I wanted to spend a few hours in a house cluttered with awful overstuffed furniture and oppressive cooking smells [Evanovich 1994, 268].

While Chandler argues that the "mean streets" shape a hard-boiled detective's (literary) character by granting him "a range of awareness that startles you, but it belongs to him by right, because it belongs to the world he lives in" (18), the overlaps between Trenton's "mean streets" and Plum's "home" in the burg decisively shape Plum's character and performance as bounty hunter. She relies on a family network and thus may not be regarded as the lonely prototypical hard-boiled detective. At the same time, she lives on her own and, initially, her social network of friends is not described in much detail. Only in the second volume do (female) friends come to play a more important role in Plum's daily life.

Transforming Genres (Altnoeder)

The contrast between "mean streets" and home is further evoked when she gradually develops a sense of character that helps her survive in dangerous territory. Plum's transition from lingerie buyer to bounty hunter illustrates her personal growth, often in humorous ways. While Plum fulfills some of Chandler's criteria for the hard-boiled detective, this element of humor emerges most clearly as Plum further exhibits several key features of the "chick." Plum's behavior merges this newly emergent popular figure in women's writing and women's literature the figure of the hard-boiled detective and illustrates new directions in crime fiction, as Plum exhibits some of the most pertinent features of both the hard-boiled detective and of contemporary, postfeminist chick culture, which mutually challenge and undermine each other's significance.

Chick Lit

Chick lit is located at the interface of post feminism and popular culture. Accordingly, it has special significance as far as its general stance on and its relationship to both popular culture and the political goals of feminism in the contemporary postfeminist age. With the landslide appearance of chick lit, triggered by the publication of Helen Fielding's *Bridget Jones's Diary* (1996), women's writing is supposed to have reached its next stage, as, for instance, Juliette Wells argues chick lit features single, mostly city-dwelling women in their late twenties and early thirties negotiating their often conflicting desires for professional and personal satisfaction (2006, 49). As such, chick lit's contemporary adaptations of both the romance and the novel of manners represent some kind of— perhaps not altogether unexpected — postfeminist venture into the field of popular culture (Harzewski 2006).

Naturally, this endeavor has sparked controversial responses. There have always been considerable tensions between feminism and popular culture, which have mainly revolved around one major conflict of interest. Feminism, throughout its heterogeneous manifestations, predominantly concerns itself with "serious" — i.e., political — goals such as, for instance, women's liberation and empowerment. Popular culture, though equally varied in its expressions as feminism, is commonly seen to be dedicated chiefly to pleasure and to entertainment. Yet, this distinction is not as rigid as this juxtaposition might suggest. In fact, post feminism aims critically — and, above all, self-reflexively — to assess the contemporary accomplishment of the feminist goals of the past three decades. As a postfeminist genre, chick lit may be regarded as the result of some of these achievements, since it portrays women's social, financial, and emotional independence, made possible by the ongoing processes of women's liberation and empowerment. Simultaneously, post feminism shifts the focus from women's oppression and seeks to re-define femininity from a more positive and multi-dimensional perspective. Cris Mazza summarizes:

> It is time to look closely at ourselves, to admit our weaknesses as well as celebrate strengths; to honestly assess what we have helped make ourselves into, rather than blaming the patriarchal world; to see how far we've come (or haven't come) since we've been aware of the feminist goals of the last three decades; and to explore all the other facets and types of experiences besides our oppression [2006, 111].

As a *post*feminist manifestation of women's writing, chick lit thus posits genre in a complex relationship with feminism and its main political objectives. The genre's affiliation with popular culture proves to be quite helpful, as popular literature represents a postmodern site of contestation in which the affirmative or subversive performance of the discursive practices of fashioning one's identity provides different ways to express the diverse experiences of feminine subjectivity. Positive evaluations of this newly emergent genre have emphasized its potential to deliver feminism — along with its social, political, and cultural objectives — from its aloof positioning in academia and render it more accessible to a wider public. Since chick lit is easy to consume and entertaining to read, it reaches a mass audience rather than the limited scope of a small circle of intellectual or academic readers. Furthermore, these two qualities help contribute to unburdening the notion of feminism of its widespread associations with dry theory. Finally, this process enables this new, popular feminist genre to relieve feminists of their reputation as humorless.

The immense success of chick lit further attests to the genre's great potential as a new form of women's writing. Throughout chick texts, the use of first-person narrative perspective gives voice exclusively to the female protagonist and thereby undermines the dominance of the male gaze commonly associated with the authorial third-person narrative perspective. Hence, chick lit provides a means to reverse gender relationships by rendering male experience the object of the female gaze. Male experience thus becomes always-already mediated through the female protagonist's perception and at least once removed from the level of the story. This narrative practice grants the female protagonist control over the narrative representation of her subjectivity. Paradoxically, however, the protagonists of chick lit are often accused of perpetuating gender stereotypes, since their performance of female subjectivity is frequently expressed through the experience of clumsiness and helplessness. Moreover, this experience is often fashioned as a spectacle for the anticipated male gaze of a potential lover. The main themes of chick lit revolve around the female protagonist's attempts to impress her love interest and to marry. As she is bound to encounter hilarious complications of this scheme, these provide a humorous stance on contemporary women's everyday lives.

Gender and the Body in Hard-Boiled Chick Crime Fiction

At the intersection of hard-boiled crime fiction and chick lit, Plum's status as a chick emerges most obviously in representations of gender and the body. Yet, in some regard at least, Plum seems to have grown beyond being a chick. For instance, Plum is divorced and claims that she does not want a man because she "had one and did not like it" (Evanovich 1994, 9). Furthermore, the prominent feature in most chick novels, the love plot, is subsumed under the professional plot. Plum's job undermines the general characteristics of the chick lit genre, since she loses her chick job as lingerie buyer and enters the predominantly male domain of bounty hunting instead. As Plum enters this hard-boiled profession, gender issues emerge on three interrelated levels: Plum's performance of her job, her own perception of her body, and the perception of her female body from the male characters' points of view. In consequence, some of the seemingly irreconcilable character traits of two popular genres merge into the tense and unstable performance of the hard-boiled chick detective.

Initially, Plum lacks not only the necessary skills, but also the equipment to perform well in her profession as bounty hunter. Hence, she turns to several male characters — such as her cop friend Eddie Gazarra and a colleague at her cousin's firm, "bad-ass" fugitive apprehension agent Ranger — to teach her the trade. This practice not only underlines her lack of experience but also alludes to prevalent gender hierarchies of hard-boiled crime, the field in which Plum has chosen her new career. Ranger particularly serves as a contrastive counterpart to Plum, since he seems to embody the stereotypical male, hard-boiled bounty hunter. Plum describes his physical appearance as follows: "His straight black hair was slicked back in a ponytail. His biceps looked like they'd been carved out of granite and buffed up with Armor All. He was around 5'10" with a muscular neck and a don't-mess-with-me body" (Evanovich 1994, 33). While his physical appearance is stereotypical of the hard-boiled genre, his performance more forcefully sheds an ironic light upon Plum's (and possibly the readership's) common perception of bounty hunting. During a joint investigation, Plum and Ranger need to break into a suspect's apartment. So Plum, perhaps rather naively, asks Ranger whether he is going to kick in a door. He impatiently retorts, "You could break your foot doing that macho shit," and ascribes her adventurous musings to "watching too much television" (Evanovich 1994, 91). In fact, he has already fetched the key from the building's supervisor and unlocked the door without causing damage either to his own body or to the suspect's property. In contrast to the stereotypical image of the hard-boiled detective, Ranger represents a less harsh and more thoughtful type of investigator, so his methods provide a subversive commentary on the hard-boiled genre's characteristic features. Furthermore, bounty hunting thus becomes a profession in which brute force is not as essential as wit. In this regard, bounty hunting appears to be a job in which women can perform as well as men.

Nevertheless, physical aspects play a significant role in Plum's performance, as both her own and other (male) characters' perceptions of her body reveal. Plum's own perception of her body frequently reflects on her appearance, and her self-conscious portrayal of her body evokes chick characteristics. For example, food is an important aspect of her life that she describes at great length. She enjoys her mother's delicious home-cooked dishes and describes meals as one of the occasions when the entire family, including Plum, her parents, and her grandmother, gather around the dinner table. These family reunions also provide a platform for negotiations of femininity across three generations. While Plum's mother tries to set her daughter up with a suitable husband over dinner and expresses her disapproval of Stephanie's new job, Grandma Mazur is eager to learn all the details of her granddaughter's professional routines and even offers to assist her in an investigation.

Furthermore, food distinguishes between the familial and single living situations, as in Plum's own single household her refrigerator is either half-empty or filled with the different kinds of junk food she likes. She nevertheless berates herself for having to struggle with her weight and, in all these contemplations, her body appears far from perfect. In fact, she muses:

> I'm 5'7" and rawboned from the Mazurs' good Hungarian peasant stock. Perfectly constructed for laboring in the paprika fields, pulling plows, and dropping babies out like bird's eggs. I ran and periodically starved to keep the fat off, but I still weighed in at 130. Not heavy, but not dainty, either [Evanovich 1995, 51].

At times, this self-conscious perception of her body ironically disrupts the unfolding events. When one of her FTAs,[4] Lonnie Dodd, attempts to flee, she "bodyslammed into the back of him, knocking [them] both to the ground. He hit with an "unh!" thanks to 125 pounds of angry female landing on top of him" (Evanovich 1994, 177). Yet, she immediately revaluates this statement by conceding: "Well, okay, maybe 127, but not an ounce more, I swear" (Evanovich 1994, 177–8). The first-person narrative voice directs the reader's attention from the actual, hard-boiled crime plot — capturing a fugitive — to Plum's body. This has the immediate effect of stalling and interrupting the growing suspense in an unanticipated self-ironic turn to the protagonist's female body. It is in this episode that hard-boiled crime fiction and chick lit clash most obviously and mutually produce an ironic commentary.

The focus of attention on Plum's body recurs throughout Evanovich's crime series and plays an important role in Plum's performance as bounty hunter. As Plum's own references to her weight range from 125 pounds to 130 pounds, her obsession with her weight reflects her own performance of gendered roles through her female body. She is unsatisfied with her body even though she weighs less than the ideal weight for her height. At the same time, the erratic references to her weight illustrate Plum's lack of care for this topic and thus subvert a stereotypically female preoccupation with the body.

Furthermore, Plum's body as well as her performance as bounty hunter are staged as spectacles for the male gaze of other literary characters, both fellows and felons, but in particular for her partner-in-arms Ranger and for her "love interest" and "prime target" of her first investigation, Morelli. Morelli and Plum grew up in the same Trenton neighborhood.

As a teenager, she fell for the town's womanizer (Morelli), which spawned a contested relationship in which they mutually take revenge. Hence, it is serendipitous that Plum's first FTA is Morelli. Morelli, a police officer, is suspected of having shot a witness during a solitary investigation. He claims his innocence despite the abundant evidence against him and has become a fugitive to solve the witness's murder. Morelli thus holds an intermediate position between felon and hard-boiled detective, which complicates his character as well as Plum's investigation. He is both her counterpart and her savior in several dangerous situations, and the task of apprehending him illustrates Plum's initiation in the trade.

Significantly, Morelli feels both professionally and emotionally superior to Plum and plays out this alleged superiority by hinting at the romantic, or more precisely, the sexual component in their relationship. He repeatedly calls Plum nicknames such as "cupcake," "sweet thing," or "babe," signaling his lack of professional appreciation. These terms instead recall their shared history and illustrate Morelli's focus on Plum's femininity in addition to her overall rather clumsy performance. Morelli's frank remarks on Plum's body not only correspond to a stereotypical, hard-boiled perception of women as objects of desire, but also they always-already judge her gendered performance. For instance, Morelli draws on their shared history to trick Plum when she more or less stumbles upon him by chance in the beginning of her investigation. She unsuccessfully tries to persuade him to accompany her to the police station, but he merely comments on her hair to critique her performance: "I like the way you've let your hair go curly … Suits your personality. Lots of energy, not much control, sexy as hell" (Evanovich 1994, 32). This remark not only renders her an object of male sexual desire ("sexy as hell") but also indicates that she simultaneously lacks and is refused agency. Their shared history has left Plum unable to keep her calm when dealing with Morelli. But, through this investigation, Plum not only acquires some essential professional skills but also learns how to deal with Morelli. Towards the end of the first novel, a remark that sexually objectifies her female body do not leave Plum as speechless or motionless as in the previous example. Rather, Morelli's final insult and his intention to break a deal they have agreed upon triggers Plum's resolution to finally best him and bring him in.

For both Mañoso and Morelli, Plum's mishaps often include episodes that expose her naked body to them. For instance, at one point, Plum breaks into Morelli's apartment after her own car has broken down to steal his car keys and "commandeer" his vehicle (Evanovich 1994, 125). When she parks in front of her apartment building, she even removes the distributor cap so that he will not be able to take it back. Morelli is naturally furious and breaks into her apartment while she is taking a shower. When he cannot find the missing distributor cap, he takes revenge by chaining her naked to the shower curtain rod with her own handcuffs. Leaving her in this humiliating situation with only a portable phone at hand, she is compelled to call Ranger to rescue her. Under these circumstances, both men make kinkily remark on her body, placing Plum in an inferior position. This not only shows the two male characters' gendered perception of Plum's body and of her performance but also illustrates the hard-boiled setting in which she needs to fend for herself and earn respect.

While these representations of the female body illustrate one of the humorous chick aspects of the Stephanie Plum series, the female body still constitutes a site of hard-boiled male violence. This element of hard-boiled detective fiction is exemplified not only in the portrayal of Plum's own body but also of the bodies of other female characters in the two first novels, *One for the Money* and *Two for the Dough*. In the first novel, Plum's confrontations with the boxer Benito Ramirez put her body in danger and her life at stake. During their first encounter at his gym in Stark Street, he physically assaults her, and she is saved only by Morelli's intervention. In the aftermath of Plum's "degrading [and] frightening experience" (Evanovich 1994, 63), Ramirez becomes obsessed with Plum and begins to stalk her, as the psychologically instable and sexually aggressive boxer does not like "having unfinished business with a woman" (Evanovich 1994, 74). In the course of Plum's investigation, Ramirez turns out to embody the toughest of the hard-boiled criminals Plum encounters. He threatens her at her own flat, standing in the hallway insulting her, masturbating in front of her door, or ringing her to make her listen to him abusing another woman.

However, her dealing with Ramirez also illustrates Plum's growing emancipation. She later makes a deal with Morelli and agrees to us her body as bait for Ramirez on Stark Street. Injured when Ramirez punches her in the face, she is able to save herself from more harm by gassing him with her defense spray. These examples of Ramirez's capacity for violence become increasingly palpable when he mutilates Lula, one of the Stark

Street prostitutes who has been helping Plum in her investigations, tying her violated body to the fire escape in front of Plum's bedroom window as a "present" (Evanovich 1994, 210). In the novel's final showdown, these atrocities are (almost) inflicted upon Plum herself, as Ramirez' trainer, Jimmy Alpha, who turns out to be the main villain, intends to have his "champ" kill Plum to save himself: "He was deadly serious. He was going to watch while Ramirez raped and tortured me, and then he was going to make sure I was mortally injured" (Evanovich 1994, 311). In this forlorn situation, Plum is saved not only by her instinct to survive — a typical feature of the hard-boiled detective — but also by her continuous training at the shooting range. Although her body is harmed when Jimmy Alpha shoots her in the leg, she manages to save her life by grabbing her gun, "blink[ing] the tears away and fires" (Evanovich 1994, 312), and thus killing Alpha before he can kill her.

As Lula's mutilation has already indicated, the threat of physical harm is not limited to the literary figure of the hard-boiled chick detective but is also extended to the bodies of other women characters to deter the detective. For instance, in *Two for the Dough*, Plum's grandmother is injured when Kenny Mancuso sticks an ice pick through her hand (cf. Evanovich 1996, 233) and is trapped in a refrigeration unit at the morgue in the final showdown. Here, Grandma Mazur's instinct and determination not only saves her but also helps Plum capture the villains. Even though issues of gender, the body, and gradual emancipation from the male domain illustrate Plum's performance as a chick, the crimes as well as the perpetrators she deals with are thoroughly hard-boiled. The perpetrators physically abuse Plum and other women, and the crimes revolve around typical hard-boiled issues like drugs, corruption, and violence.

Conclusion

In *One for the Money* and *Two for the Dough*, Evanovich merges the hard-boiled genre and chick lit. This is achieved on three intertwined levels, namely the levels of setting, of professional performance, and, finally, of issues revolving around gender and the body. For one, the author sets her novels in the "mean streets" of Trenton, which she juxtaposes with Plum's family home, the "burg." Plum thus operates at the intersection of these two settings and negotiates their differences. While her professional career unfolds in the "mean streets" and revolves around hard-boiled corruption and crime, family dinners and loyalty influence her personal life. Against this backdrop, her performance merges features of the literary figures of both the hard-boiled detective and the chick. In becoming a bounty hunter for her cousin's firm, she initially lacks control and acts clumsily. However, she adapts to this unusual profession by relying on her intuition and her wit; in fact, she outwits even hard-boiled criminals. In the end, her performance proves to be successful, and this success subverts the genres' gender stereotypes.

Gender and the body play considerably different, though equally significant, roles in both the genre of hard-boiled crime fiction and chick lit. On the one hand, Plum's own perception of her body provides an ironic, chick commentary upon the figure of the male hard-boiled detective and his flawless body. On the other hand, and in the tradition of hard-boiled fiction, her female body becomes the object of desire and of violence for male characters, both fellows and felons alike. In these multi-layered intersections of two popular genres, Evanovich challenges the traditional frameworks of both hard-boiled crime fiction and chick lit. Most importantly, her series undermines the inherent conservatism of the male-dominated genre of hard-boiled fiction with the appearance of a female detective who not only survives the challenges of this profession but also surpasses her male counterparts. Furthermore, these novels subvert the stereotypical images of women that constitute the core of contemporary chick lit through Plum's success in a tough career and independent life-style. Hence, in spite of the problematic elements inherent in the representation of the hard-boiled chick detective, such as representations of the female body as a site of male violence or gendered stereotypes, this new figure transforms both literary genres. It de- and re-constructs contemporary gender stereotypes, negotiating current perceptions of femininity and masculinity through humor. Finally, thus, the union of hard-boiled detective fiction and chick lit manifests the strategies of appropriating popular culture to serve contemporary political objectives by transforming social hierarchies from a joint popular and postfeminist standing.

Notes

1. Cultural studies has often been criticized for its allegedly exclusive focus on products of contemporary mass culture. However, more recent studies have drawn attention to a his-

torical dimension in this pertinent research strand. In this appraisal of cultural studies, this contribution follows the Birmingham tradition of the Centre for Contemporary Cultural Studies (CCCS) founded by Richard Hoggart in 1964 and an enduring influence in the field of popular culture. The CCCS dealt with a wide range of research subjects, including not only subcultures and mass media but also critical race studies and feminism, and employed an interdisciplinary methodology.

2. Developing from Tzvetan Todorov's analysis in "The Typology of Detective Fiction" (1971), this claim has been similarly argued, for instance, by Laura Marcus in "Detection and Literary Fiction" (2003). Examining the intricate position of detective fiction within the field of literature, Marcus illustrates "literary and narrative issues raised by the detective genre" (2003, 246) and to place them in their social and historical contexts.

3. Yet, there has been a longstanding history of feminist adaptations of the hard-boiled genre (cf. Walton & Jones 1999). As, more recently, post feminism has come to adopt a critical stance towards feminism and its inherent hegemonies, including those of the aforementioned adaptations, the subgenre of hard-boiled crime fiction has expanded rapidly, as will be shown in this contribution.

4. FTA is the commonly used acronym for someone who "failed to appear" for a court hearing and, hence, a denotation for Stephanie Plum's main clientele.

Works Cited

Chandler, Raymond. 1988. "The Simple Art of Murder." 1944. In *The Simple Art of Murder*, 1–18. New York: Random House.
Evanovich, Janet. 1994. *One for the Money*. New York: St. Martin's Paperbacks.
_____. 1996. *Two for the Dough*. New York: St. Martin's Paperbacks.
Fielding, Helen. 1996. *Bridget Jones's Diary*. London: Picador.
Fiske, John. 2001. "Hybride Energie: Populärkultur in einer multikulturellen, postfordistischen Welt." In *Die Fabrikation des Populären: Der John Fiske Reader*, edited by Lothar Mikos and Rainer Winter, 285–308. Bielefeld: Transcript.
Harzewski, Stephanie. 2006. "Tradition and Displacement in the New Novel of Manners." In *Chick Lit: The New Woman's Fiction*, edited by Suzanne Ferriss and Mallory Young, 29–46. New York: Routledge.
Hermes, Joke. 2005. *Re-Reading Popular Culture*. Malden, MA: Blackwell.
Hollows, Joanne, and Rachel Moseley, eds. 2006. *Feminism in Popular Culture*. Oxford: Berg.
Makinen, Merja. 2001. *Feminist Popular Fiction*. New York: Palgrave Macmillan.
Marcus, Laura. 2003. "Detection and Literary Fiction." In *The Cambridge Companion to Crime Fiction*, edited by Martin Priestman, 245–267. Cambridge: Cambridge University Press.
Mazza, Cris. 2006. "Who's Laughing Now? A Short History of Chick Lit and the Perversion of a Genre." In *Chick Lit. The New Woman's Fiction*, edited by Suzanne Ferriss and Mallory Young, 17–28. New York: Routledge.
Priestman, Martin, ed. 2003. *The Cambridge Companion to Crime Fiction*. Cambridge: Cambridge University Press.
Todorov, Tzvetan. 1977. "The Typology of Detective Fiction." In *The Poetics of Prose*, translated by Richard Howard, 42–52. Ithaca: Cornell University Press.
Walton, Priscilla, and Manina Jones. 1999. *Detective Agency. Women Rewriting the Hard-Boiled Tradition*. Berkeley: University of California Press.
Wells, Juliette. 2006. "Mothers of Chick Lit? Women Writers, Readers and Literary History." In *Chick Lit. The New Woman's Fiction*, edited by Suzanne Ferriss and Mallory Young, 47–70. New York and London: Routledge.

The Poetics of Deviance
in The Curious Incident
of the Dog in the Night-Time
BY CHRISTIANA GREGORIOU

This chapter introduces a model explicating the types and functions of deviance encountered when reading, interpreting, and reacting to contemporary crime fiction. I introduce this deviance model's application by analyzing a successful contemporary novel, Mark Haddon's *The Curious Incident of the Dog in the Night-Time* (2003).[1] This book manifests three types of deviance: linguistic, social and generic.

I have previously investigated the stylistic, socially-situated, and generic nature in contemporary American novels of this genre through an exploration of the *poetics of deviance* model. I use the term *poetics* here as well, since it etymologically suggests a study concerned with the art or theory of "making." Furthermore, these three types of analyses are connected by *deviance*, a term used here to refer to the difference between that which we perceive as normal, standard, or acceptable and that which we do not. The *Oxford English Dictionary* (OED) distinguishes *deviance* from *deviation*, defining *deviance* as the "deviant state or quality; the behaviour or characteristics of a deviant" whereas *deviation*, in this context, refers to "the action of deviating," "voluntary departure from an intended course," or "divergence" *from* a normal position. Admittedly:

> in the terms' everyday sense, "deviance" is used with a rather negative semantic prosody and evokes a defiance or rejection of whatever somebody deems normal, ordinary and perhaps mainstream, whereas "deviation" is more neutral, and only when it is linked to percentages or other independent factors does it attract a negative (or positive) evaluation [Gregoriou 2009, 28].

Although some writers (e.g., Leech and Short, 1981) have tried to make a distinction between *deviance* and *deviation* (merely preferring *deviance* for divergence in frequency from a *norm*), in linguistic and/or stylistic terms, the terms have tended to be used synonymously. I follow this tradition here. The linguistic, social, and generic aspects of deviance identified here are in fact roughly analogous to the Hallidayan (1973, 1985) model as to the metafunctions of language, a tripartite system that forms the theoretical base of his Systemic Functional Grammar. I briefly introduce Halliday's model, develop my tripartite *Deviance* model, and then relate the latter to the *Curious Incident*.

The Deviance Model

According to Michael Alexander Kirkwood Halliday (M.A.K. Halliday), the internal organization of language is not accidental but embodies the functions that language has evolved to serve in the life of social man (1973, 42–3). Halliday recognizes three principal components under the headings *ideational, interpersonal,* and *textual*:

> The ideational component is that part of the grammar concerned with the expression of experience, including both the processes within and beyond the self—the phenomena of the external world and those of consciousness—and the logical relations deducible from them. The ideational component thus has two sub-components, the experiential and the logical. The interpersonal component is the grammar of personal participation; it expresses the speaker's role in the speech situation, his personal commitment and his interaction with others. The textual component is concerned with the creation of text; it expresses the structure of information, and the relation of each part of the discourse to the whole and to the setting [Halliday 1973, 99].

These "macro-functions" of language operate simultaneously and serve for the expression of the world's content (ideational function), establish relationships between people (interpersonal function), and help organize the message through various ways (textual function). All genre literature, and crime novels in particular, are interpretable along these three coexisting dimensions, particularly with respect to deviance: "[T]he ideational function correlates to those *generic* aspects of novels [...] the interpersonal to those aspects of my framework that are *social* in nature and [...] the textual to the *linguistic* nature of any one text" (Gregoriou 2007, 153–4). Following from this, to obtain an integrated view of any crime novel, we need to investigate the text in relation to these three parallel dimensions of meaning, while remembering that certain forms of deviance are in fact the *norm*, indeed expected, in the crime novel context. When reading a crime novel, readers expect some defamiliarizing language, such as when the criminal mind is portrayed (see Gregoriou 2002 and Gregoriou 2003). Generic violations from the crime novel formula are also commonplace (see Gregoriou 2007), as are socially maladjusted characters such as traumatized detectives fighting their own demons, not to mention psychopathic murderers. Crime fiction studies have traced extensively how the detective is often equated with the criminal, who in turn becomes the detective's "double" (ffrench 2000, 225). As Joel Black puts it, the literary figure of the detective continues to be a marginal figure who frequently bears a closer likeness to the criminal he pursues than to the police officers with whom he supposedly collaborates (1991, 43). That is, detectives are often as socially estranged as criminals are. Readers only accept their unusual behavior, such as the detectives acting against the law, as it comes attached to those we take to be acceptable as "normal."

Finally, the formulaic nature of crime fiction itself presupposes that its readership does not *want* any departure from the formula and might react negatively against any such departures from the form's own deviance (Gregoriou 2007, 155). The readers' schematic expectations and even preferences are thus needed to explain their reaction to a given text. Despite certain violations being necessary for a book to prove noteworthy, too many deviations could potentially frustrate and alienate the crime reader who wants the formula.

The Curious Incident of the Dog in the Night-Time

This triangular approach to fiction is applicable to the *Curious Incident*, the 2003 Whitbread Book of the Year and the 2004 Commonwealth Writers' Prize for Best First Book. The novel takes the form of first-person, or "homodiegetic" (Genette 1972), narration, as it features a character narrating a story in which he also participates. This type of narration often converts readers to views they would not normally hold, at least for the duration of the story (Leech and Short 1981, 265). When characters are allowed to tell their own stories in their own voice, readers can be manipulated. The story's plot concerns the fifteen-year-old character of Christopher Boone, who lives with his father, seems to have a form of high-functioning autism known as Asperger syndrome, and one day discovers his next-door neighbor's dog, Wellington, dead. Since he enjoys reading murder mysteries, he decides to write an autobiographical murder mystery novel in the tradition of Sherlock Holmes revolving around Wellington's murder. The novel he writes is *The Curious Incident of the Dog in the Night-Time*. He eventually discovers that his neighbor Mr. Shears has had an affair with his mother whom he believes to be dead, having been told by his father that she died of a heart attack. His father eventually admits that he killed Mr. Shear's dog out of revenge for his wife's affair, and Chris, consumed by fear in the discovery of his dad as a killer, leaves for London to find his mother.

This brief summary reveals how this novel appeals and was marketed to a dual audience, adults and adolescents, as can be seen in that it was published simultaneously in two identical editions with different covers, one for adults and one for teenagers.[2] In relation to its appeal to adolescents, this novel adheres to several features of children's literature. Firstly, the character-narrator is young, and teenagers enjoy reading stories about other teenagers. Haddon has claimed that he wanted to write "the kind of book that the hero would read" (Haddon 2004). Also, the book's language is simple, which is one aspect of the book's appeal to younger readers (Haddon 2004). Finally, the character eventually returns to his hometown and moves into a bed-sit with his mother. As Christopher Clausen notes, children's literature typically presents the return home as the return to the place where we ought to stay or come back to, whereas adult literature sees home as the place we must escape or grow away from (Clausen 1982, 142).

The novel has received acclaim from readers and reviewers for the moving and "realistic" representation of the autistic Chris's character and worldview (Semino 2005), and the notion of *schemata* proves useful in explaining this reaction. *Schema* is a term commonly used to refer to organized bundles of knowledge in the brain that are activated when we encounter situations we have experienced previously. Having described schemata as bits of information stored in the form of packages, Mick Short uses the helpful analogy of a filing cabinet:

> When we come across a reference to a situation we have come across before, we access the relevant "file" in the "filing cabinet," which consists of an organized

inventory of all the sorts of thing related to that situation which we have previously experienced [1996, 227].

In other words, we draw information from our brain's organized inventory of schemata to interpret situations around us and in fiction. A *group schema* is one such inventory shared by many, as opposed to the inventory being idiosyncratic and individual. According to Elena Semino:

> Chris's behavior (both linguistic and non-linguistic) is compatible with a widely shared "group schema" for autistic people. He has many of the characteristics that we stereotypically associate with autism, even though no "real" individual is likely to exhibit this particular combination of characteristics [2005].

The portrayal of Chris's autistic mind may be characterized as "believable" rather than good; it is not accurate, but the depiction of autism correlates closely with the way people *understand* autism. We could hence argue for there being "fictional realism" in the depiction of autism here. Chris's portrayal is certainly verisimilar, plausible or life-like, but only in the context of fiction. I next turn to illustrate how this novel is analyzable on the basis of the triangular model of deviance.

Generic Deviance

Crime fiction typically involves the detection of a murderer in a major murder case. These novels follow detectives as they discover clues, presented to the reader in the narrative (the *fair-play* rule), about an identified set of suspects, among which is the murderer. This definition coincides with Martin Priestman's definition of the *detective thriller*, in which a past event of murder is resolved, and yet a present action of events is followed (1998, 2). Such stories are hence not chronologically ordered and deliberately withhold the killer's identity until the end to surprise the reader. The surprise at the end is a definitive aspect of crime fiction, a so-called "predictable formal term [Porter 1981, 99]," though readers do not have access to the nature of this end-surprise until the conclusion. In other words, we expect to be surprised by crime novel endings, but we do not know what form that surprise will take.

Generically, the *Curious Incident* is classifiable as a crime story. As with conventional crime stories, readers accompany Chris as he explores murder clues and attempts to trace the killer. The narrative creates suspense with its breaks from the skeleton of the plot, suspending the progress of the action. We are likely to be surprised when we find out "who did it," a character known to us from the beginning, the protagonist's father. In fact, the title of the novel is itself an intertextual reference to Arthur Conan Doyle's Sherlock Holmes short story "Silver Blaze" (1894). Also, Chris's autobiographical novel details his investigation, or detecting into a past event of murder, and reveals clues about the case as his investigation progresses. However, unlike in most crime fiction, where the detective's understanding surpasses the readers,' the readers understand things and situations where Chris cannot, mostly because of his age and condition. Cathy Emmott uses the term *frame repair* to refer to instances where "a reader becomes aware that they have misread the text either through lack of attention or because the text itself is potentially ambiguous" (1997, 225). Similarly, Dennis Porter's use of "retrospective repatterning" (1981, 87) seems to refer to this sort of repairing readers engage in, when the various hypotheses they form about the details of the crime and the killer's identity are subsequently challenged. And, it is that desire of the reader to know which of these hypotheses is right that the author requires, so that it functions as a "structuring force" (Porter 1981, 86). Invited to "read aright the signs that Christopher so often *misreads*" (Walsh 2007, 113), the reader engages in frame repair, even when Chris fails to repair his understanding retrospectively: the readers come to understand more than the detective because of Chris's autism.

As can be seen in this different relationship between reader and detective, the novel deviates from the parameters of the crime fiction genre. Unconventionally, the "detective" is a child and the victim a pet. The killing of a dog, one could argue, is less serious a "murder," something that Chris's special needs school teacher Siobhan also recognizes from the beginning:

> She said that it was usually people who were killed in murder mystery novels [...] She said that this was because readers cared more about people than dogs, so if a person was killed in the book readers would want to carry on reading [Haddon 2003, 6].

Nobody else is concerned with the discovery of the dog's murderer, and Chris shares no legal authority in trying to find out who the murderer is. In fact, when his father finds his investigative book, he hides it and forbids Chris from continuing his investigation. In addition to the deviation in the detective, the *Curious Incident* is structurally unconventional. It contains diagrams, lists, maps and pictures that do not remotely relate to the story of the crime. Various oddly prime numbered chapters (we get chapters 2, 3, 5, 7 and 11, but no chapter 1, 4, 6, 8, etc.) also digress into issues irrelevant to the central focus of a detective novel: the issue of "who did it." The narrative action is further interrupted by Chris's unnecessary self-reflection because, conscious of his condition, Chris regularly analyses his self-awareness. Finally, the murderer is revealed and somewhat punished in that Chris refuses to trust his father and leaves in search of his mother. We would instead expect a crime novel to end with the discovery of the perpetrator, but the book does not conclude with the criminal's punishment, as Chris leaves for London to convince his mother that he should live with her. Clare Walsh notes that the resolution of the murder mystery halfway through this particular novel involves a disruption of the schema for reading the crime novel, since such a resolution normally marks the point of closure. Instead, she argues, "in the *Curious Incident* [the resolution] effects a shift to an identity quest schema" (Walsh 2007, 115). At the point of resolution Chris's outlook changes and the book is less of a crime novel.

Social Deviance

Within the crime fiction parameters, Chris is an unusual detective because he is a teenager and autistic. Autism can be interpreted as social deviance in itself, as boys with Asperger's syndrome have no emotional empathy, cannot process figurative expressions, and have a tendency to use logic in handling everyday life complexity, dilemmas, and fears. In his analysis of autism's representation in literature, Stuart Murray argues that signifying autism is signifying the most radically imaginable form of personal otherness, signifying those subject to a condition that seemingly defies understanding: autism is "the *personification* of difference and otherness" (Murray 2006, 25; original emphasis). He adds that at the most extreme level of its representation, autism enables discussion about the popular understanding of the human condition because it is "the alien within the human, the mystical within the rational, the ultimate enigma" (Murray 2006, 25).

However, Chris's, and autism's, social deviance needs to be interrogated. On the one hand, he is a nondeviant autistic child. Like many autistic individuals, he does not like to be touched and reacts aggressively to this, he does not mentally age, and he shares a chronic inability to empathize with others. Again, like other autistic people, Chris also has certain obsessions; he needs to keep foods distinct on his plate and dislikes food of particular colors. Murray similarly notes that the narrative "constructs an idea of the Asperger's teenager, complete with ritualised mannerisms, love of logic and mathematics, limited emotional range and a lack of socialization skills, that itself coheres into a stereotype" (2006, 39).

On the other hand, Chris is presented as a unique and exceptional autistic child. Much like detectives are often represented functioning at a higher intellectual level than the average reader, so Chris is himself a high-achiever. He is also incredibly passionate and is talented in mathematics, even though people with Asperger's syndrome are unlikely to be as talented as Chris (see Murray 2006; Semino 2005). In keeping with many cognitively impaired characters in fiction and film, Chris is here portrayed as a noticeably gifted child, particularly where mathematics and memory are concerned. Murray refers to such characters as "super crips" and "autistic savants," most noticeably featuring in films like Barry Levinson's *Rainman* (1988).[3] Indeed, we like to read and view stories about people socially deviant, as can be seen in the popularity of the crime fiction genre itself. Even more so, in relation to autism, Murray notes that the phenomenal success of Haddon's novel has lead to what has been termed "syndrome publishing" and "autistic bandwaggonism," in both the United States and the United Kingdom. For instance, a 2005 *Guardian* article notes that Jessica Kingsley publishers, which specializes in books on the issue of the autistic spectrum, has considered nine hundred new proposals in a ten-month period following the public reception of Haddon's book. Murray adds that this identifies *The Curious Incident* as *the* contemporary marker of the details of autistic presence, a fiction that is increasingly read as being factual and as naturalistic rather than verisimilar.

Also, some of the things the character of Chris does are not in themselves deviant, but rather are made to *look* deviant because they are attached to a character who we take to be deviant. The social sciences refer to this as *labeling* (see, for instance, Holdaway 1988). For example, Chris, like many newcomers, is overwhelmed when he first arrives in London. He also defensively attacks when threatened, as do many non-autistic adults and children. Also, Chris has difficulty sleeping, as do many of us, and has problems processing new figurative expressions, such as unfamiliar idioms, as do many non-native speakers of a language. It is, in fact, easy to find the normal or nondeviant things he does deviant, because, as a *labeled* autistic individual, they are attributed to his autism rather than to his situation. In this regard, Chris is not deviant outside of a standard deviation.

Linguistic Deviance

The novel's first-person narrator is limited in his understanding of the world around him and hence is, narratologically, unreliable. Such first person narrators typically draw on reader sympathy and manipulate empathy toward themselves, particularly since readers are allowed access into their viewpoint and worldview by first-person mode definition. Roger Fowler (1977) introduced the term *mind style* to describe the phenomenon when the language of a text projects a characteristic world view, a particular way of perceiving and making sense of the world (Fowler 1977, 76, but also see Bockting 1994 and Semino and Swindlehurst 1996). I more specifically use the term *mind style* to refer to the way in which the unusualness of the language of a text relates to the unusualness of a particular character's reality, as perceived and conceptualized cognitively. The term may "now be related to the mental abilities and tendencies of an individual, traits that may be completely personal and idiosyncratic, or ones that may be shared, for example by people with similar cognitive habits or disorders" (Gregoriou 2009, 72).[4] In trying to represent the workings of the cognitively-impaired, autistic mind, the *Curious Incident* features linguistic deviance, as defined by unusualness from the sort of language conventionally found in crime novels, and as language that itself requires some deciphering.

Linguistically, the novel has attracted the attention of many stylisticians (Montoro 2005; Walsh 2007; Semino 2005). I here illustrate some of the evidence derived from this work in linguistics that accounts for the linguistic aspect of the tripartite *Deviance* model. To demonstrate, I linguistically analyze Extract 1 below, an excerpt concerning Chris's reaction to his London surroundings:

Extract 1
And then I was in a smaller room underground and there were lots of people

105

and there were pillars which had blue lights in the ground round the bottom of them and I liked these, but I didn't like people, so I saw a photobooth like one I went into on 25th March 1994 to have my passport photo done, and I went into the photobooth because it was like a cupboard and it felt safer and I could look out through the curtain[...]

And then I was in another train station but it was tiny and it was in a tunnel and there was only one track and the walls were curved and they were covered in big adverts and they said **WAY OUT** and **London's Transport Museum** and **Take time out to regret your career choice** and **JAMAICA** and [sign of British Rail] **BRITISH Rail** and [no smoking sign] **No Smoking** and **be Moved** and **be Moved** and **be Moved** and **For Stations beyond Queen's Park take the first train and change at Queen's Park if necessary and Hammersmith and City Line,** and **You're closer than my family ever gets.** And there were lots of people standing in the little station and it was underground so there weren't any windows and I didn't like that, and so I found a seat which was a bench and I sat at the end of the bench [Haddon 2003, 215–6, original emphasis].

Rocio Montoro (2005) notes the lack of modality, the presence of quasi-categorical assertions in *The Curious Incident*, and also the partial suspension of the principle of text-drivenness in text-world theory terms (see Werth 1999, 357–8). The linguistic traits of literary texts direct readers toward forming particular worlds, yet the language of the *Curious Incident*, Montoro argues, suspends the world building. Rather than helping us, the language of the text makes it harder for us to see which areas of knowledge to activate and to keep activating. The reference to the various train station surroundings, for instance, might appear important and relevant to the telling of the story, but they ultimately prove irrelevant. Extract 1 above is also epistemically non-modal, meaning that it is given in a very factual tone.

Clare Walsh also discusses the book's style, and notes the lack of cohesion between chapters, Chris's fragmented and often disjointed thought processes, and the eccentric selectiveness of his attention (2007). She also mentions his inability to distinguish between what cognitive poetics classifies as *figure* and *ground*, terms which correlate closely with Geoffrey Leech and Mick Short's foregrounding theory (1981). Leech and Short propose that we are essentially capable of seeing what is mobile and foregrounded in language in our physical environment in relation to what is static and backgrounded. Walsh adds, however, that Chris has problems with this. In Extract 1, Chris appears to have problems distinguishing what is important and worth noting from that which is not. Though at times selective, his attention can also be overwhelmingly detailed and highlights his incredible memory, which recalls an incident dating back to 25 March 1994. However, the details Chris tends to give are simply not "telling" (Walsh 2007)—they do not appear relevant. The bold typeface in Extract 1 indicates information that literally stands out but is, in effect, unimportant. In frame theory terms (see Emmott 1997, 225), one can even argue that the information is non-episodic rather than episodic. Though readers expect information that proves relevant to the telling of the story (episodic), Chris's information is, put simply, beside the point (non-episodic).

Semino further notes instances of underlexicalization in the novel, meaning where Chris lacks the specialist vocabulary to express certain concepts (2005). For instance, in the extract above, Chris refers to signs as "adverts" and also appears to be underlexicalized in his usage of "smaller room" because he does not possess the specialized term to refer to the exact type of "smaller room" in question here. Nevertheless, Semino also notes instances of overlexicalization in the novel, particularly where topics such as mathematics and formulas are introduced: "And I did some more quadratic equations like[...]" (Haddon 2003, 201). She adds that the mind style features simplistic, child-like syntax, linguistic over-preciseness, and substantial lexical repetition. For instance, "photobooth" and "underground" are repeated in the extract above, which also shows an overuse of compound sentences, the clauses of which are conjoined by "and" and "because." This mirrors the kind of syntax appropriate for a child younger than Chris. The syntax in use is additionally reflective of a meticulous reflector, yet also one who is feeling anxious over his surroundings. In addition to showing Chris's desire for preciseness, the syntax also signals his heightened stress levels here. Semino notes there is significant sentence complexity when Chris analyzes theories and details explanations: the sentences become increasingly complex when Chris explains rather than describes. Similarly, Murray adds that when Chris creeps past his father to escape the house, he displays a range of sophisticated thought processes (2006). Here, Chris can assess situations from his father's point of view, something readers have so far known him unable to do. The syntax in these contexts contradicts the simplistic one we are accustomed to Chris using elsewhere.

Semino further notes Chris's literal-mindedness, which makes it hard for him to use and process metaphor. He flouts or violates the Gricean

(1975) quality maxim, meaning that Chris constantly "says what he believes to be true" and interprets other people's language literally also, which is why misunderstandings arise. Also, she points out that Chris has problems adhering to the maxims of relevance and quantity, as in Chris's over-truthfulness, irrelevance, and over-wordiness in Extract 1. He does not appear to notice that the same sign is repeated three times, making the reader wonder if he cognitively processed the sign in the first place. Also, Chris unnecessarily relexicalizes the "seat" into a "bench" and reports too much reflection, reaction, and detail. Looking at this from the perspective of Politeness theory (see Brown and Levinson 1987),[5] Semino argues that Chris is also unable to account for other people's positive or negative face needs, which consequently makes others read him as seemingly offensive and deliberately socially deviant. Chris inadvertently attacks people's positive and negative face wants, unaware of the impact of his insults and lack of linguistic politeness markers. Overall, Chris can deal with semantic decoding but has problems with pragmatic processing.

So far, I have analyzed the poetics of *The Curious Incident* through my triangular model of deviance, a model originally devised in my study of contemporary crime fiction. To illustrate the model's interpretative effectiveness, I now examine an extract where all deviance types are evident. Chapter Seven opens with the following paragraphs:

> *Extract 2*
> This is a murder mystery novel.
> Siobhan said that I should write something I would want to read myself. Mostly I read books about science and maths. I do not like proper novels. In proper novels people say things like, "I am veined with iron, with silver and with streaks of common mud. I cannot contract into the firm fist which those clench who do not depend on stimulus." What does this mean? I do not know. Nor does Father. Nor do Siobhan or Mr. Jeavons. I have asked them.
> Siobhan has long blonde hair and wears glasses which are made of green plastic. And Mr Jeavons smells of soap and wears brown shoes that have approximately 60 tiny circular holes in each of them.
> But I do like murder mystery novels. So I am writing a murder mystery novel.
> In a murder mystery novel someone has to work out who the murderer is and then catch them. It is a puzzle. If it is a good puzzle you can sometimes work out the answer before the end of the book.
> I found this book in the library in town when Mother took me into town once [Haddon, 2003, 5].

Even though the character here frames the novel as a murder mystery, he has a noticeable tendency to digress, something generically unexpected. For instance, the detective's detailing in the footnoting is here not relevant to his task (though such footnoting is something admittedly common in certain Golden Age detective writings, including that of S. S. Van Dine's). The linguistic deviance is highlighted in the simple and concise nature of Chris's sentences together with his lexical repetitiveness. The phrases "puzzle," "murder mystery novel," and "proper novels" are repeated, revealing problems with Chris's anaphoric referencing and hence grammatical cohesion. This passage also exposes Chris's literal-mindedness and inability to decode linguistically the metaphorical expressions in the quoted excerpt though, again admittedly, in this example, his inability is reasonable. The passage also depicts his rather unusual relative terms of address: "mum" and "dad" would have been the informal and unmarked lexical choices, not Chris's use of "Father" and "Mother." He is also overly precise, such as when he unnecessarily asserts what has already been presupposed: "What does this mean? I do not know. Nor does Father. Nor do Siobhan or Mr Jeavons." The last two sentences themselves presuppose what Chris says next, namely that he has "asked them" what the excerpt means. Similarly, the detail in the other characters' description is unnecessary. Chris is presented as the kind of eccentric character that would actually obsessively count the number of tiny circular holes in someone's shoes. Overall, the narrative's linguistic deviance *alongside* his social eccentricity and digressing tendency constitutes the character as "strange."

With respect to Chris's definition of what constitutes a crime novel, he here notes crime fiction's puzzle-solving element. Though apparently literal-minded, Chris is capable of drawing on the CRIME FICTION IS A PUZZLE metaphor. In any case, Chris claims that a mystery novel constitutes a good puzzle if the reader can work out the answer. However, if the reader of a crime novel proved able to discover the identity of the perpetrator too early on, the remaining of the novel would become redundant. As Ernest Mandel claims, reading such stories is in fact not fair play but "fake play under the guise of fair play" (1984, 48). Classical detective writing, he admits, is more of "a game with loaded dice" (Mandel, 1984, 48), since the winner is predetermined by the author and, like the hunted fox, neither the criminal ever wins nor the reader ever outwits the author. The enjoyment of reading crime novels instead lies in the engagement with an intellectual game that the reader secretly wishes to lose. If the reader does "win," the book has proved itself unsuccessful in surprising the reader and hence fulfilling this vital "surprise-ending" convention. Following Chris's suggestion here, a crime novel with a winning reader would prove not only deviant but also unsuccessful.

Conclusion

For a holistic, all-encompassing view of the successful *Curious Incident*, crime fiction, or any genre literature, one needs to investigate the text's tripartite deviance, employing multidisciplinary literary analysis to do so. The *poetics of deviance* model highlights important factors contributing to the nature of any such novel's structure, themes, and language. I would even argue that the manipulation of all three types of deviance is, in fact, the key to any crime novel's success and explains why the *Curious Incident has* proved as popular as it did at its reception.

Notes

1. From this point forward, I will refer to this text as *Curious Incident*.
2. See Walsh 2007 for a discussion of this book's targeting of dual audiences.
3. Murray notes that a recent UK TV documentary of Kim Peek, the man who inspired Dustin Hoffman's character in *Rainman* was described as a "Living Google," in a clear conflation of cognitive exceptionality and modern information systems.
4. See Gregoriou 2002 and Gregoriou 2003 for analyses of *criminal mind style*.
5. Brown and Levinson propose that we employ various conversational strategies for us to achieve our goals in life, such strategies revolving around the concepts of positive face (one's want to be liked) and negative face (one's want to be independent).

Works Cited

Black, Joel. 1991. *The Aesthetics of Murder: A Study in Romantic Literature and Contemporary Culture.* Baltimore: Johns Hopkins University Press.
Bockting, Ineke. 1994. "Mind Style as an Interdisciplinary Approach to Characterisation in Faulkner." *Language and Literature* 3.3: 157–74.
Brown, Penelope, and Steven C. Levinson. 1987. *Politeness: Some Universals in Language Usage.* Cambridge: Cambridge University Press.
Clausen, Christopher. 1982. "Home and Away in Children's Fiction." *Children's Literature* 10: 141–52.
Conan Doyle, Arthur. [1894] 2000. "Silver Blaze." In *The Memoirs of Sherlock Holmes*, edited by Christopher Roden, 3–29. London: George Newnes.
"Deviance." *Oxford English Dictionary.* 2d ed. 1989 (edited by J. A Simpson and E. S. C. Weiner), Additions 1993–7 (edited by John Simpson and Edmund Weiner; Michael Proffitt), and 3d ed. (in progress) Mar. 2000- (ed. John Simpson). OED Online. Oxford University Press. Accessed November 2009. <http://oed.com>

"Deviation." *Oxford English Dictionary.* 2d ed. 1989 (edited by J. A Simpson and E. S. C. Weiner), Additions 1993–7 (edited by John Simpson and Edmund Weiner; Michael Proffitt), and 3d ed. (in progress) Mar. 2000- (ed. John Simpson). OED Online. Oxford University Press. Accessed November 2009. <http://oed.com>

Emmott, Catherine. 1997. *Narrative Comprehension: A Discourse Perspective.* Oxford: Oxford University Press.

Fowler, Roger. 1977. *Linguistics and the Novel.* London: Methuen.

ffrench, Patrick. 2000. "Open Letter to Detectives and Psychoanalysis: Analysis and Reading." In *The Art of Detective Fiction,* edited by Warren Chernaik, Martin Swales, and Robert Vilain, 222–32. New York: St. Martin's Press.

Genette, Gerald. 1980. *Narrative Discourse.* Oxford: Basil Blackwell. Translated by Jane E. Lewin. Paris: Seuil, 1972.

Gregoriou, Christiana. 2002. "'Behaving Badly': A Cognitive Stylistics of the Criminal Mind." *Nottingham Linguistic Circular* 17: 61–73.

_____. 2003. "Criminally Minded: The Stylistics of Justification in Contemporary American Crime Fiction." *Style* 37.2: 144–59.

_____. 2007. *Deviance in Contemporary Crime Fiction.* Basingstoke: Palgrave.

_____. 2009. *English Literary Stylistics.* Basingstoke: Palgrave.

Grice, Herbert P. 1975. "Logic and Conversation." In *Syntax and Semantics III: Speech Acts,* edited by Peter Cole and Jerry Morgan, 41–58. New York: Academic Press.

Haddon, Mark. 2003. *The Curious Incident of the Dog in the Night-Time.* London: Vintage.

_____. 2004. "B is for Bestseller." *The Observer.* Accessed November 2009. <http://book.guardian.co.uk>

Halliday, M.A.K. 1973. *Explorations in the Functions of Language.* London: Edward Arnold.

_____. 1985. *An Introduction to Functional Grammar.* London: Edward Arnold.

Holdaway, Simon. 1988. *Crime and Deviance.* London: Macmillan.

Leech, Geoffrey, and Mick Short. 1981. *Style in Fiction.* London: Longman.

Mandel, Ernest. 1984. *Delightful Murder: A Social History of the Crime Story.* London: Pluto Press.

Montoro, Rocio. 2005. "Curious Narrators, Curious Mathematics and Curious Representations: A Text World theory analysis of Mark Haddon's *The Curious Incident of the Dog in the Night-Time.*" Paper presented at 25th PALA Conference, Huddersfield, UK, July 18–23.

Murray, Stuart. 2006. "Autism and the Contemporary Sentimental: Fiction and the Narrative Fascination of the Present." *Literature and Medicine* 25.1: 24–45.

Porter, Dennis. 1981. *The Pursuit of Crime: Art and Ideology in Detective Fiction.* New Haven: Yale University Press.

Priestman, Martin. 1998. *Crime Fiction: From Poe to the Present.* Plymouth: Northcote House.

Short, Mick. 1996. *Exploring the Language of Poems, Plays and Prose.* London: Longman.

Semino, Elena. 2005. "Mind Style in Mark Haddon's *The Curious Incident of the Dog in the Night-Time.*" Paper presented at 25th PALA Conference, Huddersfield, UK, July 18–23.

_____, and Kate Swindlehurst. 1996. "Metaphor and Mind Style in Ken Kesey's 'One Flew Over the Cuckoo's Nest.'" *Style* 30.1: 143–65.

Walsh, Clare. 2007. "Schema Poetics and Crossover Fiction." In *Contemporary Stylistics,* edited by Marina Lambrou and Peter Stockwell, 106–17. London: Continuum.

Werth, Paul. 1999. *Text Worlds: Representing Conceptual Space in Discourse.* London: Longman.

"A Natural Instinct for Forensics": Trace Evidence and Embodied Gazes in The Bone Collector

BY LINSDAY STEENBERG

Phillip Noyce's 1999 film *The Bone Collector* introduced a fascinated public — already familiar with the forensic themed novels of Jeffery Deaver, Patricia Cornwell, and James Patterson — to a distinct forensic visual style. Preceding the influential television series *CSI: Crime Scene Investigation* (CBS 2000-) by a year, *The Bone Collector* established many of the now-iconic conventions of a new police procedure: criminalistics. Based on the 1997 novel by Jeffrey Deaver, *The Bone Collector* follows the induction of beat cop Amelia Donaghy (Angelina Jolie) into the discipline of criminal-istics, more popularly known as forensic science.[1] Her mentor and love interest is quadriplegic forensic expert, Lincoln Rhyme (Denzel Washing-ton), who she nicknames "text book guy." As Lincoln coaches Amelia in the science of detection, she becomes his stand-in at the crime scene. She embodies his gaze as he remains in the panoptic control tower of his apart-ment. In a scenario reminiscent of Alfred Hitchcock's *Rear Window* (1954), Lincoln asks her to "tell me what you see," insisting that she investigate crime scenes as his representative while remaining in constant radio/tele-phone communication. As she sees for Lincoln, he speaks in her ear, telling her what to observe and where to step. In the film, and more so in Deaver's novel, the spectator/reader audits the lessons in criminalistics' protocols and history that Lincoln gives to Amelia.

The film frames its introduction to criminalistics through the journey of a female criminalist. This focus is representative of a recent shift towards partnering postfeminist female investigators with older African American mentors. Recent films featuring this convention include *Kiss the Girls* (Fleder 1997), *Along Came a Spider* (Tamahori 2001), *High Crimes* (Franklin 2002), and *Twisted* (Kaufman 2004). Jolie's Amelia is similarly paired with Washington, whose character helps her navigate the labyrinthine world of violent crime. As one of the first forensic fictions onscreen, *The Bone Collector* codifies the visual techniques of criminalistics, particularly by highlighting the importance of physical trace evidence as the key to understanding, investigating, and recreating the criminal act. The film emphasizes trace evidence to establish a forensic gaze whose objectivity is an illusion and whose embodiment is distinctly gendered. To claim objectivity, the forensic gaze naturalizes its own processes and elides the complex power relationships that underpin it: its surveillance and disciplinary functions, its dependence on violence for its authority, and its gendered and raced hierarchical formulation.

The areas in which the forensic gaze most clearly demonstrates its ideological commitments intersect with two of the most important lessons that Amelia learns about criminalistics. Firstly, she learns about the importance of trace evidence and the necessary process of individuation that leads from the trace to the perpetrator. The codes and conventions of trace evidence reveal the surveillance function of forensics and promise to provide female experts with professional advancement and, more significantly, with personal happiness. Secondly, Amelia is trained in the practice of the forensic gaze itself, learning what to look for and why. Despite claims to objectivity, the forensic gaze is always gendered, since it is always embodied. This embodiment is made explicit in Amelia's case, as she must literally act as Lincoln's body double at the crime scene because his disability confines him to his apartment. Despite having what Lincoln describes as "a natural instinct for forensics," Amelia faces difficulties assuming the authority of the forensic gaze. These are exacerbated by and implicitly blamed on her gender.

The "One Rule to Live By"

As a forensic narrative, *The Bone Collector* marks a shift in the crime genre towards a greater focus on material trace evidence[2]:

> DAs and reporters and juries loved obvious clues. Bloody gloves, knives, recently fired guns, love letters, semen and fingerprints. But Lincoln Rhyme's favorite evidence was trace — the dust and effluence at crime scenes, so easily overlooked by perps [2006, 154].

The Bone Collector's narrative and aesthetic style reinforce Lincoln's assertion that his "favorite" kind of evidence is the most important element in a criminal investigation and that it is one of the genre's most spectacular procedures. By asserting the primacy of trace evidence, the film insists that visualization is the most important mode for analyzing a crime scene. In the forensic subgenre, everything is visualized: the crime scene, the federal database searches, the evidence collection, and even the process of laboratory analysis. This makes trace evidence spectacular and dynamic and teaches the audience — like criminalist-in-training Amelia — about the mysteries and practical potential of forensic science. This process of visualization informs not only the status of forensic science in popular culture but also the manner in which that culture imagines crime and criminality as something that can be *seen*.

Trace, as Lincoln says, is the "dust and effluence" left at crime scenes, and it represents a significant contradiction in visualizing criminal investigations because it is crucial to the process yet difficult to see. Charlie Gere connects trace evidence at the crime scene with Jacques Derrida's conceptualization of trace as something "that cannot be subsumed into either element in the binary opposition of presence and absence. The trace both is and is not" (2007, 136). The analysis of this kind of evidence is a structuring force of the criminal investigation and, through its material presence, suggests an absence and an irreversible violent act. Thus, Gere highlights the uncanny nature of the trace, whose absence in presence signals death. In *The Bone Collector*, this uncanniness is literal, signaling death's insistent presence instead of its possibility. By studying the traces left at the crime scene, the trained criminalist makes sense of absence, dust, and effluence, deducing in their connections the presence of the perpetrator.

Dr. Edmond Locard, one of the "founding fathers" of forensic science and the individual first credited with espousing the importance of trace, is mentioned consistently in both official and popular histories and in forensic fictions.[3] In *The Bone Collector* novel, Lincoln tells Amelia about Locard:

> He came up with the one rule I lived by when I ran IRD [Investigation and Resources Department]. Locard's Exchange Principle. He thought that whenever two human beings come into contact, something from one is exchanged to the other, and vice versa [2006, 155].

Lincoln posits the Exchange Principle's formulation of trace as the most important element in catching criminals. While there is no comparable discussion in the film, it proves its equal investment in Locard's Exchange Principle as the "one rule to live by" in its use of the forensic gaze and through its narrative insistence on trace as the key to tracking the criminal.

The Exchange Principle is often misquoted, and its interpretation remains a contentious issue among practicing criminalists (Chisum and Turvey 2007, 23). However, popular histories and visual culture elide this ambiguity, assuming that two people or objects exchange traces when they come into contact. Mariana Valverde argues that the Exchange Principle — and hence trace evidence — provides the lynchpin of the forensic gaze:

> The close attention to the physical traces left not only by criminal activity but by everyday activity on people's bodies and clothes, on floors, walls, gardens and objects — the key feature of the forensic gaze — is such a familiar perspective today that we tend to take it for granted that every activity leaves traces and that every criminal unwittingly sheds clues, including bits of his/her own body, which can be used to reconstruct what happened [2006, 83].

As Valverde says, modern crime stories take Locard's Exchange Principle for granted, but this foundational assumption merits further scrutiny. The trace is central to the contemporary crime procedural because it points an indisputable accusing finger at its source, so the Exchange Principle has become the "one rule to live by" when visualizing a criminal investigation. Yet, there is more at stake in reconstructing past events and identities based on object and artifact alone. Trace functions successfully in *The Bone Collector* because its collection and analysis is made visually compelling. It makes the intangible visible, and it economically visualizes the criminalist's deductive reasoning and crime solving skills. The trace also transforms the lives of those who study it. As Amelia learns criminalistics from Lincoln, she becomes a better police officer and a happier woman. Ultimately, in insisting on the importance and functions of trace evidence analysis, *The Bone Collector* frames this process as perfectly suited to the surveillance not only of the guilty but of all citizens. The ability of the criminalist to command the panoptic apparatus of trace evidence affords him or her the knowledge, status, and power to determine the signs of criminality.

The visualization of the criminalist's panoptic privileges is not without its obstacles. As Lincoln Rhyme instructs, "The essential problem for the criminalist is not that there's too little evidence but that there's too much" (2006, 140). The scale of the trace evidence itself is also an issue, as it is often small or difficult to see, such as dust, pollen, biological fluids, or minute disturbances on the surface of things. *The Bone Collector* establishes patterns for dealing with the scale of trace that have become conventional to onscreen forensic science. The film enlarges and penetrates the material evidence through extreme computer-aided close-ups, using montage and parallel editing sequences to deal sensationally and economically with the processes of collection, analysis, and hypothesis. We do not see Amelia discover, bag, and label each item of evidence; we witness only the most important discoveries. Similarly we do not watch Lincoln's lab technician, Eddie Ortiz (Luis Guzman), and his team examining every piece of trace; only the most important pieces are given screen time.

Eddie looks for what all criminalists (fictional or factual) search for: *individuated* evidence, evidence that is unusual or identifiable, which can be connected to an individual person or place. *The Bone Collector,* like other forensic fictions, features only individuated trace evidence. In the novel, Lincoln describes individuation as the "goal of the criminalist" (2006, 77). He explains that "most physical evidence can be *identified. Individuated* evidence is something that could have come from only one source or a very limited number of sources. A fingerprint, a DNA profile [...]" (2006, 77; original emphasis). Like a fingerprint, individuated trace evidence points to one specific person. However, the signature left by trace evidence is more difficult to read than the fingerprint. Establishing the perpetrator's identity from a large amount of trace evidence, *The Bone Collector* tells us, requires a more sophisticated expertise. The expert observes the most overlooked elements and prioritizes which evidence is most pertinent. Amelia and Lincoln are able to triangulate the serial killer's location and determine his personality from his preference for Victorian true crime (a publisher's logo is left at the crime scene), his knowledge of historical New York (turn of the century building materials are also left), and his understanding of forensic procedures (the evidence is staged). By focusing on individuated evidence, forensic crime stories like *The Bone Collector* can move the story forward quickly while educating the spectator and providing spectacles of science in action.

Criminalistics also promises to improve the lives of its practitioners. In a striking parallel to the Exchange Principle's assertion that every contact leaves a trace, forensic science leaves its trace on Amelia's life, transforming her personality, just as perpetrators leave traces of themselves at the crime scene. She becomes a different type of person and a different type of investigator, and the film implies that these are positive changes. Amelia struggles with the brutal violence of the crimes she investigates, but the film insists that she can overcome her doubts through criminalistics. From criminalistics, Amelia gains confidence, authority, and upward mobility. To a certain extent, her knowledge of criminalistics, and her ability to read trace evidence, protects her from the violence she investigates. At the very least, it distances her from victimhood, especially as it gives her the opportunity to save the killer's final victims (a little girl and Lincoln).

Lincoln's training helps Amelia overcome many of the obstacles the postfeminist female investigator faces to personal happiness — in particular a lack of a "work/life balance." At the start of the film, Amelia is characteristically single, unable to commit to her boyfriend, and traumatized by the discovery of her policeman father's suicide. Like many contemporary female investigators from Clarice Starling in *Silence of the Lambs* (Demme 1991) to Sara Sidle in *CSI: Crime Scene Investigation* (2000–), Amelia Donaghy deals with her past traumas and her inability to perform an "appropriate" femininity through her dedication to her job as an investigator. Through Lincoln's tutelage, she is able to come to terms with her father's death — thus beginning a pop-therapeutic healing process characteristic of postfeminist popular culture more widely.[4] The film closes with Amelia hosting a Christmas party for Lincoln and reuniting him with his estranged sister and her family. Though Amelia has been unsmiling and serious throughout the film, at this moment she is sociable, emotive, and happy. She enthusiastically performs the traditionally feminine role of supportive girlfriend and hostess. Her "healing" is demonstrated by highlighting the work/life balance missing at the film's opening. At the film's close, she is pictured outside of her work, enjoying herself and firm in her commitment to Lincoln.

Lincoln is also transformed by his contact with Amelia. Rather than suggesting that his own practice of criminalistics has made Lincoln a better person, the film dramatizes his transformation through Amelia's education and attention to him. At the start of the film, Lincoln tries to organize his own assisted suicide because he believes his disability is getting worse and his increasingly frequent strokes will ultimately damage his brain. By the close of the film, all discussions of suicide are closed, arguably responding to Amelia's chastisement: "I would've expected more from someone like you." At the film's closing party, Lincoln is no longer lying in his bed, but moving around in a wheelchair, and, for the first time in the film, dressed in a suit. Thus, Amelia's apprenticeship is doubly influential — to herself and to her teacher/lover.

As dramatized onscreen, the Exchange Principle describes the relationship of people to the objects they encounter. Criminalistics and its foundational Exchange Principle also transforms the way we, as a culture, imagine the nature of the criminal act. According to the Exchange Principle, an individual cannot leave the world untouched by his or her material presence. This means that it is likewise impossible to get away with any crime, provided there exists a trained expert who can read the trace. Because every act — innocent or criminal — leaves evidence of its occurrence, forensic trace analysis functions as a surveillance mechanism. The expert can follow a citizen's every move: which places he or she visits, who he or she sleeps with, who he or she has contact with. Through the exercise of the forensic gaze, criminalistics becomes a panoptic apparatus, tracking and watching citizens, regardless of whether they are criminals.

Yet, rather than fearing the watchful forensic eye, the citizen may be reassured by those narratives that feature it. Amelia and Lincoln are presented as virtuous and exceptionally dedicated individuals: we can trust them. *The Bone Collector* suggests that they have earned and would never abuse their panoptic privileges. The panoptic forensic eye is aimed only at the guilty, looking only for the traces of dishonesty and violence. A culture comforted by the trace has an almost pre-modern faith that "murder will out" thanks to forensic science. This reassurance, however, can be offered only in the aftermath of the crime, as the trace is retrospective rather than preventative. Despite the many reassurances offered by forensic fictions — such as closure, justice, or vengeance — the forensic gaze perpetuates rather than assuages a heightened sense of risk. Amelia may have been positively transformed by the forensic gaze, but the culture that watches, fascinated by this process, does not emerge so happily transfigured. The panoptic function of trace evidence reveals the ubiquity of violence. It propagates a chronic sense of risk to suggest constant surveillance as the only possible countermeasure. Watching for traces brings violence to our attention and reassures us that forensic science can track and punish criminals, thus legitimizing and naturalizing the practice of surveillance.

"A Fresh Pair of Eyes"

The forensic gaze is not exclusively a punitive force but is also a vehicle to visualize the process of scientific inspiration and to dramatize Locard's Exchange Principle. As one of the first visual forensic fictions, *The Bone Collector* establishes the conventions of the forensic gaze including the hierarchies on which it builds its legitimacy, the violence that is its prerequisite, and the gendered and raced assumptions that underpin/undermine its claims to neutrality and objectivity. The studied gaze of the expert is a visual anchor point for the forensic subgenre's consideration of trace. Without a guide or translator to help the audience understand the information transmitted through and by databases and archives, it loses its power to fascinate. The investigator's gaze is as important as the object or information on which he or she gazes. The shot reverse shot between findings and the eye of trained experts, often accompanied by an expository voice over, translates the clues for spectators and other investigators.

In *The Bone Collector,* Lincoln Rhyme's viewing machine exemplifies the power of the forensic gaze. He spends the majority of the film gazing at this machine as it enlarges and manipulates evidence, plots points on maps, and serves as a CCTV viewer, telephone, and access point for the Internet and law enforcement databases. It also controls Lincoln's life-support technology, his bed, and the lights in his apartment. Lincoln's internal thought processes are visually displayed by the viewing machine. As a prosthetic extension of Lincoln's gaze, the machine renders all objects accessible and legible, from trace evidence to crime scene photographs. Despite the omniscient quality of the forensic gaze, it is still an embodied phenomenon, in that it is tied to the body and inseparable from the gender and racial politics culturally inscribed on it.

The contradictory status of the forensic gaze as both abstract and embodied is evident in the complex relationship between Amelia and Lincoln's bodies and gazes. Lincoln first requests Amelia's participation in the investigation because he needs "a fresh pair of eyes." He asks her to describe everything that she sees and feels, yet he also demands that she "do everything exactly as I say." This stresses that Lincoln oversees the investigation, directing Amelia as his stand-in rather than solely training her to develop her own forensic gaze. Rather than a fresh pair of eyes, he needs a body that he can command. In this scenario, Lincoln can transcend the limitations of his disabled body through his gaze, but Amelia cannot escape hers because it defines one of her primary functions in the investigation and, perhaps, in the film. Arguably, one of the reasons why Amelia's gaze cannot be separated from her body is because she is a sexualized woman.

Amelia's gaze and her body are questioned and commented upon throughout the film. In the film's opening sequence, Amelia is the first to arrive at a crime scene where she secures the scene by stopping a train, earning Lincoln's attention and respect. But, Police Captain Cheney publicly reprimands her. He continues to criticize her forensic abilities and belittle her personally throughout the film. The film frames his disrespect of Amelia as an extension of his anger at Rhyme, suggesting that he reads her as little more than Lincoln's girl Friday. The film and the characters implicitly base their suspicion of Amelia's authority and gaze on her gender. The film repeatedly calls attention to Amelia's previous employment as a fashion model, suggesting that Amelia's beauty and sexuality disrupt the forensic investigation because her body frequently distracts her colleagues. Like many other female experts on screen, Amelia is characterized as an "unlikely" combination of a sexualized body and scientific mind. The attention given to Amelia's gendered body sabotages, or at the very least distracts from, her attempts to establish the legitimacy of her gaze. In trying to construct the authority of her forensic gaze, Amelia struggles against the objectifying male gazes focusing on her.

On the other hand, forensic fictions featuring female investigators differ from the majority of contemporary cinema in the importance, screen time, and attention given to establishing the authoritative gaze of a female character. While the female investigator's gaze is undoubtedly challenged and questioned, it marks a distinctive step towards granting female characters the power, agency, and narrative clout that the (forensic) gaze implies. Films dramatizing the forensic female gaze, from Jodie Foster's Agent Clarice Starling in *Silence of the Lambs* (Demme 1991) to Ashley Judd's Detective Jessica Shepherd in *Twisted* (Kaufman 2004), mark Hollywood cinema's experimentation with a police procedure promising access for non-traditional authority figures.

Despite his ability to transcend his body via panoptic technology, Lincoln is often challenged in a manner similar to Amelia. He is coded as "other" against a perceived white, able-bodied norm because of his race and his disability. The film, and contemporary culture more generally, assumes that Amelia and Lincoln's bodies are distractions in themselves, registering cultural baggage absent from a "neutral" white, male body. Diegetic bystanders rarely comment on the bodies of white, male experts, such as Gil Grissom in *CSI*. Comments, justifications, and explanations are reserved for those considered "different," or those bodies that seem at odds with their identities as authoritative experts. For this reason, *The Bone Collector* spends time explaining Lincoln's condition and his plans to commit suicide as well as detailing the childhood trauma that led to Amelia's career in law enforcement. Conversely, Lincoln's disability signals his superior intelligence as well as his "otherness." Because his body is immobilized, he relies almost exclusively on his gaze and his intelligence, tapping into other iconic performances of disabled crime-solvers such as Chief Robert Ironside in *Ironside* (NBC 1967–1975).

As Lincoln and Amelia's struggle for authority proves, the forensic gaze is hierarchical. Like all specialized law enforcement techniques, it proves its effectiveness by demonstrating its superiority over other crime fighting techniques — hence Lincoln's insistence that Locard's Exchange Principle is the one rule to live by. In crime films, authority is hierarchically established through its relationship to violence. In her discussion of violence and the gaze, Lisa Dickson suggests that the clinical gaze in crime films is linked repeatedly to vivisection. Although this violence is not the fault or the intention of the scientist who, after all, is searching for the victim's killer, "its (re)enactment is necessary to [his or her] epistemological quest to see, to know, trauma" (2004, 94). She summarizes: "Vision, knowledge, and violence thus act together in a necessary and contradictory relationship, because violence — enacted literally in physical wounding or figuratively through electronic penetration — is a necessary condition of the knowledge of the hidden interior of thing" (2004, 83). The dissecting gaze of the scientist revisits violence upon the corpse through dissection, by reconstructing (and frequently re-dramatizing) the original cause of death with invasive visual technologies. Amelia struggles with this violent precondition of the gaze, just as she struggles to reify her authority through it. In one sequence, Amelia is instructed to saw off the shackled hands of

sics." Her rejection of the gaze's dissecting properties is balanced by her
"natural instinct" for its preservative function. As previously mentioned,
in an early scene in the film, Amelia arrives at a crime scene alone and acts
quickly to preserve the evidence by sending a young witness to buy a dis-
posable camera. She photographs the scene methodically before the rain
washes away the evidence, even stopping a train to continue her crime
scene analysis. Lincoln celebrates Amelia's resourceful preservation of the
evidence. Here, the process of visualization is doubled, drawing attention
to itself. Not only do we see the film capture the process of criminalistics,
but within the diegesis we witness the photograph capture the trace as
part of that process. The crime scene photograph is a layered and paradoxical cinematic object that demands to be taken as truth and highlights
the visualization conventions of forensic films. In *Camera Lucida,* Roland
Barthes claims that the photograph "carries its referent within itself" (2000,
5) and this is consistently proven by *The Bone Collector*'s use of crime scene
photography as a way to signal the truth of how a crime was committed.
It carries within itself the truth of a violent crime and becomes a signal
for inarguable evidentiary fact.

In the film, Amelia cannot merely testify to what she saw. She, and
the spectator, needs the photographs as visual proof. This is a manifestation
of Barthes's argument that in the photograph, "the power of authentication
exceeds the power of representation" (2000, 89). The photos are important
because they represent a crime scene; however, this is exceeded by their
ability to denote (scientific or legal) truth itself. To uncover who committed
the crime, Amelia must have pictures of the crime scene, which is why the
film lingers on her acquisition of the camera and photographing the evidence. The photograph's ability stops time and space for future study and

122

provides what Barthes has called its "evidential force" (2000, 89). The photograph makes the aftermath of violence visible and legible. It preserves the ephemeral trace evidence — and the temporal moment — in an eight by ten glossy material object, which can be archived for future study and reference. To make this truth clear, Amelia must provide the narration for the photograph to make it legible to the general public. The photograph requires the translation of experts like Amelia who can tell us *which* specific truth the photograph authenticates.

In discussing the evidential force of the photograph, Barthes also speaks of its power to wound its spectator, which is the key to unlocking the force and knowledge contained or invoked by the photograph. This is epitomized in the treatment of crime scene photographs of the forensic subgenre. Here, the photograph of the wound itself can wound its spectators and inspectors. Wounding becomes literal as the photograph of the crime scene injures audiences because of its ability not only to signal "truth," but violent truth. The crime scene photograph represents a postmodern flattening, a compression of wounding into a single material object and frozen temporal moment. Rather than suggesting trauma is unrepresentable, forensic fiction insists that it must be represented, but in very conventional ways, such as a microscope point of view shot, a database search, or a crime scene photograph. The crime scene photograph can and must be gazed upon, read, and understood. Experienced investigators such as Lincoln are stalwart in the face of the wounding potential of both photograph (medium) and violence (content). This stoicism is reinforced by Lincoln's carer Thelma's disgust and refusal to look at the crime scene photographs. In contrasting Lincoln and Amelia's reactions to those of a "civilian," the power of the photograph to wound is clearly limited to those who are not reading it with a forensic gaze. For those that do, violence is legible and can be translated into reassurance: violence can be contained and justice can be achieved. The wound loses some of its affective potential when it is made flatly material and decipherable. The photograph in postmodernity is a paradoxical object, conflating the power to authenticate and the force to insist on materiality, yet understood — especially in the digital age — as a simulation of the real. Since the perceived ubiquity of image-editing software such as Photoshop, there is a common cultural perception that digital photographs can be doctored and faked seamlessly. Standing opposed to the mutability of the digital, is the solidity and historicity of the analogue. The eight by ten, glossy, black and white photographic print is used as a code or convention indicating a forensic truth uncompromised by the digital.

The crime scene photograph has a unique relationship to truth and authenticity. Spread across desks, stapled to police files, and on display in courtrooms, the power of the crime scene photo lies in both its indexical and authenticating value. It literally carries its referent within it — the criminal body, the corpse, or the trace evidence. It bolsters the status of the investigator who, through his or her expertise, can read all three simultaneously. The crime scene photograph also differs from other visual representations of the crime scene, such as digital CCTV footage or audio material. The photograph, as a medium, has a long history of authenticity on which it relies for its claims to truth. While CCTV footage is blurry and pixilated, the crime scene photo is crisp and analogue. Because it does not need to be "fixed," the printed photograph has a stronger claim on authentication. Evidence, as these fictions repeatedly remind us, does not lie, and thus the insistent materiality of the printed photograph is presumed to have a purer relationship to the truth.

Just as the evidence is hierarchically articulated, so too are those that process it. The authority-building mentor/student relationship is a long-standing convention of the crime genre in which older police captains have been gruffly instructing younger detectives for decades. In the forensic subgenre, this relationship has often been imaged as an older, African American father figure teaching his expertise to a younger, white female investigator. *The Bone Collector*'s partnership of actors Denzel Washington and Angelina Jolie is somewhat of an exceptional case, as Lincoln Rhyme is severely disabled and he and Amelia have an implied romantic relationship. The other films very carefully and anxiously avoid any romantic or sexual elements to the relationship by framing the older black man as a father figure. Nevertheless, however exceptional the Lincoln Rhyme/Amelia Donaghy partnership is, it still conforms to many of the conventions of the other films. Their partnership serves a similar function — providing authority for both the male criminalist and the female novice — but the partnership also marginalizes both the black man and the white woman.

The relationship between Lincoln and Amelia helps to bolster their individual authority through Lincoln's status as teacher and Amelia's eventual command of criminalistics. However, in this relationship, Amelia's knowledge is always hierarchically inferior to Lincoln's, as she remains his student and love interest rather than an equal colleague. Conversely, Lincoln's advising role to Amelia marginalizes his importance, as he becomes a supporting figure rather than a protagonist. This suggests that he can be categorized as a re-articulation of the stock character Heather J. Hicks describes as the "Magical African American Friend" (2003, 27). While Hicks uses this to describe partnerships between a white man in crisis and his helpful African American friend, in such films as *The Green Mile* (Darabont 1999), it certainly describes the many ways in which Lincoln's expertise and power are compromised and contained in *The Bone Collector.* However, categorizing Lincoln in this way does not necessarily imply that Amelia's character is granted the kind of centrality and hegemonic power of the white male characters in films such as those identified by Hicks.

Lincoln's role as "magical friend" to the apprentice postfeminist female expert registers anxieties about changing work roles in contemporary culture. As Hicks points out, the black magical man becomes a harbinger for, and a facilitator of, the marginalization and disempowerment the white man is fated to suffer in a feminizing service economy (2003, 45). This is clearly signaled in the black man's training of the white woman to enter a traditionally masculine profession like law enforcement. The partnership between an older African American mentor and a younger postfeminist female investigator is doubly threatening to white patriarchal power because it represents an alliance of those who have been excluded by it. It is tempting to read Lincoln and Amelia's relationship as a disruptive force, subverting the patriarchal power bloc of forensic scientific knowledge and the crime genre, and to a certain extent it does that. Hicks suggests that magical black men are "provocateurs, forcing latent troubles into the light of day" (2003, 51). However, because of the depoliticized nature of the relationship between black man and white woman and their double marginalization, the disruptive potential of partnerships like Lincoln and Amelia's are contained.

The Bone Collector, one of the first visualizations of criminalistics, celebrates Locard's Exchange Principle and the forensic gaze. It suggests a knowledge system free from prejudice through its reliance on material trace evidence and its attempts to construct a disembodied forensic gaze. Despite its aspirations to objectivity, forensic science onscreen exhibits conservative racial and gender politics. Furthermore, the cinematic construction of expert investigators like Lincoln Rhyme and Amelia Donaghy propagates an epistemological mechanism that is both hierarchical and panoptic. At stake in constructing and visualizing the forensic science of *The Bone Collector* is the construction of an expert knowledge. This expertise is relevant to the case and accesses wider formulations of cultural power. In setting up the conventions of forensics onscreen, *The Bone Collector* suggests that seeing is more than believing — seeing (and spectacle) is *truth*. The visual field has the power to make violence traceable, decipherable, and therefore punishable. Visualizations of forensic science in *The Bone Collector,* and in forensic fictions more widely, glorify it as a knowledge-generating system that is, literally, enlightening.

Notes

1. In the source novel, Amelia's last name is Sachs. Arguably this has been changed in the film to the much more Irish Donaghy to tap into the iconic character of the Irish-American beat cop. Jeffrey Deaver has continued to write about Amelia Sachs and Lincoln Rhyme in a series of books, focusing on crime solving via criminalistics, including *The Coffin Dancer* (1998), *The Empty Chair* (2000), and *The Cold Moon* (2009).

2. Narratives focusing on physical evidence, including the corpse of the murder victim, were certainly not unheard of at this time, for example in the novels of Patricia Cornwell. There were, however, few medical examiners, pathologists, and criminalists given top billing onscreen.

3. Generally speaking, forensic science, and indeed science in general, is charted as a discipline propelled by great men and even greater technological innovations. Legal historian Wayne Morrison has highlighted the flaws of this kind of approach, suggesting that these histories give "the false impression that criminology is our modern response to a timeless and unchanging set of questions that previous thinkers have also pondered, though with notably less success" (2006, 49). Despite Morrison's apt critique, popular histories of forensics use this very assumption to tell the story of forensics. It is precisely this popularized version of forensics that is visualized onscreen in forensic fictions such as *The Bone Collector.*

4. Postfeminist media culture champions pop-therapy as one of the key ways to re-invent oneself as a happier person — in particular a happier, more balanced woman. Therapeutic solutions are based on individual responsibility and achieving concepts such as "closure," "self-esteem," and "work/life balance." The daytime talk show, as Jane Shattuc discusses (1997), is a primary site of this process. In the crime stories featuring women as protagonists, sympathetic and authoritative men are often represented as the counsellors and overseers of this procedure.

Works Cited

Along Came a Spider. 2001. Dir. Lee Tamahori. Paramount Pictures.
Barthes, Roland. 2000. *Camera Lucida: Reflections on Photography.* Trans. Richard Howard. London: Vintage.

The Bone Collector. 1999. Dir. Phillip Noyce. Columbia Pictures. 1999.
Chisum, W. Jerry, and Brent E. Turvey. 2007. *Crime Reconstruction.* Burlington: Elvesier/ Academic Press.
CSI: Crime Scene Investigation. 2000—. Creat. Anthony E. Zuicker and Ann Donahue. CBS.
Deaver, Jeffrey. 2006 (1997). *The Bone Collector.* London: Hodder & Stoughton.
Dickson, Lisa. 2004. "Hook and Eye: Violence and the Captive Gaze." *Camera Obscura* 56.19.2: 75–103.
Foucault, Michel. 1991. *Discipline & Punish: The Birth of the Prison.* Trans. Alan Sheridan. Harmondsworth: Penguin.
Gere, Charlie. 2007. "Reading the Traces." In *Reading CSI: Crime TV Under the Microscope,* edited by Andrew Anthony, 129–139. London: I.B. Tauris.
Green Mile, The. 1999. Dir. Frank Darabont. Castle Rock Entertainment.
Hicks, Heather J. 2003. "Hoodoo Economics: White Men's Work and Black Men's Magic in Contemporary American Film." *Camera Obscura* 53.18.2: 27–55.
High Crimes. 2002. Dir. Carl Franklin. Regency Enterprises.
Ironside. 1967–75. Creat. Collier Young. NBC.
Kiss the Girls. 1977. Dir. Gary Fleder. Paramount Pictures.
Mizejewski, Linda. 2004. *Hardboiled & High Heeled: The Woman Detective in Popular Culture.* New York: Routledge.
_____. 2005. "Dressed to Kill: Postfeminist Noir." *Cinema Journal.* 44.2: 121–127.
Morrison, Wayne. 2006. *Criminology, Civilisation and the New World Order.* Abingdon: Routledge Cavendish.
Rear Window. 1954. Dir. Alfred Hitchcock. Paramount Pictures.
Sekula, Allan. 1989. "The Body and the Archive." In *The Contest of Meaning: Critical Histories of Photography,* edited by Richard Bolton, 342–389. Cambridge: MIT Press.
Shattuc, Jane M. 1997. *The Talking Cure: TV Talk Shows and Women.* New York: Routledge.
The Silence of the Lambs. 1991. Dir. Jonathan Demme. Orion Pictures Corporation.
Tasker, Yvonne, and Diane Negra, eds. 2007. *Interrogating Postfeminism: Gender and the Politics of Popular Culture.* Durham: Duke University Press.
Twisted. 2004. Dir. Philip Kaufman. Paramount Pictures.
Valverde, Mariana. 2006. *Law and Order: Images, Meanings, Myths.* New Brunswick: Routledge-Cavendish.

"Post-Modern or Post-Mortem?" Murder as a Self-Consuming Artifact in Red Dragon

BY DAVID LEVENTE PALATINUS

> If the doors of perception were cleansed every thing would appear to man as it is, infinite.
> — William Blake, *The Marriage of Heaven and Hell*

Con-Texts

In October 2002, the Brooklyn Museum of Art advertised the exhibition of William Blake's watercolor *The Great Red Dragon and the Woman Clothed with the Sun* in a press release that used the "newly released *Red Dragon* film" directed by Brett Ratner and "Thomas Harris's eponymous bestselling novel" to attract audiences.[1] By deploying the screen adaptation and the book as catchphrases to popularize the original painting, the museum's publicity suggests that the categories of "high" and "low" cannot be used any more to indicate aesthetic value judgments or a hierarchical ordering of the different layers of culture. The postmodern conception of culture seems to incorporate high and low alike — not so much as layers, but as mutually dependent and mutually reflective registers.

As Mieke Bal explains, the entanglement of "low" and "high" is intelligible from at least three different perspectives. According to the first assumption, the status of artist and his or her work can be defined in terms of "genius" and "high" or "elite" art, respectively, and the degree of aesthetic quality attributed to a work of art relies on the radical demarcation of "high culture" and other forms of art that appeal to a popular audience (cf. Bal 2006, 6–7). In response to the increasing awareness that surrounds these mechanisms of exclusion, critics after the cultural turn deliberately moved away from the works of geniuses and focused instead on the products of popular culture that were earlier discredited as "low art" to evaluate them as evidence of people's engagement with culture (cf. Bal 2006, 6–7). Bal argues that film studies gains a particular significance in this respect because when it refuses to differentiate between popular and art films in its interpretative practices, it undermines the condemnation of popular cinema as ideologically noxious. Apart from these approaches, Bal says, there is room for a third position as well, where "high art" is regarded as being part of popular culture. She claims that the high-low disjunction does not derive from the work in question but rather from our preconceptions. Culture constitutes its own works and artists, and art constitutes culture, too, by raising and addressing particular sets of questions (cf. Bal 2006, 7).

Blake's painting, Harris's novel, and the film adaptation, therefore, are caught up in an intertextual bouncing, a multidirectional movement from one to another. The meanings generated by one text are challenged, informed, and overwritten by the others. The plot of the film (and of the book) uses the ordinary patterns of the psychological thriller and the police procedural: FBI agent Will Graham (Edward Norton) returns from his early retirement to investigate a series of murders committed by a serial killer called Francis Dolarhyde (Ralph Fiennes), a mentally disturbed and schizophrenic young man obsessed with Blake's painting. Dolarhyde sees the dragon as the embodiment of ultimate corporeal beauty, perfection, savageness, and power. He has it tattooed on his back and identifies with the dragon figure in an attempt to compensate for his facial disfigurement and to repress the haunting memories of the sexual abuses he suffered as a child. In the course of events, Dolarhyde's worship of the dragon is revealed to be as much motivated by fear as by fascination, and in the end he destroys the original of the painting in the Brooklyn Museum. Blake's watercolor is presented as the embodiment of power and beauty; the villain gradually identifies with the painting until he sees himself as a powerful and fascinating work of art — as Blake's dragon incarnate. However, as the story unfolds, the painting comes to signify not only the object of desire but also the symptomatology of mental and corporeal trauma.

Consequently, the presence of Blake's painting not only provides a perfect frame for the representation of cruelty, obsession, anxiety, and perversion by virtue of its obscure symbolism and mystical apocalyptic connotations. The mingling of an artwork with the conventional thriller pattern does not simply suggest that popular culture ultimately assumes an assimilative and abusive power over the "elite." Rather, the fact that the painting is expropriated as an element of suspense also exemplifies how the isolation of high art is manipulated and repressed by the cinematographic medium. From the point of view of high art, the Blake painting is "reduced" to a vehicle of popular psychology, and thus any interpretation of either the painting or the film becomes equally simplistic and reductive. Consequently, popular cinema can be condemned as that which not only uses but abuses art. But from a phenomenological perspective, the film also exploits the blurring of the boundaries between popular and high art, testing the very concept.

Enter the Monster or Cinema, Art, and Psychosis

Blake's painting as an embodiment of psychosis also opens up a historical perspective, not only as regards the history of the psychological thriller but also that of cinema in a broader sense. As Sharon Packer notes, psychology gradually "seeped into cinema" (2007, 85) and, especially in the 1970s and 1980s, several approaches to film were to some extent motivated and informed by psychology and psychoanalysis in particular.[2] Images are much more susceptible to psychologization than texts, and the moving image itself perpetuates questions about perception and the psychology of response. The viewer's experience of his or her own body in relation to bodies on the screen and the integration of the gaze with issues of corporeality are of particular importance in regarding psychoanalysis as a possible entry-point into the realm of film. Also, the study of cinema gave a new impetus to the discussions of voyeurism, the phenomenology of the gaze, and the psychology of suspense.[3] The technologies of the cinematic image, such as lighting, camera work, *mise-en-scène*, and composition, all work towards the creation of a particular cognitive and emotional effect. As regards the entanglement of cinema and psychoanalysis, Packer approaches the question from a historical point of view:

> Cinema and psychology (especially psychoanalysis) go hand in hand. [...]
> Because cinema started at the same time that psychoanalysis was invented,

much (but not all) of our movie history mirrors the rise and fall of psycho-analysis. [...] We saw how hypnosis and behavioral conditioning, as well as drugs, drink, demons, doubles, and *doppelgangers,* played into the portrayal of the psyche and shaped the public's perception of the modern mind.

It stands to reason that psychoanalysis — and the psyche — were overrepresented in movies, not just because both were products of the turn-of-the-twentieth century, but also because psychoanalysis pushes the plot, fleshes out characters, and adds dramatic dream scenes [Packer 2007, 163].

Crime films especially adhere to this apparent psychological imperative in mapping out the anatomy of crime and in trying to decipher the workings of a criminal mind. *Red Dragon* is no exception: the portrayal of special agent Will Graham is a fictional re-investment of forensic profiling, and, indirectly, of Freudian and Lacanian psychoanalysis. The psychological thriller gives material shape to a series of questions posed by psychoanalysis, including the trauma experienced over the breaking down of the world into the orders of the symbolic, the imaginary, and the real; the trauma of the disjunction of subject and object; and the trauma of otherness and repression and of fear and desire. Accordingly, the thriller does not simply gesture at the cognitive and behavioral distortions of the psyche, but rather it shows "the reality flushed out into the open" (Magistrale and Morrison 1996, 2). It encompasses the "act of watching our collective and personal fears reworked into a narrative" (Magistrale and Morrison 1996, 3).

In *Red Dragon,* this process of self-projection is revisited through the character of Francis Dolarhyde. As a principle, thriller and horror alike build upon the existence of a being, namely a monster, that threatens to disrupt the prevailing structures of personal and social relationships. The forces the monster embodies are also contained within these structures. They are normally repressed and kept under control, but, if left unwatched, they may also become destructive. The monster in this sense emerges from within; it is not something that attacks from an outside, as its embodiment takes place on the inside. This is the reason why, in Tony Magistrale and Michael A. Morrison's words, we, as audience, watch the emergence of the monster with "a mixture of repulsion and secret identification" (1996, 4). As they write, "While part of us is appalled by [the monster's] excesses and outrages, another part gleefully identifies with its rebellion against social, sexual, and moral codes" (1996, 4). Regarding the genre codes of the psychological thriller, the opposition of the forensic profiler and the serial killer epitomizes this mixed attitude. The serial killer is presented and distanced as morally condemnable and socially deviant, whereas the profiler has to identify with the killer to understand his motifs and calculate his methods.

The beginning of the plot reveals that Dolarhyde has already murdered two families. He also displays two unusual habits that make him distinctive. He smashes the mirrors, not only in his home but also in the homes of his victims. Agent Graham also finds an explanation for the smashing of mirrors:

> Small pieces of mirror were inserted into the orbital sockets of the victims. This occurred post-mortem. Why did you put mirrors in their eyes? [...] The pieces of mirror make their eyes look alive! He wanted an audience! He wanted them all line up, watching him when he touched her! [*Red Dragon* 2002, DVD].

Dolarhyde's need for an audience implies that he takes murder to be an art form. For him murder is not merely an act of violence — a manifestation of supremacy and control — but rather it amounts to a performance, particularly a spectacle, serving as an artifact that operates primarily through the optical faculties. Therefore, Graham's finding indicates that seeing is emphasized in the film.

There is, however, another explanation for the smashing of mirrors that is psychological and physiognomic in nature. Dolarhyde lives with a facial disfigurement, a cleft lip, which he takes to be a sign of abnormality and associates with mutilation, castration, weakness, and inferiority. When he smashes the mirrors, he refuses to acknowledge the specular image as his own and tries to annul the deformity by concealing it, by rendering it invisible. As Wendy Lesser explains:

> Fictional murderers are traditionally afraid of acute sight, of accurate vision. Oedipus blinds himself after discovering he is a patricidal murderer, Gloucester has his eyes gouged out by his murderous son Edmund [...] The eye can be the inflictor of violence [and] it can be the recipient [Lesser 1995, 54].

The rejection of the self-image can be read, in this respect, as the rejection of one's own identity. As Timothy D. Harfield phrases, "The cleft lip functions as a synecdoche, as a part that not only stands for the whole, but also into which the entirety of his [i.e., Dolarhyde's] personhood is reduced" (2008, 5). Harfield sees the smashing of mirrors as "symptomatic of a kind of failed identification during the (Lacanian) mirror stage of [Dolarhyde's] development" (Harfield 2006, 6). Lacan places *the gaze* at the centre of the formation of the ego (cf. Mirzoeff 1999, 164) and defines the mirror stage as a moment in a child's development when he assumes his identity through the primordial recognition of his image in a mirror (Lacan 1977, 1–2). Lacan explains that to hold it in its gaze, the child leans forward to bring back an "instantaneous aspect of the image." He further argues that "we have only to understand the mirror stage as an *identification* [...] a transformation that takes place in the subject when he assumes an image" (Lacan 1977, 2; original emphasis). The child learns to distinguish between his or her own face and body, though the latter is given only as *Gestalt* (Lacan 1977, 2), and the image of an Other, especially that of the mother. Despite this *alienation*, as Lacan calls it, children are able to retain the integrity of their self-image because they realize that the gaze that determines the image "is outside." Thus, the child's identity is formed under the gaze of others. Harfield points out that "the shattered or fragmented mirror [...] is representative of the fragmentary gaze with which Dolarhyde was compelled to identify. Under the gaze of [...] his grandmother, Dolarhyde is refused an image of himself in the unified Gestalt of his body, and given, instead a fragmented image that reduced him to his cleft lip" (2008, 6). The importance of the self-image is revealed in retrospection when, at the end of the film, agent Graham reads Dolarhyde's diary and remarks:

> When I read his journal, it was sad. It was just so sad. I couldn't help feeling sorry for him. He wasn't born a monster. This guy was made one through years of abuse [*Red Dragon* 2002, DVD].

The other significant aspect of the mirror stage, which might eventually explain Dolarhyde's obsession with the painting, is precisely the alienation that creates a split within the subject. As Carol-Ann Tyler indicates, "The subject can never reconcile the split between itself and its mirror imago, the eye which sees and the eye which is seen, the I who speaks and the I who is spoken, the subject of desire and the subject of demand" (1994, 218). This split resides in Dolahyde's *lack* of an ideal self-image that is supposed to mark the integrity of the self. Psychoanalysis discloses the visual aspect of identity-formation and reveals that the self-image is eventually the conflation of one's own gaze directed at one's own body appearing in the mirror and the outside gaze of the Other that is posited as abject. If the mother's gaze is meant to be constitutive of this integrity, superimposed as the source of approval and confirmation, the grandmother's gaze in the film, conversely, denotes disintegration, humiliation and disapproval. It extends beyond the boundaries of the mirror stage and is used "metonymically" and stands for the "gaze of the generalized other" (Harfield 2008, 7).

To better understand the relevance of this reflective disjunction, we have to recall the distinction W. J. T. Mitchell makes between pictures and images. He describes the "picture" as "a constructed concrete object or ensemble" in opposition to the image that is "the virtual, phenomenal appearance [the picture] provides for the beholder" (Mitchell 1995, 4 n5). The gaze, for Dolarhyde, points beyond turning the picture, that is, the optical phenomenon in the mirror, into an image. When he chooses to destroy the medium, the broken mirror comes to signify the missing ideal self-image that only exists in the form of *desire*. To borrow Hans Belting's wording, the broken mirror "stages the presence of an absence" (2005, 49), and it functions as an empty frame that needs to be filled. The rejection of the specular image and the lack of an ideal imago drive Dolarhyde to search for a substitute. He chooses the Blake painting as a screen to project his narcissistic fantasies upon, thus fetishizing it and making it a vehicle of self-realization. Since the painting depicts the dragon with his back to the beholder, veiling off his face, the viewer's attention is directed to the body that displays powerful musculature, spread wings, and an emphatic tail wrapping around the female figure at the dragon's feet. The composition offers a plausible visual metaphor for the consumption of the woman in a forced interchange of gazes. The man-dragon's torso resembles that of an athlete with a proportionate anatomy, and its meticulously engineered geometry amplifies the concepts of corporeal beauty and perfection. It is, however, not so much the presence of the diabolic wings and tail that particularly strikes the viewer as monstrous as the displacement of the face. The body, in this respect, is literally de-faced. The gaze of the dragon, though only attributed, points inside the picture plane. It is fixed on the woman and directs the beholder's look to the same point. The woman, in return, gazes back at the dragon in awe and horror. The whole composition radiates dynamism, control, and a re-generative, transformative power of the spectacle that Dolarhyde associates with "art." The painting thus further complicates the pathology of sight: the dynamism of seeing implies that it is not merely the deprivation or the distortion of the face that brings about the monster, but rather the loss of one's own countenance.

Fetish, Gaze and the Pathologization of the Image in Red Dragon

Dolarhyde's obsession concerns the painting both as an art-object and as an anthropomorphic entity. He confers upon it powers that personify, or animate, the picture which, by the same token, becomes what Mitchell calls a fetish (2005, 28, 32). The painting eventually shields off Dolarhyde from his castration anxiety rooted in a childhood trauma. When the viewer first sees Francis Dolarhyde, he is already an adult, lifting weight at his workout bench in the attic of his mansion, but he can still hear the haunting voice of his late grandmother in his head:

> Oh, Francis, I've never seen a child as dirty or disgusting as you. [...] Now give me my scissors...! Take that filthy little thing in your hand and stretch it out. [...] Do you want me to cut it off?! I pledge you my word Francis: if you ever make your bed dirty again I'll cut it off [*Red Dragon* 2002, DVD].

The painting remains a fetish as long as it stages the two most fundamental characteristic features of masculinity: physical strength and sexual potency. It is in the nature of the dragon to consume the woman's body and bring his physical strength to an extreme in murder. Dolarhyde assumes the desired ideal self-image by identifying with the fetish. His identification with the dragon expands beyond the boundaries of cognitive operations into the realm of corporeality, as he also identifies with the image of the dragon in terms of physical semblance, wearing a life-size tattoo of the painting on his back.

There is another sequence in the film that marks the connection between gaze and control, murder and "art," in which Dolarhyde captures *Tattler* journalist Freddy Lounds, who, in cooperation with the FBI, published a degrading article about him. Glued to a wheelchair, Lounds represents the controlled gaze of the cinema viewer who, like Lounds, sees the tattoo for the first time. Dolarhyde threatens Lounds — and, indirectly, the viewer — to "staple his eyelids to his forehead" if he does not open his eyes and look at him. The film at this point visually juxtaposes the Blake painting and Dolarhyde's staging of the Dragon. He poses nude between Lounds and the projection screen, flexing the back muscles and imitating the Dragon's posture with wings and legs spread, actually animating the image on his back. But the tattoo is more than just a copy of Blake's watercolor. It operates as a kind of effigy which, according to Belting, "epitomizes the simultaneity as well as opposition between absence and presence" (2005, 46). The tattoo, in this case, is the mental image of the Dragon *inscribed* into a physical object, the body. In this configuration, the body not only merges with the screen, where its shadow appears as a frame but also becomes a visual metaphor in which the personified image of the Dragon steps off the screen. Consequently, the tattoo integrates with the body and becomes not just an image *on* the body but rather the image *of* the body in the fetishistic gaze. By virtue of the transfer between picture and image, Dolarhyde becomes the living personification of the *Red Dragon*. He keeps repeating the question "Do you see?" as he runs through the slides that show his former victims. Finally he turns to the journalist: "Will you tell the truth now? About my work? My becoming? My *art?*" (*Red Dragon* 2002, DVD). Dolarhyde's need for an audience explains the theatricality of the murders. As Belting emphasizes, all images "arrive with a predetermined *mise-en-scène*" (2005, 49), or staging. For Dolarhyde, murder is the art of *mise-en-scène*, in which he emerges both as *auteur* and *art-object*. On the one hand, he brings the lifeless image of the dragon into life, and on the other hand, as a living image, he exposes himself to the (outside) gaze of others. Dolrahyde's desire to be looked at and to attain and control the gaze of others may be seen as a reverberation of Lacan's famed aphorism: "In the scopic field, the gaze is outside, I am looked at, that is to say, I am a picture" (1978, 106).

If one end of relations with pictures is characterized by fetishistic iconophilia, the other end is characterized by the destructive drives of iconophobia. Fetish, for instance, as a substitute, sometimes wields so much power that it threatens to take over the place of that for which it is a substitute. Even Dolarhyde understands that the "non-gaze" of the painting controls him the same way as he wants to control the gaze of his victims. This paradox moves towards a cataclysmic peak as his relationship with his colleague and love-interest, Reba McClane, advances. In Dolarhyde's case, it is not merely the distortion of his face that brings about the monster, but rather the loss of his own countenance. De-facement, for Dolarhyde, is a self-inflected stigma that is in sharp contrast with his efforts to build up a perfect and visually pleasing body. His body-image is distorted by its own perfection and immaculacy that, retroactively, imperfects his personality. This obsession with the body-image discloses the double nature of art: generative and re-generative. The notions of beauty and perfection and the concept of the ideal are never given as absolute; they are always constructed. The integrity Dolarhyde seeks to restore, consequently, is only a fiction, and the tattooing, as the carved image of fetish, makes Dolarhyde what he beholds.

Dolarhyde's failure to come to terms with his physical condition, his scar, is highlighted in his relationship with the Reba McClane. She counterpoints Mrs. Dolarhyde, as she is not bothered by Dolarhyde's disfigurement since she lives with a disability too, having lost her eyesight as a child. She verbalizes her fascination with the man and with his physical characteristics, in particular. Reba's blindness radically repositions Dolarhyde's misapprehension of his deformity. Like the woman in the painting, she gives Dolarhyde the awe he wants, and she offers herself to him in total submission, acknowledging his strength and sexual potency. They have sex and, the following morning, the film presents Dolarhyde with his back to the camera, exposing the tattoo, as if it were to suggest that the staging of the dragon is yet incomplete. Reba's character slips out of the Dragon's will to dominate her. In fact, the dynamics of Reba and Dolarhyde's relationship posit the woman in the dominant role. She is the one who starts up a conversation with Dolarhyde in the dark room where they first meet, and her sexuality apparently subdues Dolarhyde's. In this respect, Reba can also be seen as a redeeming figure. Towards the end of the film, agent Will Graham comforts Reba with the following words: "You know, whatever part of him was still human ... was only kept alive because of you. You probably saved some lives. You didn't draw a freak. Okay? You drew a man with a freak on his back" (*Red Dragon* 2002, DVD).

At the hands of Reba, Dolarhyde's iconophilia turns into iconophobia; he realizes that he does not need to control Reba's gaze, at least not the way he did it with his former victims. As Nicholas Mirzoeff observes, "in the fetishistic gaze, reality exists but has the viewer's desire superimposed over it" (1999, 163). Since the fetish holds Dolarhyde captive, in a dramatic moment he attempts to overcome the dragon. Unable to destroy the image, he chooses to destroy the picture, the real fetish, in the Brooklyn Museum. The eating of the painting (the consumption of art) therefore prevails as a metaphor for the self-consuming nature of Dolarhyde's own art. The higher the level of perfection his art reaches, the more he loses his human self. This paradox becomes apparent when Dolarhyde makes one last desperate attempt to "save" Reba from his monstrous other. He kidnaps her and stages his own suicide, really shooting the already dead body of a former victim, but letting the blind Reba think he killed himself. He then sets his home on fire and disappears in the flames. He resurfaces in the Grahams' house where he is eventually shot in the face by Will's wife, Molly. The conclusion of the film thus deconstructs the painting's thematization of the interaction between the woman's gaze and the Dragon's countenance in an epitomic reversal of the power structures between the Dragon and his victim, the Woman.

There is, in fact, a latent irony in the portrayal of Dolarhyde that subverts his art and his interpretation of Blake. In his reading of Harris' novel, Tony Magistrale seems to retreat into defending Blake's romantic genius. He retains the disjunction between Blake and the pathological version of his art, thus detaching Blake from the novel. In so doing, he emphasizes misapprehension rather than identification in his analysis of Dolarhyde's character:

> The irony ultimately inherent in Dolarhyde's quest is that he reduces Blake's evocative symbols of the visionary human imagination to mere acts of butchery; his dragon-man alter ego revels in attacking helpless women and children who are asleep. [...] Blake's art epitomizes the positive attributes of breaking free from the oppressive social veneers of everyday life. In his need to tyrannize others in order to achieve his own freedom, Dolarhyde certainly misapprehends Blake [Magistrale 1996, 30].

In the cinematographic medium, the ideas of staging and murder are brought to the viewer at two removes. Art and gaze unavoidably constitute a difference and, as a result, a distance between the beholder (or viewer) and that which is looked at. This is symptomatic of the relation between the viewer and the cinema screen, as well. The question concerns the suspension or bracketing of this difference. No performance or staging is intelligible without a certain form of gaze. The cinematic image is also there to be looked at and the actor's bodily involvement in the staging of a character's image presupposes the superimposition of some kind of outside gaze — whether latent and attributed or apparent and distanced. Consequently, the significance of the gaze, together with the different forms of staging, resides in the ability to provide the viewers with the possibility of both immediate participation and controlled distance. In this respect, it really is true that murder as art is self-consuming, as it eventually eats up the murderer itself.

Aesthetics of Murder?

The representation of the gaze in Blake's watercolor can be read as the symptom of paralysis and, at the same time, as the manifestation of awe and fascination. As a consequence, the monstrosity of the dragon appears to be aesthetically appealing: the beauty and fear are coextensive. This coextension becomes the basis upon which the film builds its unique psychology of violence. Even though in the film *Red Dragon*, art is not normative, this does not mean art has nothing to do with social and ethical norms. The common critical stance is that crime fiction almost never challenges the social, ethical, and judicial status quo, as deviant behavior is depicted as deviant, and in the end, social justice has to be reestablished one way or another. The aestheticization of violence is not meant to decriminalize crime, but it treats violence as a "stylistically excessive" way of self-expression (Bruder 1998). As Joel Black explains, "[if] any human act evokes the aesthetic experience of the sublime, certainly it is the act of murder [and] if murder can be experienced aesthetically, the murderer can in turn be regarded as [...] anti-artist whose specialty is not creation but destruction" (1991, 14). The film, like many of Blake's works, undoes the idea of art as a beautified parallel of civilization. It promotes not simply an aesthetic but also an *aisthetic*, the attribution of "art" to *any* object.

As a consequence, when *Red Dragon* juxtaposes art and murder, it turns murder into an object of fascination, promoting a minimalist philosophy of art where the conceptualization of aesthetics is interwoven with the problematization of the sublime, the beautiful, and the repulsive. These categories are no longer intelligible in terms of binary oppositions but rather should be understood in terms of rhizomes. *Red Dragon* marks the space where the practices and the conceptualization of art are *pathologized* to incorporate the aestheticization of violence.

The main question, therefore, for Blake and for the creators of *Red Dragon* alike, is whether or not it is possible to express, represent, or embody diabolic monstrosity in an aesthetically appealing form capable of evoking fear and fascination at the same time. At stake in the intra-cultural mixing of high and popular registers is not simply the juxtaposition of high and low, ethics and nature, or, borrowing René Girard's words, violence and the sacred. At stake in *Red Dragon* is the violation *of* the sacred — with a double genitive. The sacred is always the target of violence, as in the Biblical apocalyptic narrative. Blake's painting also amplifies the sexual connotations of this violence, since the dragon's tail wrapping around the woman's body is a refined pictorial allegory for rape. Consumption therefore does not only entail the swallowing or killing of the body, but also it signifies the sexual consumption of the woman's body. The painting's ability to render an act of violence in an aesthetically appealing form highlights the other side of the double genitive: the sacred is not simply violated. It is the sacred that violates.

The nesting of the painting in the thriller-pattern can be read as a metaphor for the nesting cultural registers of the film. In this respect, the film does abuse the image, but it can only do so because the image itself embodies abuse. Consequently, the film does nothing more than offer a fiction of an art that is by definition abusive. Therefore, the double genitive indicates that violence cannot be located "outside" culture. It is not the opposite of culture, but it defines culture from within and is disclosed as a force inherent in the constitution of culture. From a phenomenological point of view, our experience and understanding of violence is pre-determined by socio-cultural, ethical, judicial, academic, and artistic preconceptions and assumptions. The phenomenology of violence also means we have to consider violence as a cultural commodity. The feat of the suspense thriller is that, by way of retaining the possibility of catharsis, it aims at an auto-therapeutic reworking of the human psyche and eventually deconstructs violence by immunizing the audience through the simultaneity of active participation and controlled distance.

Notes

1. See The Brooklyn Museum website: www.brooklynmuseum.org/press/uploads/2002_10_red_dragon.pdf.
2. Cf. Sergei Eisenstein, *Film Form: Essays in Film Theory*, trans. Jay Leyda. New York: Hartcourt, 1949; Gilles Deleuze, *Cinema 1. The Movement-Image*, trans. Hugh Tomlinson and Barbara Habberjam (London: The Athlone Press, 1986) and *Cinema 2, The Time-Image*, trans. Hugh Tomlinson and Robert Galeta (London: The Athlone Press, 1989); Christian Metz, *Psychoanalysis and Cinema: The Imaginary Signifier*, trans. Cecilia Britton, Annwyl Williams, Ben Brewester and Alfred Guzetti (London: Macmillan, 1990); and Laura Mulvey, "Visual Pleasure and Narrative Cinema," *Screen* 16.3 (1975): 6–18.

3. The most emblematic and definitive study of these questions is Laura Mulvey's "Visual Pleasure and Narrative Cinema."

Works Cited

Belting, Hans. 2005. "Toward and Anthropology of the Image." In *Anthropologies of Art*, edited by Mariet Westermann, 41–58. New Haven: Yale University Press.
Black, Joel. 1991. *The Aesthetics of Murder: A Study in Romantic Literature and Contemporary Culture*. Baltimore: Johns Hopkins University Press.
The Brooklyn Museum. 2010. Accessed February 12. www.brooklynmuseum.org/press/uploads/2002_10_red_dragon.pdf.
Bruder, Margaret. 2010. "Aestheticizing Violence, or How To Do Things with Style?" Film Studies, Indiana University, Bloomington. Accessed March 25. http://web.archive.org/web/20040908094032/http://www.gradnet.de/papers/pomo2.archives/pomo98.papers/mtbruder98.htm.
Girard, René. 2005. *Violence and the Sacred*. Translated by Patric Gregory. London: Continuum.
Harfield, Timothy D. 2010. "The Monster Without: *Red Dragon*, the Cleft-Lip, and the Politics of Recognition" Accessed March 25. http://www.inter-disciplinary.net/mso/hid/hid5/s9b.html.
Harris, Thomas. 1981. *Red Dragon*. New York: Dell.
Lacan, Jacques. 1977. *Écrits: A Selection*. Translated by Alan Sheridan. New York: W. W. Norton.
_____. 1978. *The Four Fundamental Concepts of Psycho-Analysis*. Edited by Jacques-Alain Miller. Translated by Alan Sheridan. New York: W. W. Norton.
Lesser, Wendy. 1995. *Pictures at an Execution. An Inquiry into the Subject of Murder*. Cambridge: Harvard University Press, 1995.
Magistrale, Tony. 1996. "Transmogrified Gothic: The Novels of Thomas Harris." In *A Dark Night's Dreaming. Contemporary American Horror Fiction*, edited by Tony Magistrale and Michael Morrison, 27–42. Columbia: University of South Carolina Press.
Mirzoeff, Nicholas. 1999. *An Introduction to Visual Culture*. London: Routledge.
Mitchell, W.J.T. 1995. *Picture Theory*. Chicago: University of Chicago Press.
_____. 2005. *What Do Pictures Want?* Chicago: University of Chicago Press.
Packer, Sharon. 2007. *Movies and the Modern Psyche*. Westport: Praeger.
Red Dragon. 2002. DVD dir. Brett Ratner. 2002. Universal Studios and Intercom, 2002.
Tyler, Carol-Anne. 1994. "Passing: Narcissism, Identity and Difference." *differences* 6.2–3: 212–248.

141

Revisiting Paranoia:
The "Witch Hunts" in
James Ellroy's The Big Nowhere
and Walter Mosley's A Red Death

BY MAUREEN SUNDERLAND

James Ellroy's *The Big Nowhere* (1988), the second volume of the *L.A. Quartet*, and Walter Mosley's *A Red Death* (1991), the second work in the Easy Rawlins series, are both set in America in the early 1950s and specifically engage with the anti-communist hysteria which swept America during the years of the Cold War. The Cold War culminated in a mood of paranoia, exemplified by the so-called "witch-hunts," with their obsessive search for communists or those who were termed "fellow-travellers" or "subversives." Written at the end of the Reagan era, when anti-communist rhetoric had again featured significantly in political life, the texts portray the "witch-hunts" as driven by personal vindictiveness and corruption rather than ideological beliefs. *The Big Nowhere* and *A Red Death* depict detectives forced to undertake investigations into the activities of individuals who are deemed, by the authorities, as presenting a danger to the state because of their left-wing views but who are actually revealed as only presenting a threat to corrupt individuals in positions of power.

The detectives themselves appear very differently. Mosley's Ezekiel (Easy) Rawlins, a black man who works outside the structure of the law, usually investigates events brought to his attention by friends and acquaintances in his local community, whereas the detection team in *The Big Nowhere* are detectives within the Los Angeles Police Department (LAPD) who undertake criminal investigations as instructed by their superiors.

There are similarities, however, in that all of the men have been shaped by the events of World War II and struggle with the realities of a post-war world, which they view in many ways as a betrayal of the sacrifices of the war.

James Ellroy and Walter Mosley were both born in the city of Los Angeles, often presented as the last destination of the great western migration and, consequently, as a city of strangers and outsiders. The place, and the time, of their formative years becomes the canvas for Ellroy's *L.A. Quartet*,[1] novels focused on the workings of various white detectives within the Los Angeles Police Department, and nine works by Walter Mosley, which follow the investigations of the black World War II veteran and private detective Ezekiel Rawlins.[2] Both series revisit, and attempt to reclaim and rewrite, the history of Los Angeles in the years following World War II. For Ellroy, the official history of the city, constructed on lies and hiding violence, is always false. It is essentially the story of the victors, those who have appropriated power at the expense of the weak and abused, whose stories are buried and denied. The *L.A. Quartet* presents an alternative history of the city, as the detectives of the LAPD — themselves violent, racist, homophobic, and damaged men — investigate and expose criminality at all levels. For Mosley, the black community, within which Rawlins lives and works, has been omitted from or marginalized in the city's traditional narrative. Set during the years from the late 1940s to the late 1960s, a period of momentous change in race relations in America, the Rawlins' series foregrounds that community and thus presents another alternative history of Los Angeles. *The Big Nowhere* and *A Red Death* both investigate questions about the nature of history and reality — what is eventually recorded and state sanctioned and what is ignored, suppressed, or distorted — through a re-engagement with the 1950s "witch-hunts" and the prevailing atmosphere of those years.

Fractured Masculinity in Pursuit of the "American Dream"

Mosley's choice of Los Angeles in the immediate aftermath of World War II indicates the nature of his project in re-entering the Chandlerian landscape.[3] He explicitly sets out to subvert Raymond Chandler's contemporary legacy by laying claim, as a black writer, not only to a city and period but also to the hard-boiled genre. The impact of major events, such as the assassination of President Kennedy and the early civil rights movement, are recorded from the perspective of a community whose history is absent from the Chandler narratives but which, in his desire to reclaim and retell hidden histories, is central to Mosley's work. In particular, he examines the race riots in the Watts district of Los Angeles in 1965, in which thirty-four people were killed, over two thousand injured, and almost four thousand arrested, from the perspective of the Watts community. As Easy Rawlins attempts to solve his cases, he tracks the urban landscape of Los Angeles, working and living in a number of locations from the end of World War II through to the years following the Watts riots. His narrative shows him attempting to achieve, within the city, a life that accords with many of the ideals associated with the mythology of the frontier and the settler. Embracing ideas of equality and freedom, and seeing his willing participation in World War II as part of the struggle to achieve those ideals, Rawlins continually seeks knowledge and social advancement through education. His re-location from rural Texas to Los Angeles, a city that has often been imaged as the site of the "fresh start," prefigures his attempts to achieve a home, family, respectability, and stability.

Rawlins is presented as an ambivalent character: complex and, at times, criminal and violent. His behavior may contribute to his inability to fulfill his ambitions, but the novels also make clear that his dreams are undermined and frustrated by the reality of a racist city. Despite his participation in the war, the white power structure in Los Angeles continues to confine and belittle him. In post-war Los Angeles, he is still at the mercy of white men. For instance, in *Devil in a Blue Dress* (1990), he loses his job after refusing the request of a white supervisor, the son of Italian immigrants, that he work extra time at the end of a long shift. Since he loses his job for refusing an unreasonable request and objecting to the racially humiliating comment that followed it, Rawlins understands that the dream of equality, a founding ideal of America and part of the rationale for participation in Word War II, is a delusion. Rawlins realizes that, although he is a "war hero" who has fought for the liberation of concentration camps and ideals of equality, he has less status than a man specifically linked with the recent enemies of America.[4] Rawlins's precarious financial situation in *Devil in a Blue Dress* leads to his first investigation, and his subsequent acquisition of wealth results in him being forced to take a further assignment in *A Red Death*. In both cases, Rawlins is forced into his investigations by, and on behalf of, powerful white men.

As a black veteran of World War II seeking to assert a newly confident black masculine identity within a post-war landscape, Rawlins refuses to accept the demeaning racist treatment that would maintain his employment and security. He therefore presents an inevitable contradiction because, as a private detective working in dangerous and violent situations, he represents a powerful and active masculinity, but, as a black man striving to follow an individualist approach within a white society, he is shown as vulnerable and open to manipulation. A veteran of extensive front line action, Rawlins enters his first case as a man who, having gained expertise and familiarity with killing, must now re-integrate into post-war American life. Mosley thus positions Rawlins in a wider historical context, that of the returning veteran, who, having had particular experiences of conflict and having acquired skills relating to violence and killing, has to adjust and be absorbed into suburban society. The problem Rawlins faces in re-integrating himself is that, although his recent experiences have resulted in a fundamental change in his attitudes, there has been no similar change in the attitude of white society.

When Rawlins embarks on the program of self-education, which he believes will help him to progress in post-war society, he reads W.E.B. Du Bois, "I spent the afternoon reading *The Souls of Black Folk* by W.E.B. Du Bois" (Mosley 1992, 247). Du Bois observed of black veterans of World War I, "we are cowards and jackasses if now that the war is over, we do not marshal every ounce of our brain and brawn to fight a sterner, longer, more unbending battle against the forces of hell in our own land" (qtd. in Pendergast 2000, 183). The immediate post–World War I experience for black veterans had included "the lynching of seventy-eight African-Americans during 1918" (183), and Rawlins's attempts to negotiate the post–World War II landscape and assert his version of masculinity place him in similarly dangerous situations. Throughout the post-war years, he continues to combat these situations with further assertions of his masculinity and to attempt to follow the American Dream of entrepreneurship and education. In *A Red Death*, he claims, "I suffered all of this because I wasn't, and hadn't been, my own man" (1991, 235–236). When Rawlins is forced to investigate a supposed communist conspiracy in *A Red Death*, he is once again, as a black veteran, confronted with the reality of a post-war world that remains resolutely racist. He is admitted to the ironically named "Adolf's" club only because he is accompanied by an FBI "Special Agent" (61).

During one of his frequent nightmares, Rawlins sees himself "on a great battleship in the middle of the largest fire fight in the history of the war" when his friend Mouse appears, trying to pull him from the conflict:

> "Ain't no reason t' die in no white man's war!"
> "But I'm fighting for freedom!" I yelled back.
> "They ain't gonna let you go Easy ... they have you back on the plantation 'fore Labor Day" [198].

Mouse identifies World War II as a "white man's war," and life in the post-war city appears to support this analysis. Rawlins specifically describes the aircraft factory where he works after the war as being "an awful lot like working on a plantation" (69), and the barriers he faces clearly remain unchanged. Rawlins's experiences represent a double betrayal, of the recent "fight for freedom" and of the ideals behind the frontier myth, which have been restated as the rationale for the conflict. Rawlins's dream exchange with Mouse places them on opposing sides in their engagement with American frontier mythology, as throughout the novels, Rawlins seeks social advancement through self-improvement, whereas Mouse rejects any such possibility as a lie. The investigation in *A Red Death* presents Rawlins with the possibility of a different kind of society, either driven by communist ideals or located outside of America, where racism will not define his existence. Nevertheless, he chooses to reject both alternative positions.

As Mosley presents a landscape through which his detective has to struggle to assert a new black identity, Ellroy presents a city that is being constructed, both physically and historically, as a symbol of American values and myths. Within the new city, the myth-makers present a sanitized and ethnically cleansed version of history. Hollywood movies, television, official newspaper outlets, and fantasy landscapes present a narrative in which the original move westward and the foundation and building of the city are distorted to fit an authorized official history. Throughout the *L.A. Quartet,* there is a conflict between the official and public history of the city, which is invariably shown to be false, and the city's true history, which exists in suppressed documents and buried memories. Jonathan Walker notes that, for Ellroy, "the truth has been erased from the documentary record," and his aim is to "recover history's repressed memories" (Walker

2002, 183). The official version, despite its power, is vulnerable because the truth is buried, or repressed, but never completely obliterated; it exists in secret documents and is hinted at in "unofficial" outlets. The *L.A. Quartet* employs a recurring pattern of hidden documents, files, pictures, notebooks, and videos, which emerge to reveal some repressed element of the story. The role of the detectives is to recover (and re-cover) these documents that reveal these hidden and horrific stories that build an alternative history of the city.

As the detectives work, they are written into the official versions: their roles are mythologized even as their investigations reveal the lies behind other myths. The detective team in *The Big Nowhere* is brought together to investigate communist activities and is led by Mal Considine, a World War II veteran, and Dudley Smith, the dominating violent presence of the *L.A. Quartet*. They command two other detectives, Buzz Meeks, known for his violence and corruption, and Danny Upshaw, a young, intelligent, and ambitious officer. Considine, like Rawlins, has military combat experience and has shown courage in the war. He directly experienced the horrors of the concentration camps, where he has killed a camp guard. Despite his past, his fellow LAPD officers doubt his bravery because, unlike Dudley Smith, he fails to demonstrate the violent masculinity deemed the acceptable approach of the police department. Considine represents a male fragility that is significantly different to the LAPD presentation of World War II veterans. Because he is haunted by the memories and consequences of the violence that his father, an extreme Calvinist, used to brutalize his sons if they failed to demonstrate appropriate "piety" (Ellroy 1988, 256), Considine drifted into petty crime and then into the police force. The memories of his abusive childhood and his horrific wartime experiences resurface in his brutality towards his wife, which is witnessed by his stepson. Considine's struggles with his wife focus on his determination to give her son an American heritage and future. Considine's experiences of and as a father conform to the trope of fatherhood in the *L.A. Quartet*, where fathers who perpetrate violence and create its continuing legacy are the "founding fathers" of significant dynasties and cities, reflecting American mythologizing of the "Founding Fathers" of the nation.

The official history presents a direct link between the "Founding Fathers," the ideals of the pioneer settlers, and the physical building of the city of Los Angeles. The twin frontier ideals of settlement and entrepreneurship are written into the mythology of the city, shaping the way its narrative of achievement is perceived. The contrasting, but equally important, frontier ideology of "containment" is also a central motif in the thinking of the authorities throughout the *L.A. Quartet*. As the pioneers exercised their divine right to expand, consolidating their wealth and settlements, other inhabitants of the frontier had to be contained and controlled. A parallel exists with the role of the police department, which seemingly serves not to eliminate or solve crime, but to contain it so that only some members of the community feel its impact. Dudley Smith, the immensely powerful LAPD officer and criminal mastermind, describes the police task as "the need to contain crime, to keep it south of Jefferson with the dark element" and argues that "a certain organized crime element should be allowed to exist and perpetuate acceptable vices" (Ellroy 1990, 71). Chick Vecchio reinforces this idea when he says, "Feature the word 'containment.' That's Dud's big word" (1992, 346), before describing Smith's scheme which encompasses the ownership of abandoned properties, gambling, pornography, and the selling of "dope to niggers" (346). For Smith, the investigation into communist activities is part of "containment" but his enthusiastic participation is driven less by any specific anti-communist ideology and more by the need to hide his criminal behavior. He needs to control the investigation so that he can continue to practice "containment" for personal profit.

It is clear from the outset that neither Considine nor Smith believes that the investigation has any merit in itself, but they accept their roles because both, for very different motives, want advancement within the LAPD. Upshaw also wants rapid promotion from his work with the investigative team, but he is privately obsessed with investigating the series of violent murders which are terrorizing the city and which he recognizes as the true threat to public safety. The environment of the LAPD isolates those who, like Upshaw, fail to form close emotional partnerships within the department. David Glover argues that "in the thriller male agency is staged as self-determined, active, brutal, whilst at the same time it is undercut by a profound sense of homosocial unease" (1989, 67–83). Ellroy's detectives, working in close partnerships, appear to exemplify active, violent, masculinity and Glover's "profound [...] homosocial unease." Another side of this unease can be understood from Upshaw's investigative strategy in his personal investigation. He uses a technique he terms "Man

Camera," which involves visualizing the details of a crime scene from the perpetrator's viewpoint, to enable him to identify with the killer he is hunting. He is tormented in various ways by images, from both the reality of his past and the pornography he views during his investigation. His persona as "Man Camera" makes explicit the difficulty he has in resisting the power of these images, specifically of violence and homosexual activity. The investigation into the activities of the so-called subversives results in Upshaw going "under cover" and, in this fake role, attempting to seduce one of the women under surveillance. The incident symbolizes the deception at the heart of Upshaw's life, his homosexuality, and he is so desperate to maintain his deception that, faced with the possibility that his true sexuality will be revealed, he commits suicide.

Meeks, the final member of the team, has been recruited purely because of his association with Howard Hughes. Hughes sees emerging union power as a threat to his movie empire and, as one of the powers behind the investigation, seeks to discredit and destroy the activists through establishing their links with communist organizations. Buzz Meeks's original employment, killing armadillos and Gila monsters, disappears as a direct result of the dust storms of 1931: "So he moved to LA and got work in the movies — revolving cowboy extra [...] Any reasonably presentable white man who could twirl a rope and ride a horse for real was skilled labor in Depression Hollywood" (Ellroy 1988, 27). The desert armadillos and lizards — killed first by Meeks, then the Depression, and finally by the construction of the desert highway — symbolize the environment, and people, which the growth of Los Angeles has destroyed. The original desert inhabitants, valued only because their skins can be used to make tourist souvenirs, are ultimately sacrificed to the advance of the city. Similarly, Meeks's skills with rope and horse no longer have any value other than in the unreal world of movies. His shooting of lizards and armadillos, itself a degraded version of the cowboy myth, has been replaced by his role as "cowboy extra" in films which fall victim to "the trend [...] from westerns to musicals" (27). Meeks, once an idealistic and promising member of the LAPD, has followed a similar path to degradation. With his livelihood destroyed by the change in movie fashions, his only remaining skill, how to wield "a billy club," results in his recruitment to the LAPD and, eventually, his role as a violent enforcer in the empire of Howard Hughes.

The Investigations

In *The Big Nowhere* and *A Red Death*, the detectives view the actual investigation into the likely communist activities of the subversives as something which they are forced to undertake by the authorities but which has no merit. They recognize that those being investigated are likely to be either innocent or ineffective, so the investigations are actually diverting their attentions from crimes that do represent a threat to the community. Forced into the investigations and skeptical about their usefulness, the detectives nevertheless make serious attempts to discover if there is any truth in the allegations of subversive activities. Rawlins is originally drawn into the investigation of the supposed communist conspiracy because the Internal Revenue Service (IRS), represented by the murderous Agent Lawrence, has discovered that he has failed to pay the correct amount in tax. Rawlins, faced with the prospect of being sent to prison, decides that he will kill Lawrence, but he is then offered an apparent solution to his problems. A mysterious Federal Bureau of Investigation (FBI) agent, Craxton, recruits Rawlins to what appears a relatively harmless investigation which, if he carries it out successfully, will ensure that the IRS will allow him to settle his tax affairs. Craxton asks Rawlins to gain the confidence of Chaim Wenzler, a communist and Jew, currently undertaking voluntary work in the black community. Craxton describes the communists as people who "don't believe in freedom like Americans do [but] have been peasants so long that that's the way they see the whole world — from chains" and Wenzler as "one of those communist kind of Jews" (Mosley 1991, 63).

For Craxton, the activities he wants investigated specifically threaten America, although in ways which he finds difficult to describe. The FBI is "a last line of defense. There are all sorts of enemies we have these days. We've got enemies all over the world [...] But the real enemies, the ones we really have to watch out for, are people right here at home. People who aren't Americans on the inside" (65). However, in comments that echo the operation of the actual "witch-hunt" investigations, he makes equally clear that Wenzler has committed no offence and is important only in "what he represents, the people he works with — that's what we need to know" (66). Forced to investigate Wenzler's activities, Rawlins is also drawn into an examination of the African Migration Group, a "Back-to-Africa" movement operating in the black community. The FBI views both groups as anti–American, and Rawlins, struggling to assert his masculinity and over-come racist attitudes in the post-war landscape of Los Angeles, finds himself presented with two opposing philosophies, both of which he is invited to embrace, to replace the individualist ideology of the frontier and the home-steader.

At the African Migration Group meeting, Sonja Achebe makes a speech about freedom from racism and the impossibility of achieving that dream within America, and Rawlins feels that this anti–American vision has a strong emotional attraction for him. Investigating the communists, he finds only Wenzler, an almost saintly individual, with whom he forms a real friendship. But, despite the daily abuse and humiliation that Rawlins suffers in the city, he rejects Wenzler's attempts to recruit him to commu-nism, just as he rejects the appeal of the African Migration Group. Wen-zler's experiences as a persecuted Jew in Europe have made him a communist and given him a feeling of identification with the African American community. He tells Rawlins: "Negroes in America have the same life as the Jew in Poland. Ridiculed, segregated. We were hung and burned for just being alive" (111). Listening to both Achebe and Wenzler, Rawlins recognizes that they both present "anti–American" ideologies that he could embrace because they appear to offer the prospect of a life free from racism, but he ultimately rejects them in favor of the imperfect life he faces in contemporary Los Angeles.

Rawlins's detection eventually reveals that the real purpose of the FBI/IRS investigation, which he has viewed as driven by Craxton's fanati-cism, is to cover up a series of embarrassing errors made by the authorities. The investigation results in Wenzler's death and, as a result, Rawlins briefly reconsiders his decision to reject Wenzler's political ideology. He explains his doubts to his friend, Jackson Blue, who gives him a rationale for reject-ing Wenzler's idea of the universal struggle of working people, seeing it as irrelevant to their situation. Blue emphasizes the singularity of the African-American situation, which places them outside the universal struggle Wen-zler presents. Referring to the "blacklist," where the names of those suspected of "anti–American" sentiments or activities can be published with resulting personal and professional damage, Blue describes it as:

> a list that the rich people got. All kindsa names on it. White people names [...] Yo' name ain't on that list, Easy. My name ain't neither. You know why? [...] They don't need yo' name to know you black, Easy. All they gotta do is look at

you [...] One day they gonna th'ow that list out [...] But you still gonna be a black niggah [230].

When Rawlins decides to reject the philosophies of Wenzler and Achebe, he responds to the call to return "home" by saying, "I got me a home already. It might be in enemy lands, but it's mine still and all" (221). Throughout the novels, Rawlins values his home as a place of pastoral retreat and safety, something of immense value, and he finally embraces the individualist frontier ideology, though he can recognize its degraded nature in a city territory "in enemy hands."

The Big Nowhere tracks two, parallel, investigations one into a supposed "subversive" group of minor Hollywood players who may, in some vaguely unspecified way, represent a threat to the American way of life, and the other into a series of horrific murders which directly threaten the city. The first investigation, officially sanctioned, well-resourced, supported by the most respectable figures in the city, and with apparently laudable aims, is conducted for entirely corrupt purposes and investigates people who represent no threat. The second, conducted in secret by Danny Upshaw, is individual, unofficial, and without any support. Because of the investigations, two evidence files are compiled: one substantial, powerful, and intended for publication and the other unfinished, fragmentary, and suppressed. In his mission to uncover truth, Upshaw uncovers a truth inextricably bound to the official investigation, but powerful interests mean that these results cannot be revealed. Also in keeping with maintaining powerful interests, the truth about Upshaw's death is suppressed to protect the public reputation of the police force, just as the evidence he has accumulated is suppressed to protect the reputation of powerful men within the city. Considine, viewing Upshaw's work after his death, concludes that "[t]he kid [...] would have cracked the four killings easy if the LAPD had given him an extra day or so. It was right here on page three" (Ellroy 1988, 435), but he fails to understand that Upshaw has died precisely because the LAPD could not allow him to publish the truth he is about to uncover. Upshaw's file, although unpublished, still exists to be decoded, as the official file instead is totally obliterated, destroyed by Buzz Meeks in one of the rare positive events in Ellroy's narratives.

As the investigation into the "subversives" progresses, Meeks's partners, Considine and Smith, follow their investigations onto the film set of *Tomahawk Massacre*. The studio receptionist, "a woman in a saloon girl outfit" (123) with a Brooklyn accent, tells them their suspects are cast as "the hotheaded young Indians who want to attack the fort, but the wise old chief don't want them to" (124). The suspects form part of a group consisting of "an old pseudo-Indian white man and three pseudo-Indian Mexicans" (124).

The film industry reinforces the foundation myths at the heart of American life with the frontier narrative by now almost excluding the American Indians, as their roles are reduced to meaningless stereotypes played by other races. In the *L.A. Quartet*, this is not a betrayal of the frontier dream but the realization of it. The actor Reynolds Loftis, the link between the two parallel investigations, achieved his fame in Westerns: "a tall, lanky, silver-haired man, handsome like your idealized U.S. senator" (102); his fame rests entirely on his appearance. As Loftis is one of the group being investigated, the LAPD views him as a threat, "a Communist [...] a subversive" (102), but the danger he represents is unconnected with any "subversive" activities and instead is directly related to the power of the Hollywood machine and the fantasy it creates. Loftis, enthralled by his on-screen image, has embarked on an insane narcissistic project. Finding a young man who closely resembles him, he arranges to have that resemblance increased through plastic surgery so that he is able to achieve his fantasy of a love affair with himself.

When the young man, Coleman Masskie, discovers that Loftis is actually his father, he is driven to the horrific murders that Upshaw investigates. The so-called subversive group the detectives investigate is revealed as no more than a number of ineffectual, dissatisfied, and divided individuals. Even within this group, Loftis is recognized as a weak man with a minimal role. His political activities clearly present no threat to the state but, as the clearest example of a father who literally, as well as metaphorically, scars his son, he represents a real threat that the detectives fail to recognize. His film star status has been achieved through his presentation of Western heroes, with his handsome appearance helping to create an acceptable national mythology of the conquest of the west. Loftis's obsession furthers the *L.A. Quartet*'s motif of fathers who scar and destroy their sons by attempting to make them into mirror images of themselves. As with Loftis, the instances in the novels propose that these defective fathers are nevertheless revered as representing particularly admirable examples of American masculinity. Loftis's insane vanity, fed by the Hollywood machine, leads not only to his son's murders but also to the deaths of Upshaw, Considine, and Meeks. Linked only through Loftis, the two investigations contrast in terms of their remit, resources, and power, but together they illuminate Ellroy's view of how the city creates, and publicizes, its real and false histories. The communist investigation, conducted for purely corrupt reasons, succeeds only in obscuring and restricting the criminal investigation, which ought to have been the LAPD's priority.

Paranoia in the Post-War Landscape

The landscape inhabited by Rawlins and by Ellroy's detectives is dominated by the experiences of World War II. The conflict itself functions as a more recent re-playing of the myth of the frontier conquest, since it is repeatedly presented as a fight for "freedom" and the founding ideals of the nation. The narratives deny the parallels between the treatment of "Indians," the Holocaust, and, in some respects, the position of African Americans to reinforce the identification between the victors in the war and the frontiersmen. Yet, those who actually achieved the victory for "freedom" and "equality" have to survive in the post-war world that denies those ideals. The detectives themselves have often experienced horrors that preclude them from a comfortable re-integration into post-war Los Angeles. The war comes to function, therefore, as a further symbol of betrayal. The advances into Europe of the forces of "liberation" are explicitly presented as a replaying of the advance into the American west, driven by the same apparently idealistic aspirations which are then violated. In the post-war landscape, the rise of apparently subversive and anti–American groups is presented as producing a national paranoia, which forms the backdrop to the investigations in *A Red Death* and *The Big Nowhere*. The detectives, and for the most part those who set up their investigations, appear untouched by this national mood and remain aware that the investigations are merely a cover for corrupt and criminal activities.

Those investigated by Ellroy's detectives, although representing no real threat through their political activities, are presented as weak, duplicitous, and, ultimately, responsible for murder. By contrast, the object of Easy Rawlins' investigation, Chaim Wenzler, is presented solely as a victim. In both works, the detectives resist the rhetoric of patriotism and subversion, preferring a cynicism which is justified by the revelation of the corruption actually driving the investigations. Equally, however, the detectives are unmoved by the philosophies advanced by the "Reds" they investigate, regardless of whether or not they find them personally attractive or admirable. Their prime focus is to unravel the truth behind the murders, which they see as the real crimes threatening the city. Rawlins and the detectives of the LAPD may see injustice within the structures of society, but they tackle "real crime" as something that is individual and committed for personal, rather than political, reasons. In that sense, although they appear to adopt very different approaches and views of the character of the "subversives" they investigate, both novels embody a "conservative" vision of the role of the detective. In Mosley's continuing narrative of post-war Los Angeles, the paranoia of the "witch-hunts" features as an episode, which, like many others Rawlins faces, illustrates the corruption and oppression springing from the misuse of power. Although he cannot defeat racism, Rawlins can, through individual action, defeat this particular manifestation of state oppression, which is seen as driven by weak and unbalanced individuals. Ellroy, however, depicts the Cold War paranoia as one of the building blocks of a false history, not only of the city of Los Angeles but also of America itself, which is constructed in the post-war years.

As these rewritings of the mid-twentieth century appear at its con-clusion, they provide a re-evaluative focus at the end of the century looking back over the progress that has ostensibly been made. Now able to find the personal in what had originally been disguised as political, these texts reveal the power of hindsight in uncovering the power struggles that direct the crime. Coming after the Reaganite resurgence of anti-communist rhet-oric, these texts demand careful and skeptical consideration of reopening the ideological issues of the mid-twentieth century as America moves into the twenty-first century. The returned interest in the middle of the twen-tieth century at the end of the twentieth suggests that the ideas of crime and its detection still have the same core appeal. Nevertheless, the different foci and the different conclusions that Mosley and Ellroy bring to these issues and cases show that the new direction at the end of the twentieth century is not simply new characters and new perspectives. It is also to uncover the crimes hidden in the narratives from which these texts are drawn and then diverge, re-thinking and re-engaging with the nature of history and reality and their impact of history on reality.

Notes

1. *The Black Dahlia* (1987), *The Big Nowhere* (1988), *L.A. Confidential* (1992), and *White Jazz* (1992) span the years from 1947 to 1958.

2. *Devil in a Blue Dress* (1990), *A Red Death* (1991), *White Butterfly* (1992), *Black Betty* (1994), *A Little Yellow Dog* (1996), *Bad Boy Brawly Brown* (2002), *Little Scarlet* (2004), *Cinnamon Kiss* (2005), and *Blonde Faith* (2007) span the years from 1948 to the late sixties.

3 The opening scene of Mosley's first novel in the series, *Devil in a Blue Dress*, is an explicit re-writing of the opening scene of Raymond Chandler's *Farewell, My Lovely* (1940).

4 This kind of treatment was not unusual and was deeply resented by returning G.I.s, as is evidenced by, among others, Lloyd Brown, a black veteran of World War II. Brown recounted being refused service in a restaurant in Salina, Kansas, and, with a group of his friends, watching "German prisoners of war who were having lunch at the counter [...] The people of Salina would serve these enemy soldiers and turn away black America G.I.s" (qtd. in Blum 1977, 192).

Works Cited

Blum, John Morton. 1977. *V Was for Victory: Politics and American Culture during World War II*. New York: Harvest/HBJ, 1977.

Chandler, Raymond. 2005 (1940). *Farewell, My Lovely* London: Penguin.

Ellroy, James. 1988. *The Big Nowhere*. London: Random House.

_____. 1992. (1990). *L.A. Confidential*. London: Random House.

_____. 1992. *White Jazz*. London: Random House.

_____. 1993. (1987). *The Black Dahlia*. London: Random House.

Glover, David. 1989. "The stuff that dreams are made of: Masculinity, Femininity and the Thriller." In *Gender, Genre & Narrative Pleasure*, edited by Derek Longhurst, 67–83. London: Unwin Hyman.

Mosley Walter. 1991. *A Red Death*. New York: W.W. Norton and Company.

_____. 1992. *Devil in a Blue Dress*. London: Macmillan.

_____. 1992. *White Butterfly*. London: Serpent's Tail.

_____. 1994. *Black Betty*. London: Serpent's Tail.

_____. 1996. *A Little Yellow Dog*. London: Serpent's Tail.

_____. 2002. *Bad Boy Brawly Brown*. London: Serpent's Tail.

_____. 2005. *Cinnamon Kiss*. London: Weidenfeld & Nicolson.

_____. 2005. *Little Scarlet*. London: Weidenfeld & Nicolson.

_____. 2008. *Blonde Faith*. London: Weidenfeld & Nicolson.

Pendergast, Tom. 2000. *Creating the Modern Man: American Magazines and Consumer Culture, 1900–1950*. Columbia: University of Missouri Press.

Walker, Jonathan. 2002. "James Ellroy as Historical Novelist." *History Workshop Journal* 53: 181–204.

A Detective Series with Love Interruptions? The Heteronormative Detective Couple in Contemporary Crime Fiction

BY MALCAH EFFRON

When Dorothy L. Sayers subtitled her final Lord Peter Wimsey novel *Busman's Honeymoon* (1937) as "A Love Story with Detective Interruptions," she reinforced that "[a] casual and perfunctory love-story is worse than no love-story at all, and, since the mystery must, by hypothesis, take the first place, the love is better left out" (Sayers 1947, 40). Nevertheless, many of the contemporary detective series that conform to the British Golden Age detective form have also included families and love interests.[1] However, these love interests do not contribute to the overall development of the series, instead serving as a safe haven or an unnecessary complication to a detective plot and becoming what Sayers terms "casual and perfunctory" (40). While these developments appear throughout the twentieth century, in the 1990s, Deborah Crombie developed the Duncan Kincaid/Gemma James series, which removes the "casual and perfunctory" nature of the love interest by highlighting both the male and female detectives in the investigating partnership. Sayers indicates with her subtitle that her last novel has detective elements but is predominantly about the couple, thus separating the two plotlines despite their appearance within the same text. Crombie, however, uses the detective investigation plotline as the driving force behind each novel and uses the love story to develop an overarching plot for the series: the development and progress of the professional and personal relationships of two London Metropolitan police detectives, Duncan Kincaid and Gemma James. This can be seen in the relationship cliffhangers at the end of the novels, like the partners sleeping together for the first time in *Leave the Grave Green* (1995); the discussion of Kincaid's relationship with his son Kit in *Dreaming of the Bones* (1997), *Kissed a Sad Goodbye* (1999), and *In a Dark House* (2004); the announcement of James's pregnancy in *A Finer End* (2001); James's miscarriage at the end of *And Justice There Is None* (2002); the couple's engagement in *Where Memories Lie* (2008); and their marriage in *Necessary as Blood* (2009). By developing the personal relationships through detective plots centered on their professional occupations, Crombie revises the classic British whodunit to incorporate a love plot, and in so doing, she interrogates contemporary women's advancement in both the professional and personal spaces of detective fiction.

While a woman detective is not new to detective fiction, Crombie innovatively addresses the place of the woman detective in a *heteronormative* relationship, taking her work in a new direction from her generic precursors. Kathleen Gregory Klein's *The Woman Detective* (1988) and Maureen Reddy's *Sisters in Crime* (1988) introduce the dominant critical discussions of the female detective based on their marginal — not normative — position: "the female hero is shown both to relish her independence and to seek intimate connections with others; however for that cherished independence to be preserved, the connection must fall outside the boundaries of those socially sanctioned relationships that have defined and oppressed women" (Reddy 1988, 105). Crombie's James, however, embeds herself within patriarchal structures while seeking to maintain her independence and authority in relationships. Sally Munt notes that typically for female detective protagonists, the "visceral androgyny is manifested in skill, but not appearance. Hence masculine agency is married to heterosexual femininity" (41). While Munt speaks of an amalgamation of characteristics within an individual, Crombie explores this marriage in terms of a partnership between two people, calling attention to the still dominant patriarchal hegemony at work, even in a more "modern" and happy heteronormative partnership.

Heteronormative might not seem to describe the detectives' relationships accurately, since, at least until the conclusion of the most recent novel, it has not recounted the story of a heterosexual, married couple. At the start of the series, Kincaid is divorced with no children, and James is divorced with a toddler son. Kincaid only learns of his biological son after his ex-wife's murder in *Dreaming of the Bones*, the fifth novel of the series. Kincaid and James do not live together until they have already begun an extramarital sexual relationship, James becomes pregnant, and Kincaid has taken custody of his biological son. They become engaged only in *Where Memories Lie*, the eleventh novel, and marry in *Necessary as Blood*, the twelfth novel. This novel also hints that the detectives will adopt an orphaned mixed-race little girl. With this blended family, Crombie emphatically underscores the non-normative features of Kincaid and James's relationship. Nevertheless, the heterosexual partnership that develops between the detectives nominally presents the normative family of man, woman, and children. Furthermore, Crombie's series presents men and women police detectives in a heterosexual partnership, formalizing the professional aspects of detection and stabilizing the personal aspects of union. As can be seen through the development of James's career, the detectives' consciousness of gender frequently defaults to subconscious conformity to normative values.

Crombie's examination of the heteronormative partnership addresses women's ability to pursue both a career and a family at the turn of the twenty-first century. In examining women's ability to break into the workplace in the twentieth century, research has shown that, by the late twentieth century, while external forces continue to contribute to sexist inequality in the work place, one of the strongest impediments comes from women's internalization of societal expectations. Shelley Correll argues, "gender beliefs bias self-perceptions of competence. This focus is important since presumptions of competence often legitimate inequality in achievement-oriented societies" (2001, 1724). Because women are taught to perceive themselves as inferior in certain areas, they internalize these beliefs, and this self-perception either prevents or inhibits their success in areas traditionally gendered as male. Furthermore, despite Claudia Goldin's assertion that women at the end of the twentieth century believe it possible to have both a career and a family (2004, 21), Margaret Elman and Lucia Gilbert find that "professional women must cope with societal values and with their own internalized beliefs about what is required of the 'competent professional' and 'good mother'—values which are sometimes incompatible" (1984, 317). The perception of the conflicting nature of these roles inhibits women's development professionally, as it imbues professional advancement with personal guilt and personal success with professional sacrifice. This becomes particularly apparent in the police force where, as Susan Martin notes, a "policewoman must choose between defeminization (and its emphasis on occupational role obligations) and deprofessionalization (and meeting sex role norms while on the job)" (1980, 186). By developing her divorced, single-mother detective sergeant into a married detective inspector in a dual-career family, Crombie addresses these issues throughout her Kincaid/James series, using the heteronormative relationship of her detective protagonists to examine the place and success of professional women at the turn of the twenty-first century.

While Kincaid initially fulfills the generic stereotype of the unattached detective, James must struggle with the burdens of familial obligations in her professional advancement, highlighting the double standards that remain in the professional workplace despite the advances made by women's movements. In formalizing their relationships, Crombie shows the different stresses on professional women than on their male colleagues. James's eventual promotion gives her the opportunity to direct investigations, seemingly providing her with an authoritative position. Nevertheless, in the Kincaid/James investigations, James returns to the heteronormative position of dependent woman, responsible for protecting the family rather than active participant in the criminal investigation. Nevertheless, by introducing the love narrative as a parallel — not subordinate — component to the detective narrative, Deborah Crombie interrogates women's contemporary development through the detectives' professional and personal partnership.

Career Advancement

The influence of gender in relation to professional and personal issues becomes most apparent in relation to career advancement. When contemplating a relationship with Kincaid, James is the one who feels compelled to think of the consequences beyond personal emotional entanglement. As the subordinate officer and a woman, she accepts that she will suffer consequences beyond the potential need to change partners at work, for a relationship with a superior officer will impact her authority within the workplace and, as the sole provider for her child at this point, her ability to care for her family. She hesitates in entering a relationship, reminding her superior, "'We can't do this. I've compromised myself enough already.' She took a ragged breath and added, spacing the words out as if to emphasize their weight, 'I can't afford it. I've my career to think of ... and Toby'" (Crombie 1996, 3). As she adds her son in the reasons she cannot pursue the relationship as a secondary consideration, James here puts her career ahead of her family. But as a single parent, her professional success necessarily affects her family's well-being.

By shifting from the first-person plural to the first-person singular, James highlights that the situation is particularly complicated because Kincaid is the superior in their professional relationship. An intra-office romance will predominantly have consequences for her, the subordinate woman, not for Kincaid, the superior man. By accepting a personal relationship, which should place them as equal partners, Kincaid and James problematize a work relationship that is necessarily based on rank and hierarchy. As the relationship develops and police hierarchy seeps into a gendered hierarchy enacted in the personal relationship, Crombie illustrates how, despite the seemingly "modern" relationship that Kincaid and James have, the heternormative values of Western society permeate their relationship. James becomes aware of these additional consequences to their joint professional and personal partnerships only after they become established in the personal relationship.

James's reaction is predicated not on her own emotional reaction to a personal relationship with the man Duncan Kincaid but on the effects of a personal relationship with her boss, Superintendent Kincaid. As she thus defines a personal relationship in terms of the social stigma that would be associated with dating a superior, James's perception mirrors Correll's discovery that "when gender beliefs are salient they shape behavior most powerfully by affecting people's sense of what *others* expect of them" (2001, 1697–98; original emphasis). James initially stalls the personal relationship because "of what *others* expect" a personal relationship between a superior and a subordinate to indicate. Professional expectations, as Martin suggests, mean that women within the police force still fill the same roles expected of them outside the police station, "enacting the stereotyped roles of 'pet,' 'mother,' or 'seductress'" (1994, 391). Pursuing a public personal relationship with Kincaid would suggest that James assumes the conventional roles that prevent women police from being treated as equals in the professional sphere. By emphasizing that James is the one who has to compromise to pursue a personal relationship alongside her professional career development, Crombie indicates the continual sexist inequalities toward perceived professionalism, especially in relation to career advancement.

Especially in relation to promotions, Crombie effectively articulates the complications for a professional woman, particularly one living on the borders of a heteronormative relationship. When considering applying for promotion, James weighs both the professional and the personal elements of her career:

> In the two years since she had became Superintendent Duncan Kincaid's partner, their personal relationship had sometimes strained their working relationship. But it had also enriched it — they *know* each other, could anticipate one another's ideas and reactions, and their partnership had evolved into a finely tuned and creative entity, the sum greater than the parts [...] But she hadn't joined the force to be a career sergeant. She was due for promotion, and if she didn't make a move soon, she'd be considered a non-starter [Crombie 2001, 22].

In describing her working relationship with Kincaid, James considers both her professional and personal partnerships, as the detectives' emotional connection allows the partnership to function as a unit rather than as individuals. When James considers her promotion, she weighs the costs to her career against the impact on her familial situation, highlighting Barbara Reskin and Irene Padavic's claim that "[s]ociety has given men — but never women — permission to escape from their family obligations" (154). This explains James's need to consider her family here. When considering the working relationship she would sacrifice, James still acknowledges that the comfort of the normative Kincaid/James partnership means sacrificing her own career for the sake of the partnership. Such a sacrifice is typical of the heteronormative couple in the workplace, as Reskin and Padavic find that "[u]sually it is the wives who sacrifice their careers and their earnings so the husband can advance" (1994, 153). While Reskin and Padavic's findings do not necessarily apply directly here because James's move does not directly impact Kincaid's promotion, her move does necessitate that Kincaid adjust to working with a new partner instead of continuing to rely upon her. So, by actively pursuing her own career, she affects her partner's. In breaking up her award-winning detective partnership, Crombie advocates for equal career advancement within the heteronormative pairing of the detective, breaking the professional partnership to advance James's career.

While James's concerns about promotion are not exclusively gendered, by placing this quest for promotion in relation to the professional and personal partnerships, Crombie highlights the complicated position of women in the workforce. James focuses on Kincaid's response to her decision, realizing only after her promotion that "[s]he'd been so busy worrying about how Kincaid would deal with her decision that she'd failed to take her own response to their separation into account" (Crombie 2001, 84). By indicating that James focuses on others' responses rather than her own, Crombie illustrates the trends that Reskin and Padavic outline because James is more concerned about her "family's" adjustment than her own. This highlights that traditional cultural ideologies of men and women's work still influence the way women perceive themselves in the workforce, even in the twenty-first century. However, by allowing James to realize that she has been focusing on the way others will perceive the effects of her promotion rather its direct impact on the detective herself, Crombie calls attention to how these cultural norms continue to influence women in the workplace. The problem here is not the possibility of promotion — as James is both eligible for and successful in her request — but the residual guilt that accompanies her decisions to advance her career. Since she participates in a heteronormative relationship of father-mother-children, James does not see herself as marginalized, removing marginalization as an excuse for her behavior. Instead, she must deal with her professional failure to conform to the dominant ideology's image of womanhood in which she otherwise successfully participates.

James's thoughts during the process of promotion reveal how Western cultural ideologies give women conflicting senses of who they are and how they are meant to behave. Moreover, Kincaid's account of their personal relationship indicates that the police force has not fully adapted to women's participation, as he argues their relationship had to remain a secret until she had been promoted and was no longer his direct subordinate because "for Gemma, it would have meant a permanent shadow on her career. There would always have been whispers that she'd slept her way into promotions, no matter how capable she proved herself" (Crombie 2007, 421). This illustrates how the organizing power structures in which both detectives work operate differently for each because of their respective sexes. Kincaid would not suffer any reprimand from having a relationship with a female subordinate, but the fact of the relationship is enough to scuttle the woman subordinate's respect within the department. This is particularly relevant to detective fiction because, as Martin has shown with regard to policing in the United States, when women succeed, the attitude of the men on the force is that "such successes must have been the result of using female advantage (performing sexual favors)" (1980, 100). Because Kincaid acknowledges this problem in the work environment, he is distinguished as a man who does not share these prejudices and thus as a worthy protagonist for the series. Nevertheless, as is the case with the successful policewomen in Martin's study, Kincaid's acquiescence indicates the continuing dominance of the heteronormative presumption that women's greatest power lies in their sexual control over men rather than in their ability to perform tasks as well as men. By putting these concerns in the man's mouth rather than the woman's, Crombie highlights this problem as a matter that still needs addressing to create an egalitarian society rather than simply further feminist complaints about women's positions in the workplace.

Gender Awareness

While James is normally the individual who serves to focalize the continuing heteronormative subjugation of women in the workplace, Crombie does at times allow Kincaid to understand that his sense of his own egalitarian perspective often comes from never having faced a challenge to Western gender norms. For instance, when engaged in conversation with a young female firefighter, he mentally pauses, "congratulating himself a bit because he'd never felt particularly threatened by female police officers, when it occurred to him that he'd never worked with a woman who outranked him. If he did, would he find he was a hypocrite, and a self-righteous one at that?" (Crombie 2004, 138). With this introspection, Kincaid realizes that he cannot be assured of always maintaining a gender-neutral reaction, as he has never been placed in a position where he has been subordinate to a woman and thus cannot guarantee how he would react in such circumstances. Moments such as these indicate the ability for residual latent sexism to remain even in those considered "enlightened" because the general social structure maintains social forms that allow men to feel their superiority without seeing it as a product of gender differentiation (for instance, a superintendent over a sergeant rather than a man over a woman).

By highlighting the minimal opportunities for Kincaid to feel himself in a position that does not conform to male dominance, Crombie illustrates how, despite the advances made in the mid-to late-twentieth century, women still have not progressed in the work force to a position of equality with men. Reskin and Padavic indicate that this lack of authority is often attributed to a continual difference in human capital in that "women have not yet acquired the experience and education that will allow them to rise to positions in which they can exercise authority" (1994, 95). This logic seemingly applies to James's position in relation to Kincaid, as she is both younger than and has been on the police force for less time than her partner. However, Reskin and Padavic also found that the human capital rationale is no longer valid at the start of the twentieth century, as "[w]omen have not advanced into authority-conferring jobs in proportion to their presence in the lower ranks" (95–96), indicating that at the rate of current advancement, it will be another century before there is equitable representation between the sexes in authority-conferring positions (96). As such, Kincaid's successful maintenance of his position of higher authority is still influenced by sexist ideologies, so he has never had to confront his own internalization of those policies in a meaningful manner.

Though Crombie shows Kincaid's conformity to a sex-gender hierarchy that defines men as superior to women (Reskin and Padavic 1994, 3), in defense of her character, she allows James to acknowledge that Kincaid is not wholly responsible for the sexist culture than impinges upon their partnership. After calming down from her negative response to Chief Inspector Alun Ross, the Scottish officer in charge in *Now May You Weep* (2003), James assesses the reaction in relation to her initial judgment of sexism:

> Would Ross have treated Kincaid this way, she wondered, or would Kincaid have been respected as a fellow officer — even deferred to?
> Of course, there was the matter of rank, she told herself attempting to be fair, but even that didn't excuse Ross's behavior.
> Nor was it Kincaid's fault that he was male and automatically a member of the club, she reminded herself, curbing the unjustified flash of anger she felt towards him [179].

James's initial sentiment to being shut out of the murder investigation outside her jurisdiction is to compare the way a male officer would respond to her male partner, assuming Kincaid would have received a more favorable response than she has. James rebukes herself for presuming that the respect shown to Kincaid would be because of the inherent sexism of the police force, where men are more willing to cooperate with other men than with women (Martin 1994, 390). She recalls that there is a ranking system in the police force that is not based on gender, and, as a chief inspector, Ross outranks her, but he does not outrank Kincaid, who is a superintendent. She recognizes that she operates in a hierarchical system that subordinates her without necessarily disenfranchising her because of her sex. Nevertheless, she ultimately acknowledges that ingrained sexist attitudes still play a part in her reception on the force, as she notes that Kincaid is "automatically a member of the club" because he is male, whereas she has to earn her membership, always assuming "the club" is willing to accept new members.

By excusing Kincaid from his inherent complicity in the system because of his automatic membership in the club, James notes that the systematic discrimination against women is not necessarily ascribable to the behavior of any one individual. Because of this, Kincaid, as an individual, can be excused from the instant camaraderie that Ross might show him because, just as James cannot control that others respond to her as a woman, he cannot control the way that others respond to him as a man. And, as is important in police work, using perceived gender stereotypes help make certain situations more manageable.[2] Nevertheless, while excusing Kincaid from her ill will because of his inherent ability to succeed in an area where she cannot, James's reflection on the men's club of the police force points out that this is still normative behavior within a workforce that has not fully accepted women. The problem is that the latent sexism has become carefully masked, to the point where James can neither blame Kincaid for his automatic advantages nor truly state that she is a victim of gender discrimination. Because her professional rank marks her as the inferior in the world of the police, she cannot affirmatively claim that the discrimination she feels is based on the automatic men's club rather than an officially constructed — and accepted — chain of command. This double bind suggests one of the problems with removing prejudicial concerns from the professional workplace is that they can be masked as issues of human capital rather than sexist discrimination.

In addition to allowing her characters to acknowledge the latent gendered policies influencing the professional work place, Crombie shows some gender role reversal within the personal sphere when Kincaid decides that he will do whatever he needs to keep his biological son, Kit, with him. Kincaid tells James, "I don't care what it takes, even if it means giving up the job. If we have to go away somewhere, make a fresh start" (Crombie 2004, 348). In his willingness to give up his job for his son, Kincaid makes the decision to choose his family over his career, a decision that Susan Bromley and Pamela Hewitt associate with the woman's binary options — career or motherhood (1992, 19). In keeping with this sense of role reversal, Kincaid also realizes that when he makes this bold declaration to James, she does not reciprocate with the same enthusiasm: "It was only much later [...] that the realization struck him. When he'd asked her if she would be willing to give up the life they'd built, for Kit's sake, she had not given him an answer" (Crombie 2004, 348). Because she gives no answer rather than agreeing to sacrifice her career for the sake of a stepchild, James allows herself the man's prerogative (as defined by Reskin and Padavic [1994, 154]) to place her career above her family. In this sense, these role reversals show a re-centering of gender roles within the personal relationship of Kincaid and James.

Nevertheless, these moments show the still problematic standards of gender, as Kincaid's bold statement is treated as an indicator of his superior character because he is willing to sacrifice his career for the sake of his family. Because at this one moment in his life, he is finally ready to make such a sacrifice, he is presented as a male role model. However, throughout *In a Dark House*, he has missed all the custody hearings, while James, who has no biological relationship with the child, has attended. The narrative excuses Kincaid's absences because he investigates a murder, but James is not praised for sacrificing *her* investigation to attend the court hearings. Because he is a man, this one moment of placing family over career makes him a hero in the eyes of both his son and the narrative. Furthermore, by focalizing James's lack of response through Kincaid, her inability to reject her career for her family is portrayed negatively, making James appear less caring than Kincaid because she does not state that she is willing to sacrifice her career. By not conforming to the preconceived assumption that a woman should sacrifice her career responsibilities for her familial ones (Reskin and Padavic 1994, 152), Kincaid does not support the woman detective's valuation of her career. This follows Elman and Gilbert's discovery that "[m]en, even those advocating equal opportunity, however, have difficulty giving their wives the emotional support and encouragement they themselves receive. Men are not socialized to assume supporting roles" (1984, 326). Even though not technically married, Kincaid still expects his partner to support his priorities without actively supporting hers. Though Kincaid is not presented as wanting to undermine James or her ambitions, as Elman and Gilbert note, even those men who seem to support equal opportunity are still subject to Western patriarchal ideological assumptions about the place of women and how they should behave.

Unconscious Conformity

As the cases where the detectives show awareness of sexist stereotyping still show their conformity to these stereotypes, the protagonists' heteronormative relationship leaves them embedded in the dominant Western gender ideologies. This is seen most clearly after Kincaid and James occupy the same household, behaving as a normative married couple. For instance, because she is Kincaid's personal, rather than professional, partner at the time of their Christmas visit to Kincaid's parents, his behavior in a murder investigation specifically undermines James's position as a police detective. As Kincaid's "significant other" rather than his sergeant, he forgets to include her in his unofficial investigation, assuming that she will fill the feminine position of childcare rather than contribute to the masculine position of detective.[3] When Kincaid is invited by an old schoolmate to assist in an investigation when visiting his family for the Christmas holidays, James notes that "[e]ver since they'd arrived he'd been sidelining her, treating her as if she were competent to do no more than look after the children, and she had let him because she wasn't sure of her ground. But that was going to stop this very minute. 'Don't you even think about leaving me home like the little woman'" (Crombie 2007, 218). James directly calls attention to the stereotypical assumptions about women that have created problems for their entrance into the professions, particularly professions associated with masculinity, like the police.

By reasserting herself in this moment, James shows that she has come to terms with her place both personally, in that she now is more "sure of her ground" in relation to Kincaid's family, and professionally, in that she refuses to be "[left] home like the little woman." By asserting both her personal and professional stake in the investigation, James actively redefines the situation to conform to her expectations of how her world will work rather than Kincaid's preconceived conceptions of how the world does work. This particularly undermines the sense that Kincaid is free of the gender-stereotyping traditionally associated with such perspectives, as James notices that when Kincaid works the case with his friend, he treats her as a civilian partner rather than as a fellow police officer: "Nor did anyone seem to remember that she, too, was a police officer and might have something to contribute" (Crombie 2007, 220). James has to assert her standing as a detective inspector, and with the word "too," Crombie validates James's annoyance at her relegation to the position of mother rather than — as opposed to as well as — detective. With this stance, James models an assertive form of femininity that does not allow itself to be overpowered by normative conventions, even when participating in a relationship that otherwise follows gendered norms.

While these moments show that James is the principle means through which Crombie calls attention to the continual sexist discrimination in the police force, James does not provide an exclusively independent and exemplary case of a woman in the workplace. Rather, James manipulates her personal relationship with Kincaid to influence professional investigations. For instance, James insists that Kincaid take an investigation that relates to her personal friend and then inserts herself into the investigation, angering Kincaid's current sergeant: "But by rights it should have been his guv'nor [Kincaid] in the lead, not Gemma, who had no business here" (Crombie 2008, 103). Because James uses her position as Kincaid's personal partner to have access to him as a professional partner, she deploys stereotypical femininity to gain a position that otherwise she would not be granted. Her skill as a police detective is not an issue here, as she uses her personal position to usurp the place of other qualified detectives. While this intrusion can be excused as a narrative device Crombie uses to reunite her detective team, the author refuses to allow for this excuse, as she does not ignore the conflicting behaviors of non-professional partners joining forces for a personally motivated investigation. Instead, Crombie calls attention to James's awareness of the problematic nature of her involvement in Kincaid's investigation:

> feeling a small stab of jealousy. Ridiculous, really, when the severing of the partnership had been her choice, not his, and she should consider that she had the best of both worlds now. But sometimes it seemed that the almost instan-

taneous communion they'd felt when they worked a case together got lost in
the domestic shuffle, and that it had been easier to share their disparate personal lives when they'd worked together than the other way round.

Oh, well, she'd made her bed, as her dad would say, and she doubted she'd
won any points with Doug Cullen [Kincaid's sergeant] by sticking her nose in
this case [177].

James's acknowledgment of her manipulation of the situation highlights
that she recognizes her use of her privileged position as personal partner
to control events on a professional level. She also recognizes that she had
an easier relationship when she was both a professional and a personal
partner, as the familial responsibilities of that partnership seem to overwhelm the personal elements of it. To that end, the professional relationship
seems closer and more comfortable because it unites two individuals pursuing their own vocations rather than two individuals serving others.
Because of the heteronormative assumptions about the way a male-female
partnership works in Western culture, James feels that she is given the
opportunity to regret her decision for promotion, but Kincaid, while he
might feel regret, never feels that he should not behave as he does for the
sake of family cohesion. While Kincaid's sergeant is correct to resent James
insinuating herself into their investigation and controlling the directions
they take, James's sense of her own pettiness in this relationship still calls
attention to the way women are made to question their choices of career
advancement.

Conclusion

As James ultimately falls into the stereotypical position of a woman
using her feminine wiles to achieve her goals, Crombie's series does not
ultimately present an ideal model of a woman simultaneously balancing a
heterosexual relationship and family with professional advancement. This
is particularly clear as Kincaid becomes the lead investigator on the cases,
and James's cases are left unsolved or to her subordinates while she spends
her time helping Kincaid with his. Nevertheless, as with the discussions
of the continual prejudices against women in the police department, the
failure to idealize the character indicates the residual elements of latent
patriarchal dominance within the twenty-first century workplace. Even
after the feminist interventions in the mid-twentieth century, James, the
woman, is still expected to be the primary caregiver and to make the most

sacrifices for the sake of her family rather than for her career. While Kincaid is aware of these difficulties, he is intrinsically unable to support her career as she supports his, except in the sense of indulging her in certain elements of their professional relationship to maintain their personal connection. As such, Crombie's exploration of the heteronormative detective couple suggests the continued problematic position of women's professional development — particularly in traditionally male-gendered fields like policing — in the twenty-first century because of the internalized sense of the sex-gender hierarchy. But, Crombie is still writing her series, so she could still develop James into a more dominant investigator, finding a means of bringing Kincaid in as *her* partner without him usurping the dominant position. As Crombie continues to pursue James's place in twenty-first century policing, her series will hopefully continue to reflect the development of women's professional placement in the twenty-first century.

Notes

1. For instance, Ngaio Marsh's Roderick Alleyn series, Caroline Graham's Midsomer series, P. D. James's Adam Dalgliesh series, and Elizabeth George's Inspector Lynley series.
2. Martin demonstrates that "[p]olicewomen, while not relying on male deference, do take advantage of the accepted norms of deference to a woman [and] female officers play on the fact that many [men] are terrified of women with guns, believing they are 'trigger happy' because 'they cannot fight like a man'" (1980, 176).
3. For studies that confirm these generic gendering of these positions, see Chapters Two, Four, and Eight in Reskin and Padavic's *Men and Women at Work* (1994).

Works Cited

Bromley, Susan, and Pamela Hewitt. 1992. "*Fatal Attraction*: The Sinister Side of Women's Conflict about Career and Family." *The Journal of Popular Culture* 26.3:17–23.
Correll, Shelley J. 2001. "Gender and the Career Choice process: The Role of Biased Self-Assessments." *The American Journal of Sociology* 106.6: 1691–1730.
Crombie, Deborah. 1995. *Leave the Grave Green.* New York: Avon Books.
_____. 1996. *Mourn Not Your Dead.* New York: Avon Books.
_____. 1997. *Dreaming of the Bones.* New York: Avon Books.
_____. 1999. *Kissed a Sad Goodbye.* New York: Bantam Books.
_____. 2001. *A Finer End.* New York: Bantam Books.
_____. 2002. *And Justice There is None.* New York: Bantam Books.
_____. 2003. *Now May You Weep.* New York: Avon Books.
_____. 2004. *In a Dark House.* New York: Avon Books.
_____. 2007. *Water Like a Stone.* New York: Avon Books.
_____. 2008. *Where Memories Lie.* New York: Avon Books.
_____. 2009. *Necessary as Blood.* New York: William Morrow.

Elman, Margaret R., and Lucia A. Gilbert. 1984. "Coping Strategies for Role Conflict in Married Professional Women with Children." *Family Relations* 33.2: 317–27.

Klein, Kathleen G. 1988. *The Woman Detective: Gender & Genre.* Urbana: University of Illinois Press.

Martin, Susan E. 1980. *Breaking and Entering: Policewomen on Patrol.* Berkeley: University of California Press.

_____. 1994. "'Outsider Within' the Station House: The Impact of Race and Gender on Black Women Police." *Social Problems* 41.3: 383–400.

Munt, Sally R. 1994. *Murder by the Book? Feminism and the Crime Novel.* London: Routledge.

Reddy, Maureen T. 1988. *Sisters in Crime: Feminism and the Crime Novel.* New York: Contiuum.

Reskin, Barbara, and Irene Padavic. 1994. *Men and Women at Work.* Thousand Oaks: Pine Forge Press.

Sayers, Dorothy. 1937. *Busman's Honeymoon.* New York: HarperCollins.

_____, ed. 1947 (1928). Introduction to *Great Short Stories of Detection, Mystery and Horror,* 9–47. London: Victor Gollanz.

Detective Fiction and
Serial Protagonists:
An Interview with Ian Rankin

BY SIÂN HARRIS AND MALCAH EFFRON

Ian Rankin's seventeen Rebus novels have formed a most consistently intriguing series in contemporary century crime fiction. With their multifaceted plotlines and distinctive locations, the novels combine intricate police procedurals with sharp cultural and political commentary. The protagonist John Rebus, although in many respects the epitome of the lone rebel detective, has nevertheless emerged as an endearingly complicated individual with all too human flaws and foibles. A particularly striking feature of the series has been its progression in real time. Rebus was born in 1947, made his first appearance aged forty in 1987, and sixteen books later, he was retired at sixty in 2007. The challenges posed by this real time chronology and the complexity of the characterization made Rankin the ideal writer to provide us with a creative insight into the use of serial protagonists in detective fiction.

Rankin granted this interview in early 2008, some months after Rebus's retirement in *Exit Music* (2007). We met in the Oxford Bar, Edinburgh, with the setting lending a suitably metafictive edge to the conversation that followed. Our discussion focused on how the series had developed since its conception, and how Rebus had evolved as a protagonist. The first Rebus book *Knots and Crosses* was written while Rankin was a Ph.D. student at the University of Edinburgh and was published in 1987. Rankin came to crime fiction as a relative novice, and his early characterization of Rebus was influenced by his preconceptions about the genre: "I had the notion that detectives in fiction are loners, which was handy for me because I had no training. And so if he was a loner and a maverick working outside police conventions, then I didn't have to know what those conventions actually were." While Rankin would eventually become expert in how the police operate, in the early stages of his career he lacked the resources for extensive research, and adjusted his writing accordingly: "Rebus was more like a private eye working within the police force than he was an actual policeman. He still tends to run a parallel investigation, uses his own instincts, has his own contacts." This approach is characteristic of many crime writers, who choose to avoid procedural details and focus on plot. Rankin observes that "I think a lot of the time with detective fiction, where in England you have the tradition of the amateur and in America you have the private eye, it's because in neither case do you need to know the specifics of how a police investigation works." Even now, some mistakes are inevitable, and thanks to the advent of television shows like *CSI: Crime Scene Investigation*, readers have become accustomed to the "patina of realism" and expect the same standards from their chosen fiction. Meanwhile, the brand of realism such shows promote is every bit as illusory as a classic "Golden Age" mystery. Rankin explains this dilemma: "An essential problem for any detective fiction writer is that if your books are naturalistic, they will be the most tedious books it is possible to imagine." The mundane reality of an investigation — the endless interviews, the false leads, the frequent changes in personnel — is not the stuff that good crime fiction is made of. Indeed, Rankin reports that failure to appreciate this distinction has derailed many aspiring writers with a background in the police: "Cops don't always make good fiction writers because they don't know what to leave out. They would like to write fiction, but they've got no sense of what the reader is going to get bored by." Ultimately all crime fiction is inherently unrealistic, but the pretence can be successfully maintained by a careful writer.

While Rankin's knowledge of the genre has come a long way, so too has his protagonist. Rankin talks openly about his early mistakes — he is especially annoyed that he chose a "silly, immature joke" of a name — and offers a revealing insight into the way his protagonist evolved. The early books he dismisses as "young man's books, written by a man who was much more interested in language and puzzle than what he said about the characters." Nevertheless, they were an essential part of the learning curve. In *Hide and Seek* (1991), he tested the boundaries of the crime novel and first started to think that "I could use the detective, the character, to say something about Edinburgh, and about Scotland or society or the world." While writing *Tooth and Nail* (1992), Rankin was unhappily living in London, so he took it out on Rebus by dragging him along too: "He's been my punching bag for a long time." Rankin filled *Knots and Crosses* with back-story and baggage, something he later came to regret: "If I'd known it was going to be a series, I'd have introduced that story slowly, by degrees. But it's all there in the first book. It took me two or three books until I realized Rebus was sticking around, only then did I relax and let him reveal himself to me, bit by bit." Later, he had the chance to rectify this mistake, and introduce new characters slowly into the series: "The beauty of writing a serial character is that you end up with thousands of pages, so you don't have to condense their life and philosophy into such a short space. The characters have the chance to develop." Rankin admired Anthony Powell's series *A Dance to the Music of Time* (1951–75), and, once he was confident that Rebus was in it for the long haul, he was able to create a similar narrative in which the reader can "move through life" with the protagonist. The process was one of trial and error, as Rankin adapted his protagonist to fit the books he wanted to write. Rankin also responded to external factors. In the early books, Rebus was a fan of jazz. However, this was an interest shared by Charlie Resnick, the divorced policeman protagonist of John Harvey's Nottingham dekalog, including *Lonely Hearts* (1989) and *Rough Treatment* (1990). Given the similarities between the protagonists, and the popularity of Harvey's books at the time, Rankin decided to establish some "clear blue water" between the two. Therefore, Rebus stopped listening to jazz and developed a more enduring passion for classic rock.

The turning point came with *Black and Blue* (1997), which Rankin identifies as his seminal work: "*Black and Blue* was the first book when I really felt that I knew this guy and got under his skin, when I finally felt confident about what I could and couldn't do with a crime novel. It's a bigger book than the previous ones, it's more complex and mature. It was a book that had grown up." Inspired by the unsolved "Bible John" murders that took place in 1960s Glasgow, *Black and Blue* is classic Tartan Noir and was awarded with the Crime Writer's Association's Gold Dagger. After *Black and Blue,* the scope and ambition of the writing extended, and the books took an increasingly political turn. *The Hanging Garden* (1998) draws links between Nazi war crimes and human trafficking from war-torn Bosnia. *Set in Darkness* (2000) responds to the creation of the Scottish Parliament. *Fleshmarket Close* (2004) considers the fate of refugees, and *The Naming of the Dead* (2006) was precipitated by the G8 summit. Rankin's deft treatment of these events was well received, but readers were understandably less enthusiastic when he had to respond to the Compulsory Retirement Act for the police that came into effect in October 2006. Rankin admits that he was caught out by the act, which forced him to retire Rebus at sixty rather than sixty-five. Still, there have been points throughout the series when it seemed unlikely that Rebus would make it to retirement at all: "He's not quite Bruce Willis in *Die Hard*, but he does keep coming back — probably more than a policeman would in real life. And he has faced death many times. But that's part of the game that readers like playing, the suspension of disbelief. You know he's going to make it, yet the little compartment in the back of the mind is thinking this time, he might not."

Rebus might have made it thus far, but he has not escaped unscathed. Rankin has been merciless in his portrayal of the policeman's increasing isolation: "He's married to the job, the job has been his life, lover, his companion, and every actual individual, every other person who has come across his life, he's pushed them away. I've given him nice women to play with, and it's never worked out — he rejects everybody." Rebus's old flame Gill Templer did not even appear to toast his retirement, although Rankin attributes this to fear on her part: "I don't know where she went. Maybe she stayed away because if he's retiring, she can't be too far behind. They're fairly similar ages." As well as rejecting the nice, and the occasionally not-so-nice women, Rebus is distant from his daughter and has lost most of his close friends. Rankin protests that this is unintentional: "The priest [Father Leary] died, and I was distraught. I didn't want him to die, but there he went. I don't set out to do it, but I follow the book and I had to let it take me there." Yet while Rankin claims these events are beyond his control, he also admits the method to the madness: "I removed the people around him, because I wanted to take him to that *King Lear* moment, which basically comes in *Black and Blue* when he's having a fight in the Meadows with his best friend, and he falls to his knees, sniveling and crying and bawling and all that. I wanted him to be alone, with no support. And maybe that's me punishing him, but I wanted to see what he would do once the support was taken away."

176

As Rankin's portrayal of Rebus evolved and grew darker, so, too, did his portrayal of Edinburgh. Initially, Rebus's city bore little resemblance to the actual map: "At first I went to great lengths to make Edinburgh seem fictitious. Rebus worked in a fictitious police station on a fictitious street and drank in fictitious pubs. It wasn't until some way through the series that the street he lived on was named, and the Oxford Bar was named, and I turned the fictional police station into a real one." This influx of reality received a very positive response, which Rankin puts down to the reader's desire to be deceived: "The changes give the reader a buzz, if they know that the places are real it helps them to suspend disbelief, the same goes for using real crimes." Influenced by James Ellroy's take on the under-belly of Los Angeles and Ruth Rendell's forays into the seediest parts of London, Rankin's Edinburgh emerged as a central character within the books. That character was secretive, volatile and enigmatic, with a turbulent current of darkness concealed by a façade of gentile calm. The official website of "Undiscovered Scotland" admits that through Rebus, "many people have come to know Edinburgh less as the beautiful capital of a newly reborn nation than as a starkly monochrome city of crime, sleaze and overstressed police." Rankin was quick to acknowledge the paradox: "Critics would say it's not likely to be recommended by the tourist board — like *Trainspotting*— but it has proven to be an attraction. The Rebus Walking Tour is now part of the fabric of the city, and its fun for people to arrive and to find out that Fleshmarket Close is a real street and Arbus Street Station is a real place." This level of interest has added a further dimension to the relationship between Rebus and his home city. The books have not merely reflected reality, but through their popularity, they have altered it. The Oxford Bar itself is a case in point, with framed book jackets displayed on the walls and visitors who call by in the hope that they might catch a glimpse of Rankin enjoying a pint: "There is a mention in one of the books of a writer sitting in the corner and everyone assumes that's me, but it isn't. It's a journalist I know who works in here. I just said 'the writer in the corner' and everyone assumed it was some postmodern reference."

So is there a place for postmodernism or experimentalism in detective fiction? Rankin's response is conflicted: "I love blurring the boundaries between what's fiction and what's real. I like it when a book tricks me into believing that something is real. But it's hard, for me, to see that working in a crime novel without coming across — and this isn't an academic term —

as 'wanky.'" So while Rankin admires the writing of literary innovators like Thomas Pynchon, Muriel Spark, and Italo Calvino, he remains faithful to the classical principles of his adopted genre: "There is something pure about the crime novel. The people and the structure keep drawing you back to the classic narrative of crime, investigation, solution. It's hard to get away from, because it works so beautifully well." Rankin unsurprisingly cites Agatha Christie as the supreme exponent of the form, describing the experience of "coming up against the chess grand-master when you read a book written by her, because she always knew the way that you'd be thinking, even if you knew the game you were getting into. I don't think anybody can beat her for that. I don't even try." Instead, he focuses his efforts on the content rather than the form: "What I try to bring to the genre is a sense of my time and place, what's happening politically, economically and socially. What sort of crimes emerge in our culture and what does crime say about the culture that we've become?" Rankin tries to represent his city and his characters as honestly as possible, not only for the benefit of the readers, but from a sense of duty to the individuals and the institutions that appear in his fiction: "As a writer, I've come into contact with senior police officers and politicians and people from all walks of life, and it is really important to me that I get the details of their lives right, because I'm making a very good living from telling lies about them."

Our conversation moved on to consider some of the other characters that appear in the series. A vital component in serial detective fiction has traditionally been the use of a willing assistant, to run errands, do research, and listen carefully to the detective's developing theories as to whodunit and why. Initially, it seemed that the role of Rebus's sidekick was destined for the young Detective Constable Brian Holmes, who first appeared as a useful dogsbody in *Hide and Seek*. Even without the loaded significance of his name, he seemed to be a perfect foil for Rebus, and the two developed a close working relationship as well as a quasi-paternal personal bond. However, as the series progressed, Holmes's doubts about his future with the police force compromised their relationship, and he was superseded by Detective Constable Siobhan Clarke. She joined the team in *The Black Book* (1993) and rose through the ranks to Detective Sergeant by the time of *Exit Music*. It must, we suggested to Rankin, have been quite a challenge to develop her character and integrate her so completely into the series: "Well, the challenge is the reason that I did it," he returned, "Siobhan was originally just another part of the team, but she just got under my skin very quickly. It's partly because she's the polar opposite of Rebus. She's career orientated, he's not. She's computer literate, he's not. She's young, she's female, she's got an English accent but a Celtic name, and I enjoyed the amount of sparks that were generated from placing someone like her with someone like him. She's perceptive to his influence, stepping over the lines now and again, but stepping quickly back before she can be demoted."

While Siobhan's star was in the ascendant, Holmes was written out of the series by *Black and Blue*. As Rankin pragmatically summed it up, "There was an awful lot in her character that was useful and interesting in a way that Holmes wasn't." She may have started as a foil for her difficult boss, but she grew slowly and organically into his equal. Rather than simply having Siobhan replace Holmes in the limited capacity of sidekick, Rankin used her to add depth and dimension to the character of Rebus and to the plot of the books: "I like to keep the books complex and one way to do that is to maintain more than one plot. I could give Rebus a plot and Siobhan a plot, and the fun for me, the challenge, was to see if I could tie the two plots together." It is an intriguing glimpse into a creative process that is far less circumscribed than one might assume, as he explains that the implicit connections between the plots might not register until halfway through the first draft.

Perhaps inevitably, as Rebus's retirement grew closer, many readers hopefully speculated that Siobhan could continue the series alone — a topic on which Rankin was carefully noncommittal: "She *could* carry the series, there's no doubt about that," he told us, but would not be drawn further either way. If Rankin were to use Siobhan for another book, it would make him one of a handful of male crime writers to focus on a female protagonist, and he is acutely aware of that fact. While he cited Ruth Rendell, Agatha Christie, and P. D. James as being among the female crime writers who write convincingly from a male perspective, the corresponding lack of male writers willing or able to reciprocate did not go unremarked: "There have been very few male crime writers who have written well from a woman's perspective. It is just strange, that male crime writers don't write more about women. And then you even get male readers who won't read books by women [...] It really is very strange indeed." He even questions his own success with Siobhan, speculating that she was perhaps too much like a male character: "She shies away from a love life, from friendships. She's like Rebus, she's a bit of a loner. She broods about the case, eats out of the freezer, listens to music, and goes to bed." Ironically enough, this self-perceived authorial weakness can also be read as the character's greatest asset. Rather than becoming another Bridget Jones-clone, Siobhan's ambitions and anxieties stay focused on her career rather than her personal life (or lack of one). And if Rankin could change anything about the character, it transpired that it would be her name rather than her solitary single-mindedness: "That silly name has been the bane of my life. Whenever you go outside of the UK the first question is always 'How do you pronounce that?' so I have to work that into every book and have someone mispronounce it so she can correct them." Fittingly enough, it's the exact same nominal regret that Rankin has frequently expressed about Rebus.

While the dynamic between Rebus and Siobhan is central to the narrative, an equally important relationship has flourished in the shadowy margins. Over the course of the series, Rebus and his arch-rival Morris "Big Ger" Cafferty have clashed, collaborated, and conspired, and the development of Cafferty as the serial villain has been an essential component in the development of Rebus as the serial protagonist. Rankin speaks of Cafferty with relish, admitting to a "wee gladdening of the heart" whenever the big man appears on the page. Cafferty first appeared as a very minor character in *Tooth and Nail*, but Rankin felt compelled to take him further: "I kept Cafferty going because he was fun to write about, and the books got a real lift when he turned up. He's not always there — I did send him to jail — and he's not in *The Falls* at all as a present to a friend who didn't like him, and so I said I'd write one book he's not in, but I didn't enjoy it as much as when he's present." In the best Scottish tradition of Jekyll and Hyde, Cafferty reflects an alternative version of Rebus, and Rankin evidently enjoyed writing the interplay between them: "You're never sure in the books — even I'm never sure in the books — whether they are going to become best buddies or kill each other. It could go either way at any moment, and I like that tension between them." The two characters have similar backgrounds, and despite their oppositional perspectives, similar outlooks on life. They are also increasingly isolated and overtaken by the changes in the world around them. As Rankin explains: "A cop like Rebus, thirty or forty years ago, he would have been the norm, but now you just don't get away with the stuff he gets away with — the lunchtime drinking, the physical condition he's in. And the same goes for Cafferty. He has this warped moral code that's missing in the younger, cooler villains." They are men on the verge of extinction, which explains their sense of recognition as well as their rivalry. Rankin sums them up as "two big dinosaurs facing up to each other, because they are each the last of their breed." However, Cafferty is not just a portrait of an individual criminal. He stands for what Rankin believes to be the reality of crime and the corrupt society it thrives in: "He represented all that I was trying to write about, that corruption in high places and low places. A lot of the time crime writers put a serial killer into the books to give the readers a vicarious thrill. Cafferty represents something more than that, something rotten at the core of society." Cafferty is a career criminal in a culture that enables his success and consistently fails to deliver any meaningful punishment. He is not an evil genius, or a spectacularly deranged psychopath, but an ordinary and very dangerous man: "He's not as devious or calculating as the usual serial killer in fiction, the Hannibal Lectors and people like that," Rankin stressed, "there's nothing *special* about him." In contrast to more sensational and lurid crime writers, Rankin's serial villain simply and effectively exposes the sheer banality of evil.

In the past, Rankin has had his own moments of lurid sensationalism, admitting that: "*Tooth and Nail* was my attempt at that, and a) it didn't work and b) I didn't find anything exciting in writing about that type of character." But while the quasi-Gothic goriness of *Tooth and Nail* was abandoned, Rankin has returned on several occasions to the serial killer plot. There is a geographical precedent for this, as he notes that "Scotland is plagued by serial killers. There are real life counterparts to these people, and it intrigues me that a country of five million people can throw up so many serial killers. We're good at serial killing." The sentiment is unlikely to be endorsed by the Scottish Tourist Board, but the list of Scottish serial killers is undeniably numerous and includes Robert Black, Dennis Nilsen, Colin Norris, and Peter Tobin, not to mention Bible John. Yet despite Rankin's engagement with this macabre aspect of Scottish history, the actual instances of murder in his books remain relatively low: "The investigation focuses on people who have died in the past, or there are a couple of killings in the present. Edinburgh itself doesn't have a very good murder rate, and I wanted to keep it realistic." This desire for realism has forced Rankin to consider a more diverse range of crimes than is usual in detective fiction. When writing the short story collection *A Good Hanging* (1992) he used the structure of having one story for each month of the year: "I knew damn well I couldn't have twelve murders," he explains, "there just weren't twelve murders in Edinburgh in any one given year." Therefore, Rankin had to consider the possibilities of blackmail, arson, and missing persons. As well as maintaining the realism of the series, the low body count ensures that when there is a murder, it has a real impact — on the reader, on the plot, and on the author himself. Rankin does not write murders lightly: "The significance of murder as a crime — taking away something irreplaceable from the world — it has such extreme ramifications. It's like dropping a pebble in a pond. The ripples go out from family and friends, the loved ones, to workmates, to people who just live nearby. And it says so much about the world that we live in."

It was at this point that our interview took an unexpectedly surreal turn. Given his clear sympathy with the victims of crime, we asked Rankin for his view on the popular mantra that to write successful crime fiction, one must also have some sympathy with the perpetrators: "People do say that" he replied, "and also that to be a good detective you have got to be able to empathize with the villain, that it helps if you can understand them in some way. But there's something more interesting, and I'm sure the analysts could do a lot with this: Cafferty lives in my house. In the last couple of Rebus books the description of his house fits my house to a tee. He sits in my hot tub. Why I should ally myself with the villain of the piece rather than the hero, I'm not sure." It transpires that Rankin's hot tub is something of a literary sensation in its own right, also appearing in Alexander McCall Smith's *44 Scotland Street* (2005). As our time drew to a close, the conversation therefore concluded with the unforgettable image of Cafferty and his creator sharing a hot tub.

Since retiring Rebus, Rankin has maintained an intense schedule of writing and publication. The stand-alone heist thriller *Doors Open* (2008) appeared as a serial with *The New York Times*, followed by *A Cool Head* (2008). He also collaborated with Werther Dell'Edera on the graphic novel *Dark Entries* (2009), which presented Rankin with the unusual challenge of picking up an established character — occult detective John Constantine — who was created by comic book legend Alan Moore in 1985. Meanwhile, *The Complaints* (2009) introduced Inspector Malcolm Fox, a teetotal workaholic in the unpopular Complaints & Conduct department of Lothian and Borders Police. The book was critically acclaimed, and Rankin has hinted that he may write a follow-up. Whilst many commentators have expressed the hope that this would ultimately lead to the return of Rebus, the real testimony to Rankin's powers of characterization comes from the many readers who would be satisfied simply to learn more about Fox, with or without a cameo from his predecessor. It is therefore to be hoped that the habit of serialization may remain with Rankin for some time yet to come.

About the Contributors

Sonja Altnoeder is coordinator of the International PhD Programme (IPP) "Literature and Cultural Studies" at Justus Liebig University in Gießen, Germany. She is writing a book on "Mapping London: A Transdisciplinary Approach to Representations of Urban Spaces from Modernism to Postmodernism." Her study interests include crime fiction, gender studies, postcolonialism, urban poetry, and media studies.

Malcah Effron received her doctorate from Newcastle University, England, in June 2010 and now teaches at Stevenson University. Her publications include articles in *The Journal of Narrative Theory*, *Narrative*, and *A Companion to Crime Fiction* (Blackwell, 2010). She is the co-founder of the international Crime Studies Network (CSN).

Christiana Gregoriou is a lecturer at Leeds University's School of English with an interest in the linguistic make-up of literary texts. In addition to journal articles on the stylistics of the criminal mind style (published in 2002 and 2003), she has also published "Stylistics of True Crime" (Continuum, 2007, in a volume on contemporary stylistics), *English Literary Stylistics* (Palgrave, 2009), a Crime Files series monograph on *Deviance in Contemporary Crime Fiction* (Palgrave, 2007) and a critical stylistics monograph on *Language, Ideology and Identity in Serial Killer Narratives* (Routledge, 2010).

Siân Harris received a PhD from Newcastle University, UK, in 2009. Her dissertation focused upon the Kunstlerroman narrative in 20th century Canadian fiction, and the themes of authorship and creative identity have continued to provide the catalyst for her research since then. Her interests include Canadian literature, crime, and feminist theory. Siân is currently teaching at University of Exeter, and working on the use of the female author-as-character in contemporary historical fiction.

Beth Head is pursuing a PhD at Aberystwyth University, examining the narratives of Sue Grafton and Patricia Cornwell. She has presented conference papers on both authors. She has also published several short stories in anthologies and webzines.

About the Contributors

Susan Massey was educated at the University of St. Andrews in Scotland, where she received her MA, MLitt and PhD. Her dissertation focused on the representation of masculinity in the works of Henning Mankell, George Pelecanos, and Ian Rankin. Her other research interests include seriality in crime fiction and the depiction of female masculinity within the genre. She wrote an entry on male crime writers for the Greenwood *Encyclopaedia of British Crime Writing* (2009) and has contributed to the companion volumes *100 British Crime Writers* and *100 American Crime Writers* (both forthcoming).

P. M. Newton is a Sydney-based crime writer whose first novel, *The Old School,* was published by Penguin in 2010. She was awarded an MA in writing from University of Technology, Sydney, in 2009 with a thesis on how authentic events offer new ways of reading society through crime novels. She contributed the chapter "Beyond the Sensation Novel: Social Crime Fiction — Qualia of the Real World," to *Literature and Sensation* (eds. Anthony Uhlmann et al., Cambridge Scholars Publishing, 2009).

David Levente Palatinus has a PhD from Peter Pazmany Catholic University, Hungary. He currently holds a lectureship in twentieth-century literature and film at the Department of English at the University of Ruzomberok, Slovakia. His research focuses on the meta-narratives of medicine, forensic crime fiction, and the phenomenology of perception.

Lindsay Steenberg is a lecturer in film studies at Oxford Brookes University. Her work focuses on violence and gender in postmodern and postfeminist media culture, and she has published on the *wuxia* genre, war and the art cinema, filmmaker Guillermo del Toro, and a book on crime film and television. She is writing a book on gender, violence, and forensic science in the visual media entitled *Forensic Science in Contemporary American Popular Culture*.

Maureen Sunderland's PhD dissertation examined the development of hard-boiled detective fiction after Raymond Chandler through a reading of the city, femininity and masculinity — key components of the hard-boiled genre — in four later hard-boiled writers: Chester Himes, Ross Macdonald, James Ellroy, and Walter Mosley. Another area of research interest for her is the literature of the Cold War.

Sabine Vanacker is a lecturer in English at the University of Hull. Her research and teaching interests center on twentieth-century literature, with particular attention to gender, feminist literary criticism, women's writing, and crime fiction. She published *Reflecting on Miss Marple* with Marion Shaw (1991) and has recently returned to Agatha Christie with "Guilt and Culpability in Christie's Women" (*Las damas negras,* eds. Rosa García Rayego and Josefina De Andrés, forthcoming).

Index

abduction 33, 45
abjection 37, 41, 42, 133
adaptation 6, 14–15, 16, 17, 51, 87, 96, 128, 129
aesthetics 7, 9, 10, 11, 12, 14, 15, 17, 18, 19, 114, 128, 139–140
African American 113, 124–125, 145, 151, 154, 154
agency 23, 62, 92, 120, 148, 158
Al Qaeda 26
Asperger's syndrome 103, 104
assault 32, 46, 78, 93
Auster, Paul 2
authenticity 21, 51, 122–124
autism 53–54, 64, 100–105; *see also* Asperger's syndrome
autopsy 37–38, 41–44

Bal, Meike 128–129
Barthes, Roland 122–123
beauty 120, 129, 134, 137, 139, 175
Before the Frost 51, 55, 57–63, 64
behavior 37, 40, 43, 48, 53, 54, 57, 62, 64, 67, 87, 99, 101, 131, 139, 144, 148, 161, 163, 165, 166, 168, 169
Benstock, Bernard 72, 73
Bhabha, Homi 2
The Big Nowhere 142–143, 147–149, 150, 152–154
Bill of Rights 24, 26, 27, 29, 32, 33, 34
Black and Blue 175 176, 179
Blacklist 24–28
blackmail 85, 182
Blake, William 128–130, 134–136, 138–140
The Bone Collector (film) 6, 112–126
Book of the Dead 36, 39, 42–43, 46
Boone, Christopher 100–110
bounty hunter 85–87, 89–90, 91, 95
Bridget Jones's Diary 87, 180

burg 86
Butler, Judith 62–63

Cafferty, "Big Ger" 180–182
camera 39, 43, 122, 130, 137, 149
Chandler, Raymond 9–12, 16, 17, 18, 84–87, 143, 144, 156; *The Big Sleep* 1; *Farewell, My Lovely* 156; "The Simple Art of Murder" 9, 16, 84
Chicago 21, 24–25, 34
chick lit 15, 83, 87–89, 90–91, 93–95
Christie, Agatha 2, 70, 178, 179; *The Murder of Rodger Ackroyd* 53
cinematography 122, 125, 130, 146
Civil Rights Movement 25, 144
Clarke, Siobhan 31, 32, 51, 64, 178–180
Cold War 5, 142, 155
communism 24, 27, 142, 145–151, 153–154
Conan Doyle, Arthur 67, 71, 74, 102
conservativism 21, 36, 69, 79, 83, 84, 125, 155
Considine, Mal 147–148, 152, 154
consumption 39, 64, 134, 137, 140
cop 29, 40, 45, 56, 89, 126, 174, 180
Cornwell, Patricia 1, 11, 36–49, 112, 126; *Black Notice* 46; *Blow Fly* 37; *Book of the Dead* 36, 39, 42–43, 46; *The Last Precinct* 46; *Postmortem* 36, 37–38, 40, 41; *Predator* 36, 39, 41–42; *Scarpetta* 36, 39–40; *The Scarpetta Factor* 36, 39, 46–47
corpse 9, 37, 38, 41–42, 43, 44, 72, 77, 78, 121, 124, 126
Correll, Shelley 159, 161
criminalist 5, 12, 13, 14, 19, 45, 112–118, 122, 124–126, 143
criminals 11, 14, 32, 37, 40, 41, 42, 45, 47, 52, 58, 60, 62, 75, 76, 83, 86, 93, 95, 99, 103, 109, 110, 115, 118, 119, 126, 131, 181

187

Index

Crombie, Deborah 157–171; *And Justice There Is None* 158; *Dreaming of the Bones* 158, 159; *A Finer End* 158, 162, 163; *In a Dark House* 158, 164, 167; *Kissed a Sad Goodbye* 158; *Leave the Grave Green* 158; *Mourn Not Your Dead* 161; *Necessary as Blood* 158; *Now May You Weep* 165–166; *Water Like a Stone* 163, 168–169; *Where Memories Lie* 158, 169–170

Cross, Alex 2

Cross, Amanda 10

CSI: Crime Scene Investigation 6, 11, 36, 112, 117, 121, 174

The Curious Incident of the Dog in the Night-time 16, 97–101, 103–106, 108, 110

Dalgliesh, Adam 6, 13, 67–79

daughters 13, 51, 53, 56, 59–60, 61, 63, 90, 176

Deaver, Jeffrey 11, 36, 112, 126; *The Coffin Dancer* 126; *The Cold Moon* 126; *The Empty Chair* 126

Delamater, Jerome 7

democracy 1, 23, 24, 31, 34

Derrida, Jacques 114

deviance 16, 38, 42, 43, 47, 97–99, 101, 102–105, 108–110, 132, 139

dialogic 37, 38, 39, 40, 41, 42, 46

Dibdin, Michael 22

digital 123–124

disability 16, 18, 113, 118, 120, 121, 124, 137; *see also* Asperger's syndrome; autism

Dolarhyde, Francis 129, 131, 132–138

Donaghy, Amelia 112–126; aka Amelia Sachs 126

Dupin, Auguste 66

economics 23, 46, 48, 125, 178

Edinburgh 21, 24, 29–30, 33, 34, 173, 175, 177, 181–182

education 117, 144, 145, 165

Ellroy, James 142, 143, 146–149, 152, 154–156, 177; *The Big Nowhere* 142–143, 147–149, 150, 152–154; *L.A. Quartet* 142, 143, 146–148, 153

equality 18, 24, 122, 125, 144, 154, 161, 162, 165, 167–168, 179

eroticization 39, 42–44, 47

Evanovich, Janet 6, 83–95; *One for the Money* 83, 85–86, 89–94; *Two for the Dough* 83, 85, 93, 94

evidence 92, 113–119, 122–126, 152

Exchange Principle 115, 117, 118, 119, 120, 125

fair play 101, 109

family 24, 56, 58, 63, 76, 86, 90, 94–95, 106, 117, 144, 159–163, 167–168, 170–171, 182

Farinelli, Lucy 43

fathers 13, 51, 53, 56–63, 77, 100, 102–103, 107, 108–109, 117, 124, 147, 153, 163

Federal Bureau of Investigation (FBI) 37, 43, 129, 135, 146, 150–151

felon 83, 84, 91–92, 95

femininity 10, 88, 77, 78, 90, 92, 95, 117, 158, 168–170

feminism 2, 6, 10, 38, 68, 70, 77, 83, 85, 87–88, 96, 164, 170

fetishism 14, 15, 134–137

film 6, 14, 15, 36, 46, 74, 104, 112–126, 128–141, 149, 152–153

Firewall 53, 56, 57, 62, 64

first-person 36–37, 42, 88, 91, 99, 105, 161

Fiske, John 67–68, 82

focalizer 13, 51, 53, 56, 64

forensics 1, 11, 14, 36, 41–42, 44, 68, 112–127; profiling 131–132

founding fathers 25, 34, 66, 84, 114, 147

framework 6, 7, 17, 18, 62, 83, 95, 98

frontier 144, 146–148, 151–154

future 19, 56, 70, 71, 78, 122–123, 147, 178

G8 24, 28–30, 33, 34, 176

gaze 2, 40, 42–43, 88–89, 91, 112, 120, 121–122, 130, 133–139; forensic 113, 115, 118, 119, 120, 123, 125

Geherin, David 21–22

gender 10, 16, 40, 42, 44, 49, 62, 83, 84, 86, 88, 89, 92–95, 113, 119, 120, 125, 159, 160–164, 166–169, 171; roles 85, 91, 167

genres 5–7, 9, 12–19, 36, 37, 39, 40, 41, 42, 46, 47, 49, 66, 69, 70, 75, 82, 83, 84, 85, 88, 89, 90, 94, 95, 96, 97, 98, 102, 104, 110, 113, 114, 124, 125, 131, 144, 173, 174, 178

globalization 5, 7, 11, 12, 13, 19, 23, 28, 30, 46

Glover, David 148

Golden Age 1, 13, 73, 84, 109, 157, 174

Graham, Will 129, 131–132, 133, 137, 138

Index

Great Policeman 77
gun 85, 94, 114, 171

habeas corpus 24, 32
Haddon, Mark 97, 100, 102, 104, 106, 107, 108; *The Curious Incident of the Dog in the Night-time* 16, 97–101, 103–106, 108, 110
Halliday, M.A.K. 98
Hammett, Dashiell 23, 84; *Red Harvest* 1
hard-boiled 15, 83–87, 89–96, 144
Harfield, Timothy D. 132–134
Harris, Thomas: and *Red Dragon* (book) 128, 129, 138
Harrison, John 70, 73, 77
Hausladen, Gary 21–22
hegemony 82–83, 96, 125, 158
heteronormativity 158–160, 162–164, 168, 170
heterosexuality 158, 159, 170, 171
hierarchy 10, 85, 89, 95, 113, 119, 121, 124, 125, 126, 128, 161, 165, 166, 171
"high" 128–129, 140, 181
Höglund, Ann-Britt 54, 55, 56–58, 60, 62
Hollywood 77, 120, 146, 149, 152, 153
Holmes, Sherlock 11, 67, 73, 74, 100, 102
Holocaust 154
Homeland Security 24, 26
homosexuality 148–149
Horsley, Lee 1, 20
horror 131, 134, 147, 154
humor 82, 87, 88, 89, 93, 95

identity 28, 29, 34, 40, 41, 44–45, 47–48, 82, 85, 88, 101, 102, 103, 109, 115, 116, 121, 132–133, 145, 146
ideology 23, 25, 68, 113, 129, 142, 148, 151–152, 155, 163, 165, 168
illegality 24, 33
individualism 22, 26, 27, 32, 84, 101, 104, 105, 114, 118, 145, 151–153, 155, 158, 162, 164, 166, 170, 173, 176, 178
injustice 18, 23, 27, 155
institution 22–23, 25, 26, 27, 34, 46, 68, 178
Internet 5, 119
investigation 11, 13, 14, 16, 19, 22, 23, 24, 26, 31, 44, 52, 62, 70, 74, 78, 83, 85, 90, 91, 92, 93, 94, 102, 114, 115, 119, 120, 142–154, 157, 160, 165, 167, 168, 169, 170, 174, 178, 181
Iraq 24, 26, 30, 31, 33, 46, 48

James, Gemma 157–171
James, P.D. 6, 13, 67–79, 171, 179; *The Black Tower* 72, 76; *A Certain Justice* 72, 74; *Cover Her Face* 71, 75; *Death in Holy Orders* 69, 77; *Death of an Expert Witness* 72; *Devices and Desires* 69; *The Lighthouse* 72, 73, 77; *A Mind to Murder* 73; *Murder Room* 68, 69, 77; *Original Sin* 68; *The Private Patient* 69, 72, 75, 77, 78, 79; *A Taste for Death* 72, 76
Jolie, Angelina 112, 113, 124
Jones, Manina 1, 67, 68, 96
justice 23, 28, 31, 32, 33, 44, 73, 118, 123, 139

kidnapping 24, 138
Kincaid, Duncan 157–171
Klaver, Elizabeth 41–42
Klein, Kathleen Gregory 10, 158
Knight, Stephen 1, 6, 7, 20, 21
Kristeva, Julia 41

L.A. Quartet 142, 143, 146–148, 153
Lacan, Jacques 131, 133, 136
LAPD 142, 143, 147, 148, 149, 152–155
Lavenham, Emma 73, 77
law 9, 19, 23–34, 43, 52, 84–86, 99, 102, 122, 126, 142; enforcement 46–47, 58, 119, 121, 125
Leon, Donna 21, 22
The Lighthouse 72, 73, 77
linguistics 6, 11, 16, 97, 98, 101, 105, 108, 109
Locard, Edmond 114–115, 119, 121, 125
London 30, 69, 77, 100, 103–106, 157, 175, 177; Tube bombings 28, 29, 32, 33
Los Angeles 11, 142–144, 147, 149, 151, 154, 155, 177
"low" 128–129, 140, 181
Lula 93–94

Magistrale, Tony 131, 138
Mandel, Ernest 109
Mankell, Henning 13, 50–64; *Before the Frost* 51, 55, 57–63, 64; *The Dogs of Riga* 54, 55, 61, 64; *Faceless Killers* 53, 61, 64; *The Fifth Woman* 56, 61, 64; *Firewall* 53, 56, 57, 62, 64; *The Man Who Smiled* 56, 57, 59, 64; *Sidetracked* 50, 61, 64; "Wallander's First Case" 55; *The White Lioness* 52, 55, 59, 64

189

Index

Mañoso, Ranger 89, 90–92
marginalization 99, 124, 125, 143, 158, 163
Marino, Pete 37, 39, 42–43, 46
Martin, Susan 160, 161, 164, 171
Martinsson 53–54, 57–58, 62
masculinity 10, 11, 39, 40, 42–44, 63, 64, 83, 95, 125, 135, 143, 145, 147, 148, 151, 153, 158, 168
McCarthyism 24–26
McCracken, Scott 68
mean streets 10, 11, 12, 84, 85, 86–87, 94–95
media 6, 7, 14, 15, 17, 18, 31, 47, 89, 96, 126
medium 14, 15, 123, 124, 130, 134, 138
Meeks, Buzz 147, 149, 152, 154
millennium 5, 6, 7, 9, 15, 18, 19, 31
mind style 105, 107, 110
mirror stage 133–134
mise-en-scène 130, 136
Miskin, Kate 73, 76, 78
Mitchell, W.J.T. 134–135
monster 41, 130, 131, 133–136, 138–139
Morelli 91–93
Mosley, Walter 6, 142–146, 150, 155, 156; *Devil in a Blue Dress* 144, 156; *A Red Death* 142–143, 145–146, 150, 154, 156
Most, Glenn 51, 63
Mouse 146
Mulvey, Laura 140–141
Munt, Sally 158
murder 9, 19, 22, 24, 28, 31, 33, 37, 38, 39, 45, 55, 67, 70, 71, 72, 74, 77, 78, 84, 92, 99, 100, 101–103, 108–109, 118, 122, 126, 129, 132, 135, 136, 138–139, 148, 152, 153, 154–155, 159, 165, 167, 168, 175, 181, 182
Murder Room 68, 69, 77
Murray, Stuart 103–104, 107, 110
myth 1, 146, 147, 153, 154; *see also* mythology
mythology 144, 146–148, 153; *see also* myth

The Naming of the Dead 23, 24–25, 28–33, 176
narcissism 46, 134, 153
nationism 1, 7, 12, 13, 17, 23, 24, 28, 30, 34, 69, 147, 153–154
Nestingen, Andrew 55
New York 49, 116, 182
9/11 11, 13, 21, 23, 25, 26, 28, 29, 30, 31, 32, 33, 34, 37, 46, 47, 48

One for the Money 83, 85–86, 89–94
"other" 28, 44, 47, 103, 121, 131, 133, 134, 138
Oxford 21, 77

Padavic, Irene 162, 163, 164, 165, 167, 171
panoptics 112, 115, 116, 118, 121, 126
Paretsky, Sara 6, 21, 23–28, 29, 31, 33–34, 70; *Bitter Medicine* 26; *Blacklist* 24–28; *Hard Time* 26; *Tunnel Vision* 26; *Writing in an Age of Silence* 25
partners 57, 60, 69, 91, 113, 124, 125, 148, 152, 157, 158–163, 165–171
pathology 13, 37–40, 42, 44–46, 48, 72, 126, 134, 138
patriarchy 83, 88, 125, 158, 168, 170
Patriot Act 24, 26, 27, 29, 33
patriotism 24, 25, 27
Patterson, James 2, 112
performance 41, 42, 43, 62, 86, 88–95, 121, 132, 138
perversion 26, 43–44, 46, 130
phenomenology 6, 130, 140
photograph 38, 40, 45, 73, 119, 122–124
place-based 21–22, 29
Plain, Gill 20, 39, 41, 48
pleasure 40, 60, 66, 70, 79, 87
Plum, Stephanie 6, 83–95
Poe, Edgar Allan 1, 66, 84
poetics 16, 97, 99, 106, 108, 110
police 23, 28, 30–31, 32, 33, 37, 38, 40, 42, 44, 45, 46, 50–56, 59–63, 67, 70, 73, 74, 77, 78, 92, 99, 115, 117, 120, 124, 142, 143, 147, 148, 152, 157, 159, 160, 161, 163–164, 165, 166, 168, 169, 170, 174, 175, 176, 177, 178, 183; procedurals 21, 49, 112, 120, 129, 173; *see also* LAPD; law
politics 22–23, 25, 26, 29–30, 32–34, 48, 69, 83, 87, 88, 95, 119, 125, 142, 151, 153, 154, 155, 173, 175, 178
politics of place 13, 18, 22–24, 25–27, 28–30, 32, 33, 34
popular culture 7, 15, 36, 47, 82–83, 87–88, 95, 96, 114, 117, 129–130
popular literature 9, 88
Porter, Dennis 101, 102
postfeminism 6, 10, 18, 83, 85, 87, 88, 95–96, 113, 117, 125, 126
postmodernism 82, 88, 123, 128, 177
Postmortem 36, 37–38, 40, 41
post-war 47–48, 143, 144, 145, 146, 151, 154–155

power 22–23, 24, 25, 26, 27, 29, 31, 37, 39, 41, 45, 56, 62, 70, 77, 82, 83, 113, 115, 119, 120, 122, 123–126, 129–130, 134, 135, 136, 138, 142, 143, 144, 147, 149, 153, 154, 155, 163, 164, 183
Predator 36, 39, 41–42
prejudice 125, 164, 170
Priestman, Martin 41, 49, 67, 73, 101
Prigozy, Ruth 7
The Private Patient 69, 72, 75, 77, 78, 79
profession 39–40, 72, 76, 89, 90, 95, 125, 168
professionalism 2, 3, 6, 25, 45, 46, 52, 53, 54, 56, 63, 70, 76, 83, 87, 89, 90, 92, 94, 113, 151, 157–163, 166, 168–171
psychoanalysis 2, 47, 130–131, 133
psychology 46, 64, 71–72, 74–75, 93, 129, 130–132, 139
psychopath 45, 47, 58, 99, 181

race 16, 18, 25, 27–28, 113, 119, 121, 143, 153, 159; *see also* African American
racism 2, 28, 34, 58, 143–146, 151, 155
Rainman 104, 110
Rankin, Ian 13, 18, 21, 23–24, 28–34, 51, 64, 173–183; *Black and Blue* 175 176, 179; *The Black Book* 178; *The Complaints* 182; *A Cool Head* 182; *Dark Entries* 182; *Doors Open* 182; *Exit Music* 64, 173, 178; *The Falls* 180; *Fleshmarket Close* 176, 177; *The Hanging Garden* 175; *Hide and Seek* 174, 178; *Knots and Crosses* 173, 175; *The Naming of the Dead* 23, 24–25, 28–33, 176; *Set in Darkness* 176; *Tooth and Nail* 175, 180, 181
rape 32, 37, 45, 78, 94
Rawlins, Ezekiel (Easy) 6, 142–147, 150–152, 154–155
Rebus, John 21, 24, 28–33, 51, 64, 173–180, 182–183
A Red Death 142–143, 145–146, 150, 154, 156
Red Dragon (film) 6, 136–141
Reddy, Maureen 10, 158
Rendell, Ruth 177, 179
repetition 12, 62, 67, 72, 107
reporter 25, 27, 114
Reskin, Barbara 162, 163, 164, 165, 167, 171
revenge 24, 32, 33, 92, 93, 100
Rhyme, Lincoln 112, 114, 116, 119, 120, 124, 126
Rowland, Susan 69

rule of law 24, 28–34
rules of the game 12, 41
Rydberg 53, 55, 60
Rzepka, Charles 2

Sayers, Dorothy L. 77, 79, 157
Scarpetta 36, 39–40
Scarpetta, Kay 36–44, 46–47, 49
The Scarpetta Factor 36, 39, 46–47
scenery 22, 23; *see also* setting
Schmid, David 69
science 1, 2, 9, 11, 14, 15, 19, 42, 36, 37, 42, 46, 47, 73, 108, 112, 114, 116–122, 125, 126
scopophilia 40, 73; *see also* voyeurism
Scotland 13, 23, 28–33, 51, 165, 175–177, 180–181
screen 37, 51, 113, 116, 118, 120, 125, 126, 128, 130, 134, 135, 136, 138, 153
security 23–24, 26, 27, 29–30, 31, 33, 40, 53, 60, 145
Semino, Elena 101, 107, 108
serial killer 37, 41, 44, 46, 47, 48, 58, 61, 116, 129, 132, 181
serialization 13, 24, 36, 51, 64, 67, 68, 75–76, 77, 173, 175, 178, 180, 181, 182
series 6, 10–18, 36, 41–42, 51–55, 58, 59, 61, 63, 64, 66–68, 70–77, 79, 83, 85, 91, 93, 95, 112, 126, 142, 143. 156, 157, 158–160, 164, 170, 171, 173, 175–180, 182
setting 11, 12, 16, 21–22, 68, 69, 75, 84, 85, 93, 94, 98, 173; *see also* scenery
sex-gender hierarchy 165, 171
sex offenders 24, 31, 32
sexism 1, 2, 37, 75, 159, 162, 164–166, 168, 169
sexual abuse 93, 129
sexual assault 32, 46, 93
sexuality 38, 40, 42, 43, 47, 48, 84, 92, 120, 124, 131, 135, 137, 140, 149, 159, 164
Short, Mick 100, 106
Silence of the Lambs (film) 117, 120
slavery 28, 34
Smith, Dudley 147–148, 152
Soitos, Stephen 1, 20
spectacle 15, 38, 89, 91, 116, 126, 132, 134
spectator 112, 116, 119, 122, 123; *see also* viewer
style 97, 98, 105, 139
subgenre 14, 83, 84, 96, 114, 119, 123, 124
surveillance 73, 113, 115, 118–119, 149

Index

suspense 91, 101, 130, 140
Sweden 23, 54, 58, 64
symbolism 31, 131
Symons, Julian 1, 2, 20

technology 6, 11, 14, 15, 49, 119, 121
television 6, 14, 36, 74, 75, 82, 90, 110, 112, 146, 174
terrorism 23, 24, 27, 28, 29, 30, 32, 46
third-person 36, 37, 38, 39, 42, 51, 88
thriller 51, 69, 101, 129, 130, 131–132, 140, 148, 182
Todorov, Tzvetan 96
tourists 149, 177, 181
trace evidence 82, 113–119, 122–125
traditionalism 14, 19, 40, 47, 48, 69, 95, 117, 120, 125, 132, 143, 159, 163, 169, 171, 178
trauma 25, 27, 46, 48, 99, 117, 121, 123, 129, 131, 135
Trenton 85, 86, 91, 94
truth 14, 25, 108, 122–124, 126, 136, 146–147, 150, 152, 155
twentieth century 5, 9–13, 16–19, 48, 131, 155, 157, 159, 165, 170
twenty-first century 5–7, 9–19, 155, 159, 160, 163, 170, 171
Twisted 113, 120
Two for the Dough 83, 85, 93, 94

United Kingdom 13, 29, 30, 50, 104
United States 7, 11, 13, 36, 37, 46, 48, 64, 104, 164

victim 31, 32, 37, 38, 39, 40, 42, 43, 45, 46, 74, 75, 84, 102, 117, 121, 122, 126, 132, 136, 137–138, 149, 154, 166, 182

Vidocq, Eugène 1
viewer 130, 134, 135, 137, 138; *see also* spectator
villain 84, 94, 129, 180–182
violence 12, 25, 26, 36–38, 42, 44, 61–62, 67, 93, 94, 95, 113, 117, 118–119, 121, 123, 132, 139, 140, 143, 145, 147, 149
visual 6, 14, 17, 112–116, 119, 121, 122, 124–126, 133, 134, 135, 136, 149
voyeurism 39, 44, 130; *see also* scopophilia

Wallander, Kurt 13, 50–64
Wallander, Linda 13, 51–53, 55, 56–63
Walton, Priscilla 1, 67, 68, 96
War on Terror 11, 12, 30, 46
Warshawski, V.I. 6, 21, 24–27
Washington, Denzel 112, 113, 124
Watson, Victor 66, 67
Watts race riots 144
Wesley, Benton 37, 43, 46
Western 10, 11, 23, 31, 32, 42, 149, 153, 161, 163, 164, 168, 170
Whiting, Frederick 47, 48
witch hunt 142, 143, 150, 155
World Trade Center 5, 11, 27
World War I 145
World War II 11, 12, 143–147, 154, 156; *see also* Holocaust

Ystad 50, 51, 52, 54, 56, 59, 63

Žižek, Slavoj 63